THE FARM

BY

JEFF MCENTIRE

To Robert,
for always being there when the road was rough
and the ghosts of the past came calling.

PROLOGUE

I t was nearly two a.m. on a Sunday, early in September, in the Blue Ridge Mountains of North Carolina. A light rain had begun to fall on the emergency vehicles parked outside the Crawford's house in the Forest Hills neighborhood, giving the already garish pulsing blue and red lights in their yard an even more surreal quality. Inside, as a paramedic bandaged thirteen-year-old Jack's arm at the kitchen table and a female police officer with a pen and pad patiently asked him questions, the conversation in the foyer between Jack's parents, Tucker and Penny, and their neighbors, Paul and Melanie Redmond, grew heated.

"I don't understand why he won't tell them where Andy is." Mel said, her voice shaking.

"He doesn't know," Penny replied, clearly frustrated. "I know you're scared, Mel, but for the third time, he said he doesn't know. He said he didn't see Andy again after he wandered off from the fire. He just heard him..." she trailed off.

1

"Scream?" Melanie said, finishing the sentence as she dissolved in tears, burying her face in her hands.

Paul put his arm around her and shook his head. "What the hell were they doing way down there anyway? It's miles down to the river. We've told them a hundred times to stay away from that goddamn farm. And at night? Jesus!"

"Did you know they were going camping?" Mel demanded.

"Of course not," Tucker said, trying to remain cool. "He told us the same cock-and-bull story Andy told you. Jack said he was staying over at your place to play some stupid video game."

"Yeah, Andy told us he'd be over here," Paul said. "Even said you guys were making snacks for them."

Something about that made Mel sob again. "They should be out there looking for him!" she snapped. "They're wasting time!"

"Please, keep your voice down, Honey," Paul said, "They've got people ready to go, but they've got to know where to look."

"I just think Andy would never have done something so reckless on his own," Mel said, glaring at Tucker and Penny.

"That's not fair, Mel," Tucker said, his cheeks flushing. "Jack's not to blame here. We're all in pieces over this, but Jack didn't twist Andy's arm into doing anything. Andy's always the one asking if I'll take them to shoot the rifle."

As soon as he said it everything stopped, as if the air had been sucked out of the room.

Paul worked his jaw. "Damn it, Tuck, tell me they didn't have that rifle out there with them."

"Hell, no. I've got it locked in a closet in the back. I've told them both it's strictly off limits."

But even as he said it, they could see the rising fear in his eyes.

"Good Lord," Penny said, putting a hand to her mouth. "Tuck, you better go and check."

"I swear, it's locked up," Tucker said, his voice trailing off.

"Go check it," Paul said, his voice hardening. "I'll go with you."

The two men disappeared down in the hall, leaving Mel and Penny in the foyer. Mel began pacing.

"I hate those things," she said, almost to herself. "We've told Andy we don't want him anywhere near them."

"I know. I wish he'd get rid of it." Penny said, trying to be supportive. But as she watched her son talking to the officer in the next room and studied the expression on his face, she sensed that something was not right, and a deep feeling of dread crept over her. She had seen that look before.

Just then both women turned as their husbands appeared from the bedroom at the end of the hall and in an instant, the contrast in their expressions confirmed everyone's fears. Tucker was ashen and looked stricken with guilt. Paul was furious.

"It's gone," Paul said, cutting his head toward Tucker. "So much for being locked up."

Penny looked at her husband in disbelief. "Tuck?"

3

"My key is gone," he said. "He must have taken it."

Mel groaned and put her face in her hands. "Oh my God, something happened to him out there. I knew it."

Penny tried to reassure her. "Don't jump to that conclusion, just because..."

"It's his fault!" Mel growled, pointing her finger at Jack. "Can't you see that little shit is lying about what happened out there?"

"Hey!" Paul barked. "That's enough!"

Then the others waded in, and a full shouting match broke out in the foyer.

In the kitchen, the officer who had been sitting opposite Jack was just finishing up her questions and looking back over her notes as the paramedic closed up her kit.

She looked up at Jack and locked eyes with him. "Jack, I need to know that you're telling me truth about all this, and that you've told me everything."

Jack's lower lip quivered and his eyes were wide. Tears streaked his dirty cheeks.

He swallowed hard. "Yes, it's the truth. And I told you everything. I swear."

The officer put a hand on his knee. "Okay," she said. "We're going to..."

Just then, the officer broke off and looked away, obviously concerned by the rapidly escalating argument in the hall.

"I'll be right back," she said, standing up and heading in to talk to the parents.

As he watched her go, the raw fear and deep sense of shame that gripped Jack were nearly overwhelming. He had never felt more miserable and alone in his life. Partly because he knew that he would never see his best friend again, but mostly because he could not bear to think about what he had done. He knew that he had not told them everything about what really happened to Andy.

...not nearly everything.

CHAPTER 1

*C**lick-click.*

Jack Crawford bolted upright in his bed, in the semi-darkness of his room and looked at his phone. It was eleven forty-five...again. He closed his eyes for several seconds, listening, but he did not hear it again. Maybe he had not heard it at all. Maybe he had dreamed it, but mercifully, he could never remember his dreams. Maybe it had been the icemaker dropping a fresh set of cubes. Hell, it could have been anything.

Just then he realized that his sheets were soaking wet with sweat.

"Jesus," he whispered. It had been bad before, but not like this.

He rubbed his hands across his face and got out of bed, shuffling into the kitchen and pouring a class of water before sitting at his breakfast table and staring at the cardboard box that sat in the middle of it, still untouched. The box contained what few personal belongings he had had room for, as a public school teacher, in his impossibly crowded classroom. They consisted of some office supplies the school system was too cheap or too broke to provide, the remnants of his emergency pharmacy (antacids, pain relievers, and antihistamines), some lunch containers, a travel umbrella, and a pair of framed photos he had kept tucked away in his desk.

One of them was of his parents. It was the last one taken of them together, before they split up. It was the last reminder of the time before everything went to hell. The other one was the only known photo of him and Andy, taken at a cookout in the Redmond's back yard when they were eleven. They were in bathing suits, side-by-side, grinning from ear to ear, soaked from running repeatedly through a sprinkler. It hurt him every time he looked at it so he kept it in a drawer, face-down, but he owed it to Andy to keep it and to look at it now and then, as if there was any chance he could forget.

He had made it through another school year, but barely. Before the teachers left for the summer, Bob Woodall, his principal, had pulled him in for a one-on-one and had not pulled any punches. Woodall had spelled out the issues documented in his mid-year Performance Improvement Plan (the dreaded PIP) and lamented the "marginal improvement" Jack had made on several of these, including tardiness, and apparent distraction and disorganization in the classroom. When Jack had pointed out that the majority of his students had scored in the 90th percentile or higher on the mathematics portion of their PSATs,

Woodall had begrudgingly admitted that the problem was less about academic performance than about perception. There was he insisted, a perception on the part of students, their parents, and some of the faculty that Jack's behavior in the classroom was troubling and reflected poorly on the school and on him personally. Woodall had suggested that Jack take the summer and consider his options, including "getting some counseling," but he had made it clear to Jack that if he opted to return, he would be on probation with no more strikes left. If any further issues were reported, he would not allow Jack to finish out another school year.

The conversation had humiliated Jack, but he had heard it all before, more than once. At least Woodall, unlike other bosses from his disjointed and spotty work history, had not pegged him for drinking on the job. Jack had grown adept at concealing it and had mercifully maintained enough self-discipline to pull back before he became obviously physically impaired.

Rather than giving in to his urge to punch Woodall in the mouth, Jack had stiffly thanked him and promised to consider carefully what they had talked about. He heard himself promise that, should he decide to come back, there would be no further issues.

Bullshit, he thought, replaying the conversation in his mind as he got up and traded his water for a shot of vodka in a tumbler. Who was he kidding? He had no intention of going back to that school in the fall. And although Jack had not said anything to Woodall at the time, he had been in counseling for years, for all the good it had done him.

He had been through half a dozen counselors in the last twenty-three years, and few of them had lasted more than a year, most not that long. At first, Jack had lashed out at the counselors and the process itself as little more than a rote academic exercise. For most of the early years, Jack had pushed back on the idea that he even needed counseling, and each time a personal crisis had compelled him to start seeing another therapist, he had unconsciously begun looking for reasons to abandon the process. As the years progressed, however, Jack had gradually revealed more details in these sessions about the trauma surrounding the loss of his childhood friend, the dramatic unravelling of his life that followed, and the ultimate breakup of his parents, culminating in his complete estrangement from his father.

But despite the glacially slow progress he had made, he knew there was a darkness at the core of his psyche that he had never revealed to these people, no matter how sincerely they tried to help him. He knew there was a truth he had never allowed himself to reveal to anyone. One he had walled off so completely, that he would never allow himself to replay it in his waking mind, much less tell a stranger about it. The better therapists had sensed that guilt and shame were at the root of Jack's issues, but before they could steer him too close to the demons that lurked there, he would find a reason to stop attending the sessions. It had been a repeating cycle, until recently.

Until the dreams, and Millie Braxton.

He had stumbled upon Millie's name entirely by accident, six weeks earlier when he had begun having strange, frightening dreams about the past, about Andy and The Farm. Despite all his waking efforts to bury his childhood memories, the dreams had dragged him back and replayed that awful night, only with horrible embellishments that only nightmares can conjure up. He had often bolted awake at night in a cold sweat, with his chest heaving, and been unable to get back to sleep. And disturbingly, as if his nightmares and his body clock were conspiring to play a cruel joke on him, he had repeatedly awakened from the nightmares at 11:45 p.m. The same time, possibly to the minute, when it had happened that night.

Most disturbing of all had been the clicking. The unmistakable and unique double-click sound made by the cricket-clickers that he and Andy had used so often to communicate during their adventures. The small, ingeniously simple, thumb-sized device which relied on a coiled strip of metal to produce its sharp, signature click-click sound, had originally been designed for US troops in World War II to identify friend versus foe on the battlefield. After the war, what became known as the cricket-clicker, or simply the cricket, had remained popular as a training tool and a novelty, even to present times. Jack and Andy had purchased theirs at an army surplus store and had begun using a call-and-response pattern during games after dark, in an era before cell phones and GPS, to locate and identify each other. They had prized their crickets and always carried them, at least until the night his childhood ended. Jack had started to throw his away several times after Andy disappeared, but something had stopped him each time, and he had finally put it away in a shoebox of memorabilia instead, where it still remained buried somewhere in his closet.

At first the hauntingly familiar click-click noise had appeared in his dreams, but as the days had passed and the dreams had grown more intense, more terrifying, Jack had begun to doubt that the sound was part of his dreams. He had been increasingly certain that the sound was coming from somewhere in his house.

As he had so many times in his life, Jack had leaned heavily on alcohol to blunt the ragged emotions and anxiety that came from stirring up the past. But as his nightmares had become more frequent, and the booze had followed suit, he had begun slipping at work, failing to show up on time or in a couple of cases, at all, struggling to teach through a bad hangover, and often losing his train of thought in the classroom. All just as final exams and the end of the school year were in sight. But despite his personal issues, Jack had not been blind. He had seen the way his students looked at him, heard the tone of their parents' voices during parent-teacher conferences. And he had felt the sting of the disapproving glances of his fellow teachers in the lounge or in the hallways.

Just as he had felt the situation slipping beyond his control, he had overheard two women talking in the produce section of the grocery store. One was telling the other about a counselor she had been introduced to named Millie Braxton, and about how unlike other therapists she was; frumpy, somewhat disheveled, completely casual, and entirely unpretentious. She described the woman as "a uniquely genuine person," and something about that phrase piqued Jack's interest. The woman told her friend that even the therapist's house reflected an unconventional, non-conformist philosophy. In the middle of an east-coast suburban neighborhood, the woman lived and worked in a house that most closely resembled a traditional terra-cotta, adobe dwelling one might see in rural New Mexico. Rather than a grass lawn, the house was surrounded by an expansive rock garden, filled with cacti of all varieties, with a scattering of desert shrubs and grasses. She described the therapist's home as "shockingly refreshing."

The conversation had compelled Jack to do something he rarely did; approach a stranger and strike up a conversation. The woman had been reticent to engage with Jack at first, but his genuinely apologetic and sincere demeanor had been disarming enough that she was at least willing to give him one of her Millie Braxton's cards.

A week and half before his last day as a faculty member at Jefferson High, Jack had endured a wretched sleepless night that left him at wits-end. The next morning, he had called the number on Mille's card, fully expecting to get an answering service or a voicemail greeting. Instead, a woman with a husky voice and a warm, casual tone answered.

"Hello, this is Millie."

Jack had hesitated and nearly ended the call, but made himself push ahead.

"Ah, hi. My name is Jack Crawford. You were referred to me by someone, and I wanted to see if you're accepting, ah, new clients."

"Nice to speak with you, Jack," Millie said. She coughed a smoker's cough and cleared her throat. "My schedule is pretty full, but I do have a couple of open slots. Let me get my book."

She stepped away from the phone and Jack heard rustling and what sounded like a dog shaking its collar, then she was back.

"My sessions are an hour, and it looks like I have Tuesdays at four, and Fridays at eleven-thirty open. I do have a Wednesday evening slot at seven for people who can't make daytime appointments. It was booked, but I had a cancellation. Will any of those times work?"

The familiar irritation that Jack felt at the whole cycle of therapy started to creep back into his mind as she spoke, but he tried to stay focused on the nightmares and how close he had come recently to losing his tenuous grip on his job.

"If the Wednesday evening at seven slot is open, that would work best. I guess just schedule for this week and then, maybe we'll see where it goes from there?"

"Certainly, Jack. I never schedule more than an initial intake visit for new clients right out of the gate. We need a chance to get introduced, and for you to see if going forward feels like the right thing for you."

Refreshing, Jack thought. *At least she didn't push for a weekly obligation.*

"Thanks, that sounds good," Jack said. "You're off of Peace Street, on Harrison?"

"Yes, number 308. You can't miss the house. It looks like it belongs in Albuquerque." She chuckled and coughed again. "You can just park in the driveway."

Jack smiled a wry smile. *I like her already.* "Okay, great. See you on Wednesday."

His first session with Millie had immediately put Jack at ease, and the words he had overheard in the grocery store, describing her as "shockingly refreshing," could not have been more apropos. Her home did indeed look like a Navaho dwelling that had been transplanted from the New Mexico desert to suburban North Carolina, which had a surprisingly disarming effect on Jack, easing the tension and giving him a sense of being far removed from his day-to-day. She greeted him like an old friend at the door, and looked almost exactly like he had pictured her; short, heavyset, big warm smile, tussled hair, and dressed like someone who was kicking back on a lazy Saturday afternoon with a glass of wine.

Nothing about the inside of her home resembled a counseling practice. The multi-level home had a casual, lived-in, mid-century-modern décor, with a quirkily eclectic blend of Art Deco and traditional furnishings. It reminded Jack of the houses he'd seen on old 1970s TV shows, but with a southwestern flavor. Original art decorated the walls, and various colorful pottery pieces and sculptures were displayed on tables or stands. Plants of all sizes and shapes were scattered around the room, including several potted cactus gardens. The house had offset levels between some areas, and the living room had wall-to-wall bookshelves on two sides, the kind you mostly only saw in libraries. The seating area of the living room was in a rectangular area, two small steps lower on all sides than the rest of the room. It was unlike anything he had seen before, but Jack liked it. Two armchairs, a wicker chair, and a well-worn leather loveseat were spread around the seating area. A large Golden Retriever was stretched out, napping on the loveseat, and took no notice of Jack.

"That's Siggy," Millie said, flopping down in one of the armchairs. "Short for Sigmund. Just move him if you'd rather sit on the sofa."

"Sigmund," Jack repeated, grinning despite himself. "No, this is fine."

"Would you like anything to drink, Jack?" Mille said. "I'm having some mint tea."

"Ah, no, but thanks. I'm good."

In all the therapy sessions he had ever been to, Jack's hands had grown uncharacteristically cold and clammy, but as he leaned back in the leather armchair and looked at the kind, patient expression on Millie's face, he realized that his hands were warm and dry. It was a little thing, but spoke volumes.

"I guess if you were referred by one of my clients, then you're familiar with what I do?" she began.

"Yes, I think so."

"Good. Well, before we start, I should tell you that there's a reason I'm not working in a counseling practice. Probably several reasons," she chuckled. "Mostly because I don't subscribe to traditional counseling models and I believe in a more holistic approach. Unlike a lot of people in my line of work, I believe there is more to be gained by a genuine conversation between two people than by a scripted bunch of questions."

Jack nodded. "I couldn't agree more."

"Okay, with that said, tell me a little about why you called me, and what you're hoping to accomplish, if we go forward."

Suddenly, Jack felt a flood of emotion rising up from somewhere deep inside him, and a hard knot formed in his throat. Despite his best effort to hold back, he felt his eyes begin to water and his lip began to tremble. He gripped his knees tightly and tried to speak.

"It's okay, Jack," Millie said softly. "Whatever you feel and whatever you say, it's okay here. This is a safe place."

Jack nodded and took a couple of slow breaths. Then, before his formidable array of self-defense mechanisms could intervene, he looked Millie in the eye and spoke.

"Do you believe in ghosts?"

Millie studied him for a moment, then smiled. "Yes, as a matter of fact, I do."

Jack wiped his eyes with the back of his hand and leaned forward.

"I don't mean old bad memories that stay with you, although, God knows I've got a truckload. I mean actual ghosts. The kind that some people see."

Millie waited patiently for him to finish his thought.

A pain Jack had been fighting off for decades slammed into him, and he felt hot tears running down his cheeks as his voice began to tremble.

"The kind that comes out of the dark places in an old house and takes your best friend, right in front of you, while he's screaming for your help. And instead of helping him, you just run away." Jack sniffed. "That kind of ghost."

Mille looked at Jack with kind, wise eyes and an expression of infinite understanding.

"Yes, Jack, that kind."

A sense of relief washed over Jack, but he remained cautious.

"Are you bullshitting me?" he asked. "It's okay, I'd just like to know."

"No, I think you'll find I don't believe in bullshitting people. Nothing to be gained. When you get a chance, take a look at some of the books in my collection. You might be surprised at some of the titles. To say I have an open mind might be a bit of an understatement."

"Thank God," Jack said, rubbing his eyes.

Millie took a sip of her tea. "You've been carrying that around for a very long time, haven't you?"

Jack nodded. "Longer than you can imagine."

"Well, congratulations. It feels good to give yourself permission to let things out, doesn't it?"

He nodded again. "Yeah, there's so much I haven't talked about for years. So much I haven't ever talked about. Ever."

"Then maybe that's the best place to start," she said.

CHAPTER 2

His first session with Millie had, by any reasonable standard, been a breakthrough for Jack, and his sense of relief at finally bringing his tortured childhood secret out into the light had been indescribable, but the peace it brought him was short-lived. The day after he thanked Millie and asked her to book him for a weekly Wednesday evening session, Jack experienced a frightening escalation of incidents relating to his past, to The Farm and Andy. The nightmares grew more frequent and more intense, with images so jarring that they carried into his waking mind, and the cricket-clicker was almost always there, with a new urgency, as if demanding a response from him. Several times during the day, as he went about chores and errands, he had been startled by what he was certain was the sound of the cricket. Only it seemed louder and closer than before.

But most disturbing of all, Jack had seen a faint, blurry shape, roughly resembling that of a person, in two photos he had taken of his living room. The first time, he had thought it might be dirt on the camera lens, but the shape had appeared again after he carefully cleaned the lens. When Jack had opened the photo app and looked through his phone he saw nothing but the room, but when he had taken the photo and opened it from his library, the hair had gone stiff on his arms. The shape was there again, only it had moved from the corner of the room to a position by the arm of his sofa, closer to where he was standing.

Jack had felt a creeping suspicion that by opening the long-locked door to his dark past, he had released something terrifying into the present; something that didn't belong there. His trips to the liquor cabinet had become so frequent that he stopped putting the bottles back at all, leaving them instead in disarray on the kitchen counter. *Easy access.*

Through it all, by some miracle, Jack had made it through the end of the school year, albeit barely and in a blur of caffeine and booze. It had been ugly and he had been reprimanded but he had done it. During that week he had tried twice to see Millie again on an emergency basis, but her schedule had been fully booked. She had been apologetic but up-front about her policy of not seeing clients on an ad-hoc basis. She had explained that working out of her home, it was the only way to ensure some separation between her personal and professional lives.

It was still dark outside on Tuesday morning, and after an-other rough night, Jack shuffled into his kitchen and turned on the coffee maker, massaging his irritated eyes with his fingertips. Though he felt weary and emotionally bruised from recent events, he was deeply grateful that the school year had ended when it did. On top of work pressures, the anxiety and exhaustion of dealing with his past had pushed him to the edge. Now, without the usual burden of lesson plans, teaching six classes a day, and endless hours of grading papers, he might have a fighting chance. Fortunately, he had elected to have his paycheck spread over twelve months, rather than just the nine months that made up the school year, and while that left him with less each month, it meant he did not have to take summer work. That would leave him mercifully free to focus on confronting whatever was happening to him, and hopefully, with Millie's help, find something resembling a solution.

One more day, he thought. *Tomorrow is Wednesday.*

The trashcan under the sink was overflowing, and after stuffing it down with his foot and tying the drawstring, he turned on the floodlight and carried it out the back door, to the large rolling bin at the back of his driveway. He lifted the lid and threw it in, and as he turned and started toward the house...

Click-click.

Jack froze in his tracks. The sound had come from behind him, and it was close. Very close. The hair on his neck stiffened and he felt a cold sweat break out on his forehead.

Click-click. Again.

Despite his fear, Jack braced himself and turned around, fully expecting to see Andy, or some terrible thing resembling Andy,

21

standing behind him holding the cricket in one rotting hand. Instead, he saw only the wooden enclosure and the top of the bins that it concealed.

Click-click.

The sound was coming from behind the enclosure, in the darkness where the floodlight could not reach. Jack gritted his teeth and felt a tremor in his arms.

He took a small step toward the enclosure.

Click-click.

He stopped again and licked the sweat off his lip.

"Hello," he said quietly. "Is someone there?"

He waited several seconds in silence. There was no response. Only the chirring of the crickets all around him.

He turned around again, wondering if he could be losing his mind.

Click-click.

A rush of fear coursed through Jack and he walked faster away from the bins, toward the lighted house.

Click-click.

Jack bounded up the steps and back into the kitchen as his fear and frustration boiled over and he rummaged through the junk drawer until he found the Maglite flashlight he kept there. He turned and walked back out the door and down the steps.

Click-click.

Click-click.

The clicks were coming faster now, more urgently.

Click-click.

Pushed beyond the point of caring, he hurried across the driveway and around the wooden enclosure.

Click-click.

He shone the bright light into the dark area behind the fencing, ready to swing it like a club if necessary, but there was nothing there. The concrete ended and gave way to a narrow strip of woods that separated his driveway from the neighbor's yard.

Still tense, Jack swept the flashlight around the whole area, but there was nothing out of the ordinary. Confident that he had not imagined the sound, Jack had an idea. The one way he could know for sure. He went back to the house and down the hall, to the closet in the spare room, turning on lights as he went. At the back of the closet, behind the shoes and stacks of old work papers, Jack found the shoebox with a faded Converse logo on it. The one he knew contained the few items he had kept from his childhood. Seeing the painfully familiar contents of the box, Jack felt another flood of emotion. There was his shark's head PEZ dispenser, some arcade tokens and miscellaneous old coins, including a buffalo nickel and some wheat pennies. There were several arrowheads he and Andy had found at The Farm, as well his pea shooter, a cap gun, and a scattering of baseball cards. There were also folded and yellowed newspaper clippings that Jack had no need to examine. He knew all too well what they contained. Some were covering Andy's disappearance and the investigation, and others covered the Juvenile Court hearing that followed, to determine if Jack should be charged with murder. Perhaps morbidly, he had also kept the wrist-band from the hospital, when he had attempted suicide, nearly a year after Andy disappeared. Under the newspaper clippings, he found the cricket. The metal on the small rectangular device had a mottled patina of oxidation, and the oval, thumb-shaped depression in its top, which triggered its signature sound, had been worn bare from so much use during those early years.

It felt odd in Andy's adult hand, but he put the box down and hurried with it through the kitchen to the back door. He opened the door and looked out across the driveway, to the trash enclosure.

He held the cricket out in front of him and pressed the button.

Click-click.

The noise was louder than he remembered.

Pushing back the objections of his rational mind, Jack held his breath and waited for a response.

Click-click.

Jack went rigid and whirled around, his blood turning to ice. The response had come, but not from the darkness at the back of the driveway. It had come from behind him, in his house.

"Fuck this," Jack said, looking at his jacket on the peg by the door, and his car keys and wallet on the end of the counter. He hurriedly grabbed all three and went out the back door, locking it behind him. *Like it matters*, he thought darkly. As he climbed in his car and backed out of the driveway, he did not know where he would go, but it would be anywhere but there. Even if he had to drive around until the sun came up, it would be a small price to pay. One thing was clear; whatever this was, it was coming to a head.

Half an hour later, as the sun was beginning to brighten the horizon over the east side of town, Jack sat in his car at the back of a McDonald's parking lot, drinking a large hot coffee and trying to decide what the hell was happening to him. Maybe there was some truth to the old cliché about the past always catching up with you. It felt like he had spent half of his life trying to outrun it. All he had ever wanted was for it to stay in the past; to leave him alone and let him have a life. But the harder he had tried to build one, the more the past had crept in like water into the foundation of house. It didn't take much, but given enough time, cracks would form and the house would collapse. Jack took another sip of his coffee as he watched the growing line of cars in the drive-thru, and marveled at the trail of wreckage he had already left in the wake of his relatively short life; more jobs than most people twice his age would ever have, four badly failed relationships, including one engagement, and a half dozen more cringe-worthy misadventures in the online dating scene.

Who had he been kidding?

The jarring events of the last few weeks along with his conversation with Millie had finally convinced him that, one way or the other, the past would have to be reconned with. And while he had always chalked his occasional nightmares up to the normal venting of subconscious pressure, like steam escaping from a volcano, this was something else. Most people would have assumed they were hallucinating; that the pressure had become too great, pushing their mind over an invisible edge into the early stages of psychosis. But he was not most people.

For him, belief in the supernatural world was not an abstract idea, a hypothetical musing based on what he wanted to be true. He may have only been thirteen, but he had seen it up close, there in the darkness, and watched it take his friend. There was nothing hypothetical about it for Jack. Not believing was not an option, nor could he blame it on psychosis. He had to accept that whatever was happening was real, but that left the frightening question of what he was dealing with. Was it a ghost? Was it Andy's ghost, or something much worse?

It was then, as Jack pondered possible answers to the question, that he realized he had never allowed himself to think about, much less articulate, the most disturbing thing of all. He had assumed all these years that Andy had died that night; that whatever dark thing had been living in that hole in the wall had killed him. But as Jack stared at the stray coffee grounds in the bottom of his now-empty cup, he realized that nobody had ever proven that. Andy's body had never been found. After nearly a year, they had declared him "presumed dead" and held a memorial service, after which they had buried an empty casket in Oakmont Cemetery, beneath a headstone that read, "Beloved Son, Gone Too Soon."

But now Jack wondered. Hearing the cricket-clicker, just like when they were kids, made him wonder, maybe for the first time whether Andy had died at all that night. The possible implications made his skin crawl.

If he didn't die, what happened to him? Where has he been all these years? And what if he's not Andy anymore? If he's not, what is he?

The sun was fully up now, and Jack shook off the chill that was settling over him as he started his car.

One more day.

The following evening, Millie asked Jack to sit in the reclining armchair, explaining that she was going to have him try some relaxation techniques and then guide him through a free-association memory exercise. This would, she said, not be a question and answer session. Jack would be the narrator and there would be no judgement and no interruptions, save Millie telling him when they needed to wrap up.

She turned off most of the room lights and dimmed the one remaining lamp, then asked Jack to close his eyes. There was a faint but pleasant smell of essential oils, patchouli and lavender, and the gentle babbling of a table-top water fountain somewhere close-by. And there was Millie's voice walking him through relaxation of the muscles in his face and head, his neck and shoulders, and continuing all the way to the soles of his feet and his toes. Jack had never felt so relaxed.

"Now," she said, in the same quiet, calm voice. "With eyes still closed, staying fully relaxed and safe, I want you to take me back to those days with Andy, and your time at The Farm. Let your mind see your surroundings, and hear the sounds. Let your mind remember everything. Describe it to me as we go. If you're not comfortable, we can stop at any time. Does that sound okay, Jack?"

Jack nodded.

"Okay," she said. "Start wherever you like."

And in his relaxed state, Jack let himself begin drifting back into the recesses of his memory, to the fall of his thirteenth year. Slowly, images and sounds began to fill his mind and Jack knew beyond a doubt that he *did* remember.

He remembered everything.

CHAPTER 3

As afternoon turned to evening in the Blue Ridge Mountains, a thin veil of clouds muted the fading light in the western sky, leaving a pale glow over the high ridges that surrounded the remote river valley. Autumn had come, and the lush hardwood forests that usually blanketed the rolling mountains had shed their brightly painted leaves and now stood like an endless sea of skeleton soldiers, their bony arms reaching skyward and rustling in the easterly breeze.

Andy and Jack had cobbled together a small fire in the wide flat area by the river and tried to make jokes as they sat by their packs and finished the last of their Twinkies and Kool-Aid. Occasionally they sneaked uneasy glances up the hill behind them, to the darkened frameless windows of the old abandoned house and the dilapidated outbuildings that made up the rest of The Farm. They had been best friends since elementary school but they were officially teenagers now, and neither one of them dared admit to the other that they were scared or that they were having second thoughts about their mutual dare.

It was a meandering two-hour hike from their neighborhood to the valley, but they had made it many times and spent entire afternoons exploring there, hunting Indian arrow heads in the rich soil that carpeted the fields on either side of the river and shooting rusty cans on old fence posts with Jack's father's twenty-two caliber rifle. They had even summoned the courage to go into the old shell of a house that remained, cautiously inspecting its rooms, wondering who might have lived there and what had happened to them. Mostly they had speculated about what a farm would be doing there in the first place, in such an isolated valley, with no access by road and no other civilization for miles in any direction.

Even on sunny blue-sky days, there had always been something strange about the silence and stillness that permeated the valley. There was an air of melancholy about The Farm itself, unlike any other place the boys knew. Whenever they wandered too close to the house or among the outbuildings and the groves of trees that now grew around them, the boys had an uneasy feeling that made the hair on their arms stand up; a feeling that they were not alone. It was as if they were intruding in a private place where they didn't belong. Neither of them had said it, but they both had a sense that The Farm did not want them there.

They had joked many times that they should camp out in the valley, and on several occasions, Andy had suggested that they spend the night in the old house; "the whole night," he would say. Jack had always said he was full of shit, accusing him of big talk and of being too chicken. But even the idea of it had frightened Jack, and he was always glad to change the subject.

But the morning Jack's father had slapped him for saying "the F-word," he had cried bitterly in his room and had taken it out on Andy at school. When Andy had said that the upcoming weekend would be a perfect time to camp out in the valley and had suggested yet again that they try to spend the night in the house, Jack had turned on him. He had called Andy a pussy and said he was too chicken-shit to spend the night in the house. Jack had dared his friend to do it.

The wounded expression on Andy's face felt like a knife to Jack's gut, but he was too angry to back down, and he watched Andy's disbelief turn to anger.

"Fuck you," Andy had said. "I'll do it. But I don't think you will. I think you're the one who's chicken. I dare you back. This Friday night. Mom and Dad are going to some party and they won't care as long as I tell them I'm staying at your place. Then we'll see who's a pussy."

Before Jack could even think, he had blurted out, "You're on. But you'll be the one running out of that house, back to mama's titty."

He had been shocked at himself but too proud to take it back, and Andy had stormed off. They had not spoken all the following day, but late that afternoon resentments had faded and they were talking again about preparations for their camping trip, despite the fact that both boys secretly dreaded the implications of the dare.

Now, as Jack poked the coals of their small fire with a crooked stick, they saw the first fireflies begin to blink on and off around them across the field.

Andy spoke first. "I guess we better get up there before it gets any darker."

"Yep," Jack said, still looking at the fire. But his gut was in knots. Every time he looked at the dark frameless windows of the abandoned house, they looked like hollow eyes watching him. He could almost feel a presence in the house waiting for them.

"You ready for this, Bro?" Andy said, standing up and putting his supplies back in his pack.

Jack felt his resolve crumbling, but didn't want Andy to see. As he half-heartedly got his supplies together, he tried to think of a reason to back out, but after the things he had said to Andy he couldn't.

"Let's do this," he heard himself say.

"You got plenty of shells for that rifle?" Andy asked, nodding in the direction of the twenty-two. "We might have to shoot-a-bitch." Neither of them laughed at the joke.

As they made their way up the rocky path from the river toward The Farm, the house and the surrounding outbuildings were already beginning to fall into shadow. Jack felt his mouth going dry and his tongue sticking to the roof of his mouth.

"Deena knows about this," Andy said, as they neared the crumbling front porch of the house.

"Are you serious?" Jack said.

Jack had always found Andy's younger sister Deena cute, but annoying. She was two years behind Andy, and would badger them to be included in whatever they were doing, but Andy was constantly brushing her off, sometimes cruelly so.

"Yeah, she heard us on the phone. Asked me if she could come along. Can you believe that? She would have pissed herself."

"You know she's going to tell your mom."

"I don't think so. I lied and told her we were planning another trip in a few weeks, and if she'd keep her mouth shut, she could come along on that one."

"Did she go for it?"

"Oh yeah, she..."

Just then a familiar groaning sound came from the old house and both boys looked up at the ancient tin roof. They knew the sound by now, but had never gotten used to it. As the breeze rustled the pale white birch trees clustered around The Farm, the tips of their bony branches raked across the rusty metal roofs of the buildings and produced a steady chorus of blood chilling sounds, from scratching and creaking, to long agonizing groans and even an occasional high-pitched scream.

It was nearly enough to send Jack in the other direction, back to the relative safety of the fire.

Instead, they continued into the house, skirting the wrecked steps and the holes in the porch boards before stepping through the doorway. The front door had apparently fallen off years earlier, and lay in the grass in front of the porch. There was no furniture in the house and the walls were cracked and mottled, mostly bare, with patchy remnants of faded floral wallpaper. Even though the doors and windows in the two-story house had long ago been stripped of frames and glass and reduced to open holes in the walls, the breeze outside never made it into the house. The air there was still and musty.

Andy turned on his flashlight and pulled the small lantern out of his pack, as Jack set his pack and the rifle down in the middle of what was once the living room.

"This is some shit, isn't it?" Andy said.

"Yeah, pretty hard-core." Jack replied, but he could not muster a smile.

As the glow from Andy's lantern bathed the room in yellow, they rolled out their sleeping bags on the floor and sat down on them. Darkness was falling across the valley, and as the crickets' chorus filled the night air, they could barely see the white trunks of the birches outside. Doorways on two walls of the living room led to what would have been a kitchen and a bedroom, both now empty and dark, with only boards, shards of dirty glass, and old rusty scraps of metal scattered on the floor. The lantern's light did not reach into these empty spaces that flanked the room, and Jack could not keep his mind from conjuring images of what might be hiding in there.

Andy pulled out a couple of cans of Mountain Dew and gave one to Jack.

"Hey, why don't we go check it out?" Andy said, waving the flashlight around them.

Jack felt his stomach clench.

"I don't know," he shrugged, trying to appear casual. "We're here, aren't we? What's the point?"

"Awe, come on," Andy said, egging him on. "Hey check this out. I'm armed. I snuck it out of my dad's closet."

He reached into his pack and pulled out a metal tomahawk with a leather handle. One side of the head was a traditional blade, but the other was a wicked diamond shaped point, honed to a razor's edge.

"Damn," Jack said, and let out a breathy whistle.

"My dad got it from one of his buddies who was in Vietnam. It's a combat tomahawk, but the modern kind. The guy told my dad that this spike would go right through a metal helmet and straight into a guy's brain. Killed 'em dead."

"Jesus," Jack said.

Andy took a long swig of his Mountain Dew and grinned. "I'm going. You can stay here if you want."

He set his drink down and picked up the flashlight. With the light in one hand and the tomahawk in the other, he started into the adjoining room, scanning the floor and walls as he went.

"Yeah, okay," Jack said feebly, forcing himself to stand and follow Andy, turning on his own light as they went. He could hear Andy's feet crunching the bits of wood and glass ahead of him.

"Nothing in here," Andy said, standing in the middle of the room and holding out his arms. "How about the bedroom?"

"It's just an empty room," Jack said, but followed along, spinning around every few steps and shining his light behind them as they moved through another doorway and into the other room.

"All clear down here," Andy said, turning and heading back to their makeshift camp.

For a moment, Jack felt a wave of relief, but then he saw Andy look at the stairs, and knew in an instant what he was thinking.

"Come on, Andy," Jack pleaded. "Don't go up there."

"You dare me?" Andy had a wild look in his eyes, as if he didn't give a shit, and Jack was shaking.

"No, I don't dare you. You can't see shit up there, even with a flashlight. We've never been in the attic."

"So?" Andy said, pointing his light up the dilapidated steps and into the darkness above.

What they called "the attic" was actually a jagged four-foot-wide hole in the back wall of the large upstairs room, that stretched from floor to the ceiling. It was one of the most disturbing anomalies of the house, because the hole was not a doorway. It appeared that something many years earlier, had broken through the wall. And though they had never ventured into the darkness beyond, they could make out a large, empty space with what looked like strange graffiti on the walls. It was as if someone had sealed off a large, perfectly usable portion of the upstairs. But what had always frightened them the most about the attic, was the scattering of ragged plaster and wood in the floor of the room, as if something had broken out...from behind the wall.

"I'm not going," Jack said, turning and taking a step back toward the sleeping bags. "Don't go. It's stupid."

Andy made a low clucking noise and grinned at Jack. "Who's chicken now?"

"I don't care," Jack said, resigning himself to defeat. "You go."

As Andy shrugged and started up the stairs, gingerly stepping around the few broken boards, Jack reached into his pocket and took out his cricket.

"Hey," he said, and pressed the button. *Click-click.*

Andy stopped and took his out of his pocked. He clicked a response, then continued to the top of the steps and out of sight. Jack could hear his footsteps on the ceiling above him, crossing the room, then silence. After a few moments, Jack's fear welled up and he clicked the cricket. A couple of seconds later, he heard a muted *click-click* from above him and felt his fear ease, but only slightly.

"All clear here," he heard Andy shout. "Come on up."

Jack licked his lips and shone his light up the steps, then started up. The wind outside had picked up and as he emerged into the upstairs, the screeching and groaning noises of the dead branches on the tin roof above them was amplified by the empty space, and echoed all around them. Jack felt his heart pounding in his chest as he shone his light through the gloom to the back wall, where Andy stood waiting for him in front of the gaping black maw of the attic.

"Come away from there," Jack said, almost whispering. His hand was trembling as he tried to keep his light trained on Andy.

"It's cool," Andy said, holding one hand out beside him. "Nothing to..."

A loud bang on the roof made both boys flinch and duck. Jack cried out.

They exchanged glances, then Andy laughed. "That scared the shit out of me. Must have been something falling on the..."

Jack stopped hearing Andy and his eyes grew wide as they fixed on something emerging quickly from the darkness of the attic, behind his friend. Jack tried to cry out but his voice caught in his throat as his mouth gaped. He couldn't breathe. A pale white face with dead eyes and skin that looked like the belly of a fish moved up behind Andy and reached for him with two bony white arms and skeleton fingers.

Andy froze and went silent, alarmed at the look on Jack's face.

Jack felt his knees buckling as the thing in the attic grabbed Andy around the chest and throat. In the beam of Jack's light, Andy screamed and thrashed to get away.

But Jack was paralyzed with fear and could not move, his mind unable to grasp what was happening.

As the dead white thing pulled Andy backward, into the inky darkness, he screamed Jack's name over and over, begging him for help. Instead, Jack turned and bolted in sheer terror, struggling to breath. He jumped halfway down the aging steps, barely missing a hole, and sprinted out the front door of the house into the night, as Andy's agonizing screams echoed behind him.

Jack ran like a wild animal away from the house, tears running down his face, straining to see by the light of a half-moon as he tore through tree branches and briars. The image of Andy's face contorted with fear, screaming for help with one hand outstretched, was burned into his mind. When he reached the fence-line that marked the edge of The Farm, he stopped and doubled over, his breath coming in great gasps as the first wave of guilt hit him like a freight train. What had he done?

"Oh my God," Jack groaned as he looked back toward the house.

All the windows were dark, except one. There was a glow from one upstairs window, the one closest to the attic. A sob escaped Jack's throat and he shook all over as he thought about

Andy's flashlight. Andy had dropped it and it had rolled across the floor.

His mind was racing now. What had just happened? What was that God-awful thing? What should he do? Maybe he could go for help. But it was dark and his house was miles away. It would be hours before he could get anyone. By then it would be too late.

Briefly he thought about going back, but quickly abandoned the idea. He had left all his things, all Andy's things, even the rifle, but what did it matter? Andy was gone. He cried bitterly at the thought of it.

On impulse, Jack pulled his cricket out of his pocket, and in a shaking hand, held it out and pointed it at the house. *Click-click.*

A moment passed, but there was no response. Then the light in the upstairs window went suddenly dark.

A whimper escaped Jack's throat and he turned and ran.

In the quiet of Millie's living room, she handed Jack a Kleenex and watched him with kind eyes as he sat up in the recliner.

"How are you feeling?" she asked.

Jack wiped his eyes and shook his head. "I don't even know. Like a douchebag, a coward."

"You know that you were only thirteen, right?" she said.

"I know, but who does that?" he said, looking at his hands as he balled up the tissue. "What kind of an asshole just leaves his best friend to..." He trailed off.

She let him sit with his thoughts for a moment.

"Is this the first time you've talked about what really happened?"

He nodded. "Yeah. It is. In twenty-three years."

"Why do you think that is?"

Jack shrugged, "I couldn't bring myself to tell everyone what I'd done, especially his parents and his sister, Deena. I hated myself for it. And I knew they would call me crazy and say I was lying. I never have told anyone until now. So, I just made up a story that he wandered away from our campfire and never came back. I said that I heard him scream from somewhere far away, but I could never find him. I told that bullshit story so many times that I almost started to believe it."

"Under the circumstances, maybe that was understandable," Mille said.

He chuckled darkly and looked up at Millie. "But you know what the hell of it is?"

"What?"

"Most people never believed my story anyway, even the made-up one. Andy's parents were convinced that he had been killed with my dad's rifle, and that I had either done it, or was lying to cover up some kind of stupid accident. They even tried to have me criminally charged with Andy's murder."

41

"That must have been awful at that age."

"Awful doesn't even begin to describe it," Jack said. "But that's a story for another time."

Millie smiled. "We are nearly at the end of our time, but you should be proud of what you accomplished here tonight. What you did took courage."

Jack raised his eyebrows. "Courage? Maybe not the best choice of words. But thanks. It did feel good to say it."

"Courage is appropriate, I think," she said. "When you wall something off for that long, it takes an act of courage to tear down the wall."

"Maybe so," he said, standing up and getting his jacket.

"We'll talk more next week, but I would like to ask," Millie said, standing with him. "What do you think you saw in the dark that night?"

A chill crept down Jack's spine as he slipped his jacket over his shoulders.

"I wish I could tell you." He said. "I thought about it for years, but there were never any answers. Maybe the devil? Maybe some kind of ghost or malevolent demon, who the hell knows? Nothing I was willing to go around talking about."

"And what do you think has brought all of this up, after all these years?" she mused.

"Andy," Jack said, smiling darkly and turning to the door. "I don't know how, but I think he's come back."

CHAPTER 4

That night, for the first time in weeks, Jack did not reach for a bottle.

He felt as if he had been wrung out, like a dirty dishrag, but he also felt a deeper sense of relief than he could remember. His whole life, Jack had heard people throw around the word "catharsis," but he had never been able to relate. Maybe this was what they meant. Whatever the case, he didn't want to blunt the powerful, but oddly peaceful mix of emotions with alcohol.

As he stood at the sink in his boxers and a t-shirt, pouring a glass of water, Jack looked out at the parking lot and the dumpster at the back, and felt the chill again as he wondered about Andy; not the laughing, joking Andy from when they were kids, but whatever version of Andy had begun showing up in his dreams and his life, wreaking havoc with his sanity.

Despite what he had accomplished with Millie that night, the discussion had not answered his most troubling and urgent questions: was he being haunted by a ghost as retribution for what he did? If so, was it really Andy, or something else, maybe something darker and more sinister? If it was Andy, and he wasn't there to exact revenge, why was he showing up now? Why had he waited twenty-three years? Was it possible that Andy was trying to communicate with him? If so, why?

But apart from the other questions, his discussion with Millie had resurrected the most disturbing unanswered question of all. It was the one Jack had been most afraid to face—the one that had made him build such an impenetrable wall in the first place. What was it that he had seen that night at the farm, in the darkness behind the shattered upstairs wall? What was the thing with the dead white face that took Andy?

Perhaps he had made himself bury it, but now, as he stood in his kitchen, looking out at the night and wondering when he would see or hear Andy again, he remembered that on the morning after that awful night, he had promised himself and whatever forces in the universe might be watching, that one day he would find out.

Click-click.

Jack sat up in bed, feeling groggy and thick headed, but he knew he had heard it. It had come from the living room. He crawled out of bed and shuffled to the door of his bedroom, staining to see if anyone was there, but it was as if a fog had settled in his house.

"Andy?" Jack said. His voice sounded oddly hollow. "Andy, are you there?"

Click-click.

It was closer, but Jack could not see.

Then something moved in the fog.

Jack looked down and realized that he had the cricket in his hand. He held it up and pointed it at the living room.

Click-click.

There was no response. The fog was drifting across the floor and onto his bare feet and he felt a chill. He stepped into his living room and walked toward the kitchen through the fog. When he reached the sink, he heard something move behind him.

Click-click.

Jack turned and Andy was there; thirteen-year-old Andy. But his skin was a pale bluish-grey, and his eyes were cloudy white, with wide, dark circles around them. His mouth was crudely sewn shut, with some kind of ragged string, and dried blood had clotted around the threads. He looked pleadingly at Jack with wide eyes and held out his hand. In it, Jack saw a small glass bead with multi-colored, zig-zag stripes around it.

"What is it?" Jack asked softly.

Andy nodded at the bead and pushed his hand toward Jack.

As Jack reached for it and picked it up in his fingers to inspect it, something dark moved, like a trap-door spider, out of the fog behind Andy and grabbed him, disappearing the way it had come and pulling him with it.

Jack screamed and sat up in bed, shaking all over and dripping with sweat. The clock said eleven-forty five.

"Jesus, Christ," he said, cradling his face in his hand as his heart pounded in his chest.

He looked around his darkened bedroom, half expecting to see Andy there.

"What do you want from me?" he groaned.

This time, there was no response.

Jack slid to the side of the bed and turned on the lamp. He squinted against the light and looked down at his phone, then froze.

For a moment he didn't grasp what he was seeing. His heart skipped a beat, then began racing. Beside his phone, he saw a brightly colored glass bead. The one from his dream. Still disoriented, he struggled to wake up and remember. Had he absentmindedly picked up the bead somewhere the day before and dropped it into his pocket? Maybe from the parking lot of the gas station when he stopped to tank up on his way home? If he had seen the bead before going to sleep, his subconscious could have woven it, along with all his recent thoughts of Andy, into the hellish nightmare.

No, that was not right. He blinked and stared again at his phone, and at the bead. He distinctly remembered looking down at the phone just before bed because he heard the ding of a pop-up news alert. In his mind, he could still see the phone lying on the table. There had been nothing beside it. Apart from the phone and the lamp, the table had been bare.

No, the bead had not been there.

Briefly, Jack wondered if someone could have come into his house in the night, but quickly dismissed the idea. He always locked the doors, and if someone *had* broken in, the last thing on their to-do list would have been leaving a memento on his bedside table.

That only left one explanation and it scared the hell out of him, partly because if it was true, then whatever remained of Andy had somehow reached into the real world—into his world. But also, because it was clear in his dream that as gruesome and shocking as Andy's appearance had been, he had not come to harm Jack. Rather, he had been trying desperately to communicate with Jack, and tell him something important.

Jack reached slowly for the bead, but stopped his hand inches from it and hesitated. A deep foreboding came over him and he had a sense that, not only was the bead significant in ways he could not yet understand, but that by taking it he was making a commitment. He was making a promise to Andy to go wherever it took him—to do whatever was required. And while he had no idea what that journey might involve, he was darkly certain where it would eventually lead: back to The Farm, where it all began. He shuddered at the thought.

What if he did go back and couldn't cope with what he found there? What if all of this was a trap, a trick to get him to open a door that was never supposed to be opened? His instincts told him he was right to be afraid, that there was real danger down that road. But at the same time, he felt that this was a second chance to do the one thing he had failed so miserably to do as a kid—to help Andy.

This time, come hell or high water, he wasn't going to run.

"Okay, Andy," Jack said quietly, as he picked up the bead. "I'm in."

By some miracle, after splashing water on his face and crawling back in bed, Jack had been able to get back to sleep for a few hours. Now, he sat at the kitchen table with a cup of coffee and his laptop, holding the unusual glass bead up to the light and rolling it slowly around in his fingers. His first impression was that it was handmade and very old. He wanted to clean it to get a better look through his magnifying glass, and as he carefully wiped it with a wet cloth, he realized that it had a thin layer of dirt caked on it in places. It was not like the dust that would accumulate on an object that sat forgotten in storage for years. This was dirt, dark dirt, like you would find in a forest or a farm field. No, Jack thought, this bead had been buried somewhere at one time. But where? And why had it been so important to Andy that he have it?

Jack retrieved his old-school, Sherlock Holmes-style magnifying glass from the desk drawer and carefully inspected the bead. There was nothing obviously significant about. It was undeniably beautiful and expertly crafted, with colors that were still vibrant despite its apparent age. He was no craft jewelry expert, but his ex-fiancée had been an enthusiast, and had taken him through countless galleries and shops. He did not remember ever seeing anything like it.

On a chance, he took a closeup photo of it and loaded it into a Google image search. A dozen hits came back immediately, with images that were remarkably similar to his bead, only with subtle variations in pattern, color combinations, and density of stripes, but all clearly identifiable as belonging to the same style. According to the referenced articles, they were called chevron Beads, and if the one he held was an original, it was far older than he had imagined and extremely rare. An article by the Fernbank Museum in Atlanta, Georgia said that the beads were first produced in Venice in the late fourteenth century. Crafted by artisans, they were made from many-layered rods of colored glass that were sliced into uniform segments and shaped using a fiercely guarded and long-secret process that produced their unique patterns. The beads were so valuable, that they were later used as the primary trading currency of Spanish explorers with the Native American tribes in the southeastern United States in the 1500s.

It had been widely accepted by historians and archaeologists of the last century that Spanish explorers such as Hernando De Soto had traveled through the southeastern states, but for decades there had been no definitive means of knowing exactly where they had been and which groups of Native Americans they had interacted with. Over time, chevron beads were discovered at a growing number of Chockowan settlements excavated across the southern states, with a strong concentration in the Blue Ridge Mountains of western North Carolina. They would eventually become such a reliable indicator that Hernando De Soto had visited a particular location, that they became known as "De Soto's calling card."

As Jack read, glancing now and again at his own chevron bead, a small light began to glow in the back of his mind. Even as kids, he and Andy had known that Randall County had been home to a large number of Chockowan Indians in the past. That was why arrowheads, spearpoints, and pottery shards were so plentiful in some of the river valleys and farms in the area. Jack thought again about the arrowheads he had collected with Andy on The Farm and wondered about the bead. Had it come from The Farm as well? Or maybe from the neighboring fields? If so, then according to the museum article, it would mean that Hernando De Soto's expedition visited the valley in the 1500s. It was an amazing idea to think about; Spanish conquistadores with their armor, muskets, and horses camping alongside a large, thriving Chockowan settlement, all in the same place where he and Andy had played as kids.

But somehow, Jack knew there was more to it than that. There was a reason it was so important to Andy, and he had to know what it was.

Jack's phone startled him out of his thoughts and he cringed when he saw "Mom" on the display. Like most times she called, he was struck by the sudden inevitable wave of sadness he felt seeing her name. He loved her in his own way, but he secretly dreaded the uncomfortable blend of guilt and sentimentality that he felt talking to her. He had always known she loved him and supported him in whatever ways she could, but like his relationship with his father, Jack's relationship with her had been forever changed by the ordeal their family had endured during what he now thought of as, "the dark time." His parents' fighting had steadily escalated after the incident with Andy, and when he had been a Sophomore at Randall High School his parents had separated and later divorced, largely because of his father's drunken and abusive behavior. It had culminated that year in his mother throwing his father out of the house and taking out a restraining order against him. Tucker Crawford had broken off all contact with his family after the divorce, save for a monthly child support payment, and Jack never saw him again. After Jack graduated from high school, his mother had bought a condo and moved to the nearby mountain town of Blowing Rock.

Four years later, after graduating from Appalachian State University in Boone, Jack had moved halfway across North

Carolina to get away from Benton and all things related to his childhood. And the older he had gotten, the more painful he found associations with the past. Sadly, that had included his mother. Even though his relationship with her had survived relatively intact, his feelings towards her were complicated and he found himself reflexively letting her calls roll to voicemail more often than not.

This time however, something prompted him to take the call.

"Hi Mom," Jack said, trying half-heartedly to sound upbeat.

"Hi Jack," his mother said. She had been crying.

Suddenly alert, Jack sat up in his chair.

"Mom, what is it? What's wrong?"

She sniffed and cleared her throat. "I got an email yesterday that Mel Redmond passed away on Wednesday."

"Oh, no. I'm so sorry to hear that," he heard himself say, a little too mechanically. The truth was, Jack was shocked but oddly not surprised by the news, and in his heart-of-hearts, he felt nothing at her passing. Of all the people in both his and Andy's families, Andy's mother, Melanie, had been the most profoundly changed by the tragedy. She and Jack's mother had been as close as sisters in the years leading up to the incident, but like so many other things, their friendship had turned sour in a matter of a few short hours on the night Andy disappeared. Mel Redmond had blamed Jack right out of the gate for what happened, at first implying that he was somehow involved, and later accusing him directly of murdering their son. She had even blamed Jack's mom and dad for negligence where the rifle was concerned and she demanded that the local District Attorney charge Jack with Andy's murder. In the interest of fairness, a judge had ordered a hearing in juvenile court to determine if there was probable cause to bring criminal charges, but when it had become clear that there was a complete lack of evidence that a crime had been committed, particularly a murder, the case had been quietly dismissed. Mel Redmond had remained outraged and broken over the incident, sliding into worsening depression over the years and from what Jack had understood, into heavy-duty prescription medications and alcohol to dull the pain. Sadly, it had taken a civil action to stop her from leveling accusations against Jack and his parents online in later years.

As an adult, Jack had come to understand how desperately a grieving parent who has lost a child needs someone to blame, whether that person is responsible or not, and in Mel Redmond's case, that had been Jack. Their families had broken off contact as well, apart from what was necessary to navigate the legal action, and that had been mostly through attorneys. Jack had felt sorry for Andy's sister Deena during the whole ordeal. Probably as a self-defense mechanism, she had become withdrawn and detached from the entire incident. He had rarely seen her after that night, but she had avoided eye-contact with him at school and Jack remembered thinking that she looked sad and ashamed, much like he felt at the time.

Hearing about the death of Mel, Jack could not help wondering where Deena had ended up, and how close she had been to her mom.

"What happened?" Jack asked.

There was a pause.

"Mom?" Jack said.

"The article said it was an accidental overdosed, but someone else told me it was suicide."

"Damn, that's awful," Jack said, again somehow not surprised. "Did she still live in town?"

"Yeah, she moved to those condos out on Greenway Road a few years after she and Paul split up, and she has been there ever since."

"Where did Deena end up?"

"I haven't seen her in years. I read somewhere that she lives near Asheville, maybe Black Mountain? I think she owns an antique dealership." Jack's mother sighed. "Poor child, she had it rough."

"No doubt," Jack said. *Didn't we all...*

"Anyway, I just thought you might like to know. I assumed you wouldn't be interested in coming to whatever service they have."

Jack frowned. A part of him bristled that she would even hint at the idea, given the way the woman had treated him and his family for so long.

"Yeah, that would be a hard no for me," Jack said, trying his best to be patient.

"I know, I understand how you feel. I just wish things could have been..."

"Listen, Mom, don't go down that road. It's water under the bridge and there's nothing to be done now except move forward." Jack marveled at the irony of his own words, in light of the entire week he had just spent deep-diving into the past, with no end in sight. But he had no intention of mentioning anything about it to his mother. That time might come, but it was not now.

"You're right. I know you're right," she said.

"Have you seen Ellen or Ruth lately?" Jack asked, eager to change the subject.

"Ruth and Tom are out west visiting their oldest son and his wife. I think they're going to do some travelling while they're there. But I met Ellen this past week for lunch. She's still working for the county and said that..."

"Hey, Mom, I'm really sorry, but I need to run. I've got someone coming in a few minutes to fix a leaky sink, and I need to clean up the kitchen," Jack lied. "But I appreciate you letting me know about Mel."

"Oh, okay, well good luck, sweetie." She paused. "I'd love to see you if you get a chance to come up this way, now that school is done."

Yeah, it's done all right, Jack thought. "I don't know, Mom, I've got a lot of stuff to do around here, but if it looks like I can make time, I'll shoot you a text."

Jack was immediately relieved to end the call, but found himself curious about Andy's sister, Deena. He had, on occasion over the years wondered where she ended up and how she came to see the whole incident as an adult, with the benefit of hindsight. Even as a child, Jack sensed that, unlike her parents, Deena felt a degree of sympathy for him, even if she had been afraid to tell him.

As he picked up the chevron bead again and looked at it, he wondered now if his instinct about her had been right. If so, there could be a chance, however remote, that she would be willing to talk to him. He had no idea what he would say to her if he got the chance, but she was the one other living person who knew Andy the way he did, so it might be a chance worth taking.

Jack got another cup of coffee, opened Google Maps to show the western end of North Carolina and opened the calendar on his phone.

CHAPTER 5

It was a beautiful morning as Jack drove west on I-40, away from the metro-traffic crush of North Carolina's Research Triangle, heading toward the far western end of the state and the Blue Ridge Mountains. The familiar highway would take him through just over two-hundred miles of rolling fields and lush green woodlands that blanketed the landscape between the cities and towns he would pass along the way: Burlington, Greensboro, and Winston-Salem, and later Statesville, Morganton, and Marion in the foothills of the Blue Ridge. Finally, he would travel up twelve miles of hair-raising switchbacks on one of the steepest sections of I-40 east of the Mississippi, known by locals as "the Asheville Mountain," on his way to the tiny picturesque town of Black Mountain.

Jack had made a two-night reservation at the Hampton Inn, and even if he took his time on the drive, he would still likely have time to kill in town before check-in, so he was in no hurry. Completely unsure whether he would be able to find Deena, and whether she would even speak to him if he did, Jack had set his expectations low. But he had not packed light.

A couple of days before the trip, Jack had been wrestling with the idea of making a detour on the way back, and taking Highway 201 up to Benton. For what exact purpose, he was not sure. At first, he had rejected the idea as suicidal, convinced that the psychological hit he would take would send him into a dangerous tail-spin, but something in the back of his mind told him it was important; that he should at least pack some extra things, just in case.

As he had rolled the idea over in his mind, he had thought about the house he grew up in—the one where it all happened—and wondered what it would be like to drive by and look at the place again after all of these years. He thought how strange it would be to see someone else living there. On a whim, he had called his mother back and asked her if she had any idea who owned their old house.

She had taken a few moments to answer, and her reply had left Jack reeling.

"Jack, sweetie, you do."

It had been like someone sucker-punched him in the face. For a moment he was sure he had misunderstood.

"What?" was all he could manage.

"I'm sorry, I probably should have said something before now, but I guess I thought you weren't ready to know about it yet."

"What the hell are you talking about?" Jack had asked, deeply confused. "You sold the house twelve years ago."

His mother sighed. "No, Jack, I didn't. I started to. God knows I couldn't live there anymore, but the more I thought about it, the more I thought you might want to have it someday. I don't mean to live in of course, but the town has grown so much and it's going to be worth a lot one day. I guess after everything that happened I wanted you to have something for it. Like an investment."

"Shit, Mom. Are you serious? How did you manage that? Who's been living there, keeping the place up?" Jack was trying to get his head around the news.

"I got an attorney to help me work it out. It's technically in a trust of some kind, so I've been the one managing taxes and such. I guessed at the time that you wouldn't want any part of it, but time changes your perspective, and I hoped there would come a day when you would see it as a good thing. I hired a man and his son to keep the place up, and they've been looking after it ever since. The father passed a few years back, but the son still looks after it."

"Jesus," Jack said. "So, it's just been sitting there empty all these years?"

Jack's mother began to cry.

"Hey, it's okay, Mom. I'm not mad, just kind of freaked out," he said, trying to reassure her. "That's huge. I appreciate it, I really do."

"Okay, I'm glad," she sniffed.

"Thanks, Mom. I mean it."

"You're welcome, dear. I've got the paperwork in my safe-box. I can send you a copy anytime you like. And if you ever decide you want to go and check on the place, the key is under that fake rock beside the flower bed."

It had taken Jack a couple of drinks and several hours to absorb the shock of his mother's bombshell news, but as he considered the ramifications of it, taken along with the timing of his trip and Andy's most recent appearance, his mind was made up; regardless of what happened in Black Mountain, he would travel back to Benton afterwards, come what may.

Between spotty clouds in the afternoon sky, the sun felt warm on Jack's face as he stood at the corner of Gregson and Main, in the quaint downtown of Black Mountain. Like so many small towns in the Blue Ridge, Black Mountain felt like a throwback to an earlier, simpler time, but with a quirky modern flare. An eclectic assortment of shops and restaurants, each with their own distinct character and charm, were scattered among the modest grid of intersecting streets that made up the downtown. A railroad track ran through the center of town, carrying freight trains and an occasional Amtrack west from Old Fort to Asheville and on to Tennessee.

After negotiating an early check-in at his hotel, Jack hadn't bothered unpacking his bag before rechecking directions on his phone and heading out on foot. Now, as he scanned the shop signs on Gregson Street, he finally saw what he was looking for about two thirds of the way up the block, "Stella's Antiques."

Jack's nerves had begun to kick in and as he started down the sidewalk in the direction of Stella's, part of him wondered if he had lost his mind. He didn't even know what Deena looked like after so many years, much less what kind of person she had grown up to be. He realized he knew nothing about her. It was the longest of long-shots, but nothing ventured, nothing gained. At least that's what he told himself.

As he approached the wide glass storefront, adorned with a beautiful set of colonial-era pewter kitchenware, he noticed a white cat with black spots sitting in the corner of the window, watching the street with a vaguely disinterested expression, slowly flicking the end of its tail. Jack stopped and put his hand up to the glass in front of the cat, but it took no notice, raising one paw instead and starting to lick it.

You're stalling, he told himself.

Jack heard a ding as the shop door opened and an older woman with a cane emerged, holding a small bag in her other hand. He held the door open for her and managed a faint smile as she thanked him and passed. His felt his pulse quicken as he stepped inside, immediately struck by the elegant, yet comfortable atmosphere of the shop, and of the obvious quality of the items they had on display. This was no junk shop.

He saw a woman facing away from him, behind a small counter at the center of the store. She had shoulder-length blond hair, and wore a smart crème jacket and a skirt that came to her knees. She appeared to be filing a sales slip.

Trying to appear calm, Jack cleared his throat and the woman startled, spinning around with her hand on her chest.

"Oh, you scared me," she chuckled, breathlessly.

Jack knew immediately that she was not Deena Redmond; she was far too young.

"Sorry," Jack said, holding up a hand. "I didn't mean to scare you. I guess you didn't hear me come in."

"Not at all. What can I help you with today?"

"I was hoping to talk to Deena Redmond? Sorry, I'm not sure whether her name is still Redmond. Does she own the shop?"

The woman smiled politely, but appeared guarded. "Are you a friend of Deena's?"

Jack shrugged. "Deena and I were kids together, in Benton. She was my neighbor."

The young woman's eyes lit up and her expression softened. "Wow, really? That's amazing."

"I haven't seen her in a very long time, but I just heard that her mother passed away. I was in the area and just wanted to stop by and say how sorry I am."

"I know she would appreciate that. I'm Tanya, by the way," she said, holding out her hand. "I work for Deena three days a week."

"Jack," he said, shaking her hand.

"Well, unfortunately she's not in today. She would normally be, but she needed a few days off to plan for the service. I think she'll be going back home for it. Anyway, I'm filling in some extra days this week."

Disappointed, but feeling like he had nothing to lose, Jack decided to press her.

"Too bad. Hey, I'm only going to be in town for a day and I'd hate to miss her. I'm not sure exactly where she lives. Any chance you could give me her address? I would really appreciate it."

Tanya looked skeptical. "I'm not sure she would want..."

Jack thought quickly. "Does she still hate to be called Dee? People tried to nickname her that when we were growing up and it used to really piss her off."

The smile returned to Tanya's face and she nodded. "Yeah, she does. It's probably the quickest way to get on her bad side." She considered Jack for another moment. "You know I'm sure she wouldn't mind for an old friend. She's over on Hawthorn, up the hill a few hundred yards. House number three-forty-four, on the right. It's got colonial blue shutters and door, and a big wind chime on the front porch."

She handed jack one of Deena's business cards as well as one of her own.

"Thank you so much," Jack said. "It was so nice to meet you. This is an amazing shop, really beautiful things."

"Thanks, we like it," Tanya said. "Take care. And if you're ever in the market for something special, stop back by."

"Absolutely," Jack said, backing out the front door and taking a deep breath as he started down the street.

The part of him that had been dreading the conversation was relieved, but he was also confident that Tanya was already calling or texting Deena to let her know he was coming. Whether that would work for or against him remained to be seen. Her mother's passing would almost certainly make the disturbing conversation he was anticipating even more precarious.

As Jack found Hawthorne Street and walked north, the relatively flat streets of Black Mountain's modest downtown began to climb into the hilly neighborhoods that bordered it on two sides. Despite his anxiety, the breathtaking beauty of the mountains on a sunny autumn afternoon brought a rush of nostalgia flooding back from his younger years growing up in Benton, and he was reminded how much he missed living in the mountains.

A few minutes later, as he walked through a curve, Jack spotted house number three-forty-four ahead of him on the right. A young, attractive woman with short chestnut hair, wearing Khaki capris, a white cotton shirt and sandals sat in a wicker chair on the front porch.

Deena Redmond was waiting for him.

Jack felt his already nervous stomach knot up and his mouth go dry. Part of him wanted to throw his hand up, but he didn't want to seem overly familiar. If this was Deena, she was not smiling.

He stopped at the mailbox directly in front of the walkway that led to the front steps, and as he looked up at her, she stood up and walked to the edge of the porch, thrusting both hands in her pockets. Her eyes were red and she looked anxious and tired, but Jack recognized shades of the eleven-year-old he remembered.

"Hi Deena," Jack said. "It's Jack. Jack Crawford. I guess Tanya let you know I stopped by."

Deena regarded Jack for a moment.

"Yes, she did. I was kind of shocked, really. I wasn't sure I believed her at first. It's been a very long time."

"Yeah, it has," Jack said, hoping he hadn't made a terrible mistake. "Look, I apologize for showing up unannounced. I wasn't trying to ambush you, really. I was just in the area and Mom mentioned recently that you live here. She also told me about your mother passing, and I wanted to stop by and say, well, just say how sorry I was to hear it."

"Thanks," she said quietly, studying him for a moment. "I'm kind of surprised, with everything that happened, that you'd go out of your way to do that."

"I know what she thought of me," Jack said. "I always knew, but I guess the more years that passed and the older I got, the more I understood why she felt the way she did. I've been thinking a lot about the past lately, and I guess as much anything, I wanted to do it for you."

"I appreciate that, but you should know that we weren't close, me and Mom. You probably remember how things were in high school; well, they only got worse from there. I'll just leave it at that."

"I do remember," Jack said. "I always hated that for you."

"Likewise. I know your dad was no picnic either."

Jack snorted, "Jesus, that's putting it mildly. I was glad to see the back of him."

Deena looked down and shuffled her feet. "Listen, Jack, I really appreciate your stopping by, but I'm kind of busy. The whole thing with Mom has kind of thrown everything off and I'm trying to make arrangements and get ready for a trip to Benton tomorrow afternoon."

Jack saw that if he didn't speak now, he would lose his chance.

"Yeah, of course. I completely understand, it's just that I was hoping...I was hoping to get just a few more minutes of your time. There's something else I wanted to talk to you about. Something important."

Deena winced and he saw a shadow of frustration and skepticism creep across her face.

"What is it?" she asked, as if bracing for a sales pitch.

"I know it's terrible timing, but some things have happened lately that have got me really rattled. Some things relating to the past. Relating to Andy. And I wanted talk to you about them."

She massaged her forehead in silence for a moment, as if trying to muster patience.

"Listen, if this is part of some kind of twelve step program you're doing, making amends for the past; I'm just not sure I can help you right now."

"No, it's nothing like that," he said, taking a deep breath and a couple of tentative steps in her direction. "There's some things I realize now that I need to tell you about, things that happened back then, with Andy. Things I never told anyone at the time. Not our parents, not anyone. But something strange and kind of frightening has been happening lately, and it's all coming back up, and I think you may be the only one I can talk to about it."

Her face grew dark. "What do you mean, things you never told anyone? You mean you were lying back then about what happened to Andy? Lying the whole time, to the police, to everyone?"

A knot had sprung up in Jack's throat as he felt the conversation falling apart.

"Only about part of it," he stammered. "I left part of it out."

"How convenient for you," Deena said, her voice rising. "You mean the part where you shot Andy by accident?"

"No," Jack insisted. "That's not it."

Her voice was shaking with contempt and disbelief. "You know, maybe mom was right about you the whole time. Maybe I was the asshole for feeling sorry for you. And here I was thinking it was kind of you to come all this way and track me down for condolences when you really came looking for me to confess? After twenty odd years of lying?"

"You don't understand," Jack pleaded.

"You know what? Fuck you for whatever you did, and for showing up here. And you can give your confession to someone else; it's twenty-three years too late for me."

As she turned on her heel and walked toward the door, Jack panicked.

"I didn't kill Andy," he called after her, "But I saw what did."

Deena stopped walking and turned slowly around.

"What did you say? What do you mean, 'what did?'"

"Please," he said, walking to the foot of the steps. "If you'll just give me five minutes to explain. Five minutes, and after that I'll leave if you want me to and never come back. But something is happening; something strange that I can't explain and I don't understand, at least not yet. And it's all related to Andy. I know this is all out of the blue, but you're the only other person who really knew him. Please."

She struggled for a moment, considering his request, then turned back toward the door.

"Five minutes," she said over her shoulder as she walked in the door and left it standing open. "Then I want you gone."

Jack's heart leaped into his throat as he walked up the steps behind her, crossed the porch, and stepped through the door.

CHAPTER 6

Deena's house was as tastefully adorned as her shop, and equally comfortable, with aged hardwood floors and a scattering of decorative rugs in the hallways and great room. He followed her into the living area, in front of a row of floor-to-ceiling windows that looked over a large deck, with a stunning view of the mountains as a backdrop.

She sat down and pointed to a chair opposite her. "Sit if you like."

Jack's pulse was pounding as he sat down and he wished badly that he had a drink.

Her eyes bored into him. "What did you mean out there?"

He knew that as hard as it would be to tell her everything, it was his only chance of gaining her trust and possibly her insight. But he also knew that there was an equal chance she would think he was deranged, sadistic, or both, and throw him out. He braced for either outcome.

"When I said I left some things out back then," he began, "I didn't mean that I did something to Andy. I would have never have hurt him. And there was no accident. Despite what everyone believed, we never even shot the rifle that day. I didn't lie to cover up something I did. I lied because of what I didn't do, and because of what I saw. Even as a kid, I knew that nobody would believe what really happened, so I made something up. I still think nobody would believe it."

"Try me," Deena said, crossing her arms. "From where I'm sitting you've got nothing to lose."

Jack looked toward the windows as he tried to decide where to start.

"Okay. You went with us one time to The Farm, didn't you? The time we took a bucket to pick blackberries and ended up eating them all?"

Deena's eyes suddenly teared up and she wiped them with her hand as she nodded. "Yeah, I actually do remember that. I had a stomach ache when we got back and spent the rest of the afternoon in the bathroom. Why?"

"Do you remember the old house, and the other outbuildings? The shed and the barn?"

"Sort of. I remember they scared me. Everything about that place was creepy. I remember begging Andy to leave, but the two of you wanted to poke around in the house. I think I waited outside."

"Well, Andy and I always thought the place was haunted. I mean, that's what thirteen-year-old kids would normally say, but we really did. We always thought something was watching us when we were there. Something that wanted to hurt us. Anyway, we had dared each other for a long time to spend the night in that house, and that's what the camping trip was about. We were going to prove who was the bigger...chicken," Jack said.

Deena stood up and walked to the window, fanning her eyes with one hand.

"I don't know if I can do this," she said, looking out at the mountains.

"I'm sorry," Jack said. "I know this is hard, but if you'll just hear me out. I think it's really important."

"Important to who? You?"

"Important to Andy," Jacks said.

Deena turned to look at him. "Why did you say that? What do you mean, important to Andy?"

"Please, let me explain and maybe you'll see what I mean."

"Do you want a drink?" She said, walking suddenly across the room toward a cabinet on one wall. "Sorry if you're on the wagon, but I've got to have something."

"God, no," Jack said, relieved. "I mean, yes please, that would be great. Whatever you've got. Rocks or neat is fine."

She poured them each a shot of Grey Goose vodka over ice in a tumbler and handed one to Jack as she went back to her place by the picture windows.

"Go ahead," she said, taking a big sip of her drink.

Jack knocked back his drink in two gulps and forged ahead with the story of what had really happened at the farm that night, in as much detail as he could remember and leaving nothing out, despite his urge to hold some of it back.

Deena paced as he talked, stopping to refill hers and Jack's drinks in silence partway through. As he reached the part where he and Andy set up their sleeping bags in the downstairs of the house, she looked especially anxious. Dreading what came next, Jack steeled himself and described how he and Andy had taken their flashlights and explored the empty, decrepit rooms of the downstairs, and then how Andy had suggested they go upstairs and look in the attic.

"What was the attic?" Deena asked. "You said it like it was something bad."

Jack exhaled, glad that he had a couple of drinks in him. He did his best to describe the oddly placed wall in the upstairs of the house, along with the large misshapen hole in the center of it.

"We called it 'the attic,' but that's not really what it was. I think now, that someone built it long after the house was built, like they wanted to wall off part of the room for some reason. There were no windows behind the wall and no light ever got in.

That was the part of the house that scared us the most. Maybe because the flashlights wouldn't light up whatever was in there for some reason. Or maybe because we heard strange noises in there, in the dark."

"Was the hole where a door used to be?" Deena asked.

"No," Jack said. "I've thought a lot about it over the years, and I don't think the hole was supposed to be there at all. From the shattered wood laying around in the floor, and the jagged edges of the hole, it looked like something had broken through the wall – violently."

Deena shuddered. "Okay."

Jack continued, telling her how much Andy had wanted him to go and look in the attic, and as he said it, he felt the all too familiar wave of shame return as he admitted that he had been too scared to go. He had stayed downstairs while Andy explored. Jack told her about the cricket-clickers and how he had listened to Andy's footsteps on the ceiling above him, and then Jack had heard him calling to come upstairs, that everything was clear.

As Jack talked, Deena kept glancing at him, sensing that something bad was coming.

"Stop," she said, holding up her hand. Jack saw that it was trembling. "Before you go on, do you swear, I mean fucking swear to me that you're telling the truth this time? If this is any..."

"I swear," Jack said, leaning forward in his chair and locking eyes with Deena. "On my mother's life, it's the truth. Before I go on, you need to know that."

"I need to sit," she said, walking to the chair opposite Jack and sitting on the edge of it.

"Do you want me to go on?" Jack said.

She propped her elbows on her knees and clasped her hands together into a double fist.

"Yes."

It was Jack's turn to stand and pace, as he felt himself beginning to sweat.

"Okay," he said.

Without giving himself time to back out, Jack described going up the rickety stairs of the old house and shining his light on Andy. And then, as Deena watched with wide, disbelieving eyes, he described how the pale dead thing had come out of the darkness and grabbed her brother.

A whimper escaped Deena's lips and she clenched her hands even tighter as Jack told her about Andy screaming for help as it pulled him away into the inky black of the attic; and Jack's voice broke as he confessed to her that he had run. Instead of trying to help Andy, he had run for his life.

Jack felt tears on his cheeks and turned away as he told her about hearing Andy calling him. He pushed to the end, telling how he had finally stopped and tried the cricket one last time, and how he had seen the light in the upstairs window go out.

When he turned back around, Deena was looking at him, shocked and disheveled. Her eyes and her cheeks were wet and her hands were trembling, but she did not speak.

Jack walked back over and sat down, wiping his face with his hands. "I ran all the way home in the dark that night. Got torn up by some barbed wire along the way apparently, and didn't even know it. I knew nobody would believe me if I told them what really happened, so I just made something up, something that sounded possible. I've been wrecked by what happened that night."

Deena was still watching him in silence, and he felt miserable with shame as he saw the pain in her eyes.

"Say something," he said softly. "I understand if you don't believe me."

"I don't know what to believe," she said, standing again and walking back to the windows. "About any of it."

"If you don't think I'm completely crazy, that's at least something," Jack said.

"No," she said, staring out at the mountains. The sun was sinking low in the sky and the shadows across town were growing long. "I'm wondering if I am."

"Why?" he asked, as he looked up at her.

When she turned around, her expression was strangely numb.

"Because that's exactly what Andy said happened to him."

The empty tumbler slipped from Jack's hand and bounced hard on the rug at his feet, but he didn't notice.

"What?" Jack gaped. "What do you mean?"

Deena walked back over and sat across from Jack. "He didn't say it, exactly, more like he showed me. I've been dreaming about Andy for a while now. I don't know why. Some of it is horrible. I'm not sleeping."

Jack was gaping at her now. "I can't believe this," he said. "Me too. That's why I'm here."

"It's like in the dreams he's showing me things," she said. "In that damned house. But in the dreams he can't talk because his..." she broke off and choked back a sob.

"Because his mouth is sewn shut?" Jack said, as their eyes locked with dawning realization.

"We're having the same dream, aren't we?" she said.

"Maybe," Jack said. "No, not exactly. I'm not seeing scenes from the house, but maybe that's because I was there. But I'm seeing Andy, and his mouth...he looks like that in my dreams too."

"What you told me just a minute ago," Deena said, almost in a whisper. "It's exactly what I saw in the last dream I had. Exactly. It was like he wanted me to see it. Jesus, I just thought it was some awful nightmare. If I had known..." she broke off again and grimaced. "So that...thing from my dream. You're saying that was real? Like really real?"

Jack nodded. "Yeah. You can see why I wasn't in a hurry to tell anyone."

"What do you think it was?" she asked, seeming almost afraid to know.

"I have no idea. That's part of what I want to find out."

Deena clenched her eyes tightly shut and shook her head. "I can't fucking believe this."

Jack reached over and handed her his unused napkin and she wiped her eyes.

"Why is this happening?" she said.

"I think Andy, or whatever he is now, is trying to communicate with us. I thought it was just me, but now that I know he's coming to you too, I'm even more convinced."

"Convinced of what?"

"Convinced that he's asking for our help. I think it has something to do with The Farm and what happened that night, but I don't know what or how."

Jack stood up and pulled a folded envelope out of his pocket.

"In the last dream I had, Andy gave me something. He put it in my hand." As he was speaking, Jack was opening the envelope, and he noticed that Deena sat bolt upright and was staring at the envelope with wide eyes.

"And when I woke up, I found this on the bedside..."

Before Jack could finish and pull the chevron bead from the envelope, Deena ran from the room, down the hall and into what he assumed was her bedroom. She came running back down the hall a moment later with something in her hand.

"I'll show you mine if you'll show me yours," she said, out of breath. There was no humor in her voice.

As Jack pulled his bead from the envelope and held it up, Deena rolled her hand over and opened it. She held what was clearly another chevron bead, nearly identical to Jack's, in her palm.

"I'll be goddamned." Jack said, utterly astonished. "He gave you one too?"

"Yes, in the dream, just like you said. But I have no idea what it is and how it ended up outside of my dream, in the real world, on my table."

"I can tell you the first part," Jack said, carefully taking the bead from her hand and comparing it to his. "I've been doing some reading. They're called chevron beads, and they were originally made in the late 1400s and early 1500s in Venice, from layered glass rods. They were very valuable and Spanish explorers used them as currency to trade with the natives on their expeditions through the southeastern states."

"Okay," she said, looking back and forth between the beads.

"The big Spanish explorer who came through this area was Hernando De Soto," Jack continued.

"I've heard of him," she said. "In history class."

"For decades, they had never been able to uncover exactly where De Soto went when he traveled around the southern states, but someone finally figured out that these beads were the key. They learned that everywhere the beads turned up, De Soto had been there. It was so consistent that they started calling the chevron beads "De Soto's signature."

Deena looked confused. "Alright, so the beads point to De Soto. What does that have to do with Andy, and The Farm?"

"I haven't figured that out yet, but Andy and I used to hunt arrowheads and spear points down there in that valley. We found a lot of them and I kept a few. I did a Google image search on some of them a few days ago, and they're Chockowan. They could easily have been from the same time period."

"So, if the beads are from The Farm, that would mean that maybe the Chockowan lived there back then and De Soto stopped there, maybe traded with them?"

"That's what I'm thinking."

She hung her head. "I just don't understand why it would matter, I mean to Andy, if it's really him. In the dream it was almost like he was desperate for me to have it."

"I know," Jack said. "That's why I think he's asking for help. He can't tell us what he wants to tell us, so he's trying to show us."

Outside, the sun had disappeared behind the mountains and only the dim glow of twilight shone through the living room windows. Deena realized that she had lost track of time.

"God, it's late," she said, pinching the bridge of her nose. "I don't know what to do with any of this. First Andy, then mom, now you." She took the bead in her fingers. "And this."

"I know it's a lot," Jack said. "I'm sorry for dropping it all on you, especially now, and for taking up so much time. I appreciate you talking to me about it, really."

"What are you going to do?" she asked, looking very tired again.

Jack shrugged. "I guess I'm going to keep trying to figure this out. I teach high school, and I'm off for the summer, so I've got some time. Since Andy's come back, I'm not sleeping much, so I'm going to try and help him. It's the least I can do."

Deena cocked her head. "What do you mean, 'he's come back?' We're talking about dreams, aren't we?"

Jack looked at her with a faint, sad smile as he reached into his pocket. When he pulled out the cricket-clicker, he could tell that she recognized it from the one Andy had.

As she watched, mildly alarmed, Jack held up the cricket and pointed it across the room.

Click-click. The sharp popping sound echoed off the wooden floors in the large open space.

Deena froze, staring at the clicker with wide eyes, realizing at that instant what Jack was doing.

Click-click, from somewhere down the hall.

Deena screamed and jumped up, taking several steps backward toward the darkened windows. She was shaking all over.

"Oh, my God," she said. "What was that? Was that some kind of trick? I swear to God…"

"It's okay," Jack said, lowering the cricket and standing up. He walked over to her and put a hand on her shoulder. "It's not a trick, I promise. It's Andy. I don't know how, but it's like I can communicate with him, just like when we were kids. I've been doing it for a couple of weeks now. I still can't get used to it."

"Jesus," she shuddered. "You mean he's…here? Now?"

"I don't know," Jack said, feeling more tired than he could remember. "Maybe? Maybe his spirit? I can't explain it, but I've been pretty freaked out, honestly. Anyway, that's why I said that he's back, because in some way, he really is."

Badly shaken, Deena looked between Jack, the cricket, and the hallway to the back of her house.

"Can we talk to him?" she asked, almost whispering.

"He can't talk, remember?" Jack replied. "I think that's why he's using the cricket."

She choked back a sob, and Jack could tell she was crushed by the thought of her brother with his mouth sewn shut, trying to ask for their help.

"What do we do?" she stammered. "What are we supposed to do, if he's…"

"I'm going back to Benton," he said. "When I leave Black Mountain. I can't take much more of this, so I'm going back there and try to get to the bottom of it."

Deena's nerves had frayed. "No, I mean now. Tonight? I can't sleep after that! You can't just do that and expect me to be okay."

"I'm sorry. You're right, that wasn't fair. I wanted you to understand, but I shouldn't have done that."

"Well, you have to stay," she said, grasping for something to hold onto. "Or I'm leaving for the night. I'm not staying here by myself with that..."

"You know whatever this is, it's not going to hurt you, right?" Jack said.

"Well, something sure as hell hurt Andy," she said, looking nervously down the hall again. "So, I'm going or you're staying. What's it going to be?"

Jack was caught off guard and felt his pulse quicken.

"I can stay, if you like," he managed. "I'll sleep on the couch if that will help. I've got a room at the Hampton Inn, but it's not a big deal."

"Would you mind?" Deena asked. "I'm sorry to ask."

"No, it's not a problem. I don't mind." Jack hesitated. "I take it you live alone? I mean, just not wanting to take anything for granted here."

"Yeah, just me." She said, glancing toward the bedroom. "Has been for several years now. I was married once, but it didn't work out."

"Sorry to hear that," Jack said. "I never made it that far. An extended engagement a few years ago that fizzled out. That was as close as I've come, but what do you do?

"Nothing you can do, except get on with it," she said. "That's what I always say."

Deena walked over to the dining room table and stood looking down at the papers and file folders that were haphazardly scattered there. Jack had not noticed them before.

"I just don't think I can deal with this anymore tonight," she said, tapping one of the file folders with her finger.

"What is it?"

"Family stuff, my mom's will, real-estate papers for the house in Benton, and the condo, and God knows what else. I'm trying to get organized for the trip over there tomorrow, but I'm too tired to focus."

"Want some help?" Jack said. "I might not be able to do much, but if you need to get it done tonight, I could order a pizza and keep you company. I did kind of wreck your afternoon, so it's the least I can do."

She scratched her head and stared at the pile of papers, then looked up at him and shrugged. "Why not? That actually sounds pretty good. I would appreciate the company, and maybe thinking about something else for a little while." Deena managed a weak smile.

"You sure you don't want to go out and get something?" Jack asked.

"I'd much rather do that, but I've just got too much to go through. There's years of shit in these folders and multiple versions of things. Unfortunately for me, she was always updating and adding documents. And there's the service coming up next week."

"Say no more," Jack said. "I'm on it, just tell me who in town delivers and what you want on it."

"Veggie on thin crust from Antonio's is what I usually order," she said, sitting down at the table. "But if you're a meat-eater, they can do half-and-half. There's a number on the fridge and I've got Diet Coke, white wine and Stella to drink. I hope that's okay."

"Perfect," he said as he took out his phone and headed to the fridge.

CHAPTER 7

Two hours later, Jack and Deena sat across from each other at the still-cluttered dining room table finishing the last two pieces of pizza, Jack with a Stella and Deena with a glass of white wine. Organizing the files had been a welcome distraction for them both, and as if sensing it was best, they had made a point of avoiding any discussion of Andy or the past.

The files and miscellaneous papers were now loosely organized into keep, shred, and trash piles, along with a more urgent action-needed pile, for bills, correspondence, and tax forms. Deena had also managed, with Jack's help, to finish drafting the eulogy for her mother to post on the funeral home's website.

"You know, that's pretty rich," Deena said, grinning as she finished a bite of pizza and reached for a napkin.

"What, is?" Jack asked as he leaned back in his chair, enjoying the nice buzz that had kicked in.

"You helping write Mom's eulogy. She would just roll right over."

Jack grinned. "Yeah, I thought about that, actually. A little ironic for sure. But you have to admit, what we came up with was pretty damn eloquent, especially given, well you know."

"What a bitch she could be?"

Jack raised his eyebrows. "Ouch."

"You know it's true," Deena said, pushing the empty pizza box away from her and sipping her wine. "That woman was a piece of work."

They sat in silence for a few moments, each in their own thoughts, and Jack felt better than he had in a long time. Finally, he pointed at the piles with his nearly empty Stella bottle.

"Do you have what you need for tomorrow?"

"I think so. I'll probably need a couple more photos for the service, but I can probably get them from her albums. She had the newer stuff from her phone in cloud storage, but she never got around to digitizing the old stuff." Deena propped her elbow on the table and rested her head in her hand.

"God, I'm dreading dealing with all her stuff and trying to sell that condo. I'll be running the roads between here and there for months." She sighed and waved away the topic. "Anyway, enough about her. I want to hear how you ended up teaching math, but I'm going to have to take a rain-check. I'm beat. If I don't get at least a little sleep, I'm going to be no good tomorrow."

"Good idea," Jack said.

She stood up and gathered the pizza box and plates. "If you're still good with the couch, I'll bring you sheets and a pillow. I think I've got some of those travel packs from the dentist office with extra tooth brushes."

"Thanks, sounds good."

On her way back from the kitchen, Deena stopped and put her hand on his shoulder.

"I just wanted to say, I appreciate your stopping by, and I'm sorry for what I said. I'm not usually like that."

"Thanks," he said, putting his hand on hers. "You've got nothing to apologize for. This is a lot to deal with in the best of times. But I appreciate it. I'm glad I came."

She smiled and headed down the hall, turning on lights as she went.

Jack opened his eyes. He was on his back looking up at a grey, angry sky with rain clouds building and a rumble of thunder in the distance. He looked around and beside him and was horrified as he realized he was naked and lying on a pile of dead bodies in a field. Blood ran freely across the tangle of brown arms and legs that surrounded him, and the glassy vacant eyes in the broken faces of the men, women, and children stared back at him, unseeing. Jack's heart was pounding in his chest, but he couldn't move, and it was then that he noticed the soldiers. They were white men with beards, wearing animal skins and carrying swords and lances. When they reached the bodies, they began thrusting their weapons into them in a last, cruel attempt to ensure they were dead. Jack tried to be as still as a stone. *Play dead*, his mind screamed. *Make them think you're dead and maybe they won't...*

But it was too late. The angry bearded face of a man appeared directly over him, looking down at him, and Jack saw the man's eyes grow wide with fury as he realized that Jack was still alive. Jack saw the still bloody gash across the man's face as he bared his teeth and raised a bladed lance high above Jack's chest. Jack tried to scream but no sound would come as the lance came crashing down...

Jack bolted awake and sat up in the darkness, his chest heaving.

He tried to shake the terrible images from his mind as he looked around him, but he was in a dimly lit room he did not recognize, and for a fleeting moment he had no idea where he was. As his mind cleared, he remembered the previous evening. He was on Deena's couch, in Deena's house. Gradually his breathing returned to normal, and it was then that he looked over at the recliner in the corner of the room and saw Deena curled up there asleep on her side under a thin blanket. She must have been too scared to stay in the bedroom, he thought. *Welcome to my world.*

As he watched her sleeping, he felt bad for her. Bad that she had been in the blast-radius of everything that happened back then, bad that she had lost her big brother and that her mother had gone off the rails and now, apparently killed herself, and bad that he had brought it all back and laid it in her lap. But despite the guilt, a part of him was selfishly but profoundly relieved that he wasn't in it alone anymore.

Jack quietly got up and went into the kitchen and poured himself a glass of water. He sat back down on the couch and looked out at the hazy glow of the streetlights and the blinking yellow traffic lights from the deserted downtown streets below them.

Deena stirred and sat up, pulling the sheet tighter around her. "Mind if I have a sip of that?"

Jack walked over and handed her the glass. She took a drink and handed it back to him.

"Want a glass?" he asked.

"No, I'm good."

He sat back down on the couch. "Couldn't sleep?"

She sighed. "Not back there. My mind did a number on me. I kept imagining Andy standing over me, looking down at me. And I couldn't stop thinking about that, whatever the hell it was in that attic."

"I'm sorry. I was afraid that might happen," Jack said.

"I came in here, thinking there was safety in numbers. I think I slept for a while, then had another damn nightmare."

"Me too," Jack said, shaking his head. "This is getting mental."

"You were groaning in your sleep," she said. "I started to wake you up, but I didn't want to startle you."

"I wish you had," Jack said. "It would have been better than my dream."

"I'm almost afraid to ask."

"I was lying in a pile of dead bodies," Jack said, sipping his water. "Hoping the guys with the spears wouldn't notice I was still alive, but one of them saw me and came over and stabbed me in the chest."

Deena cringed, "Jesus, that's terrible."

"What about you?" Jack asked.

"I was locked up in that attic place, in the old house," she said. "It was almost totally dark and I was desperate to get out, but the walls were completely sealed. And then I realized there was something in there with me, some kind of monster, and I knew it was coming for me. I started screaming and woke myself up, thank God."

"Holy crap," Jack said with a shiver, "I don't know which one was worse."

"Do you think he's making this happen?" she asked.

Jack considered her question. "I didn't at first, but I do now. I think he's showing us things because there's something important he wants us to know. I just can't figure it out, at least not yet. That's why I'm going back to Benton. I don't know what's left of The Farm after all these years, but I feel like he wants me to go back there. I feel like that's where the answers are."

"Are you sure that's a good idea?" she asked.

"No," he said. "I'm not sure it's a good idea at all. But I owe it to Andy. I know that sounds whacked, but that's how I feel."

They sat in silence for a few moments and Deena got up and went into the kitchen. She poured herself a glass of water and got a Tylenol bottle out of the cabinet, popping the top and swallowing two of the capsules.

"Want some company?" she asked, looking back at Jack.

"Are you serious?" Jack asked, immediately conflicted over the idea.

"I'm going to be in town for mom's stuff anyway. I think I'd like to come along if that's okay. Maybe I need answers too. Maybe just closure. Who the hell knows?"

"I mean, sure, if that's what you want. I'd love the company, but after twenty-three years I don't have any idea what we'll find. And after some of what's been happening, I'm not entirely sure it will be safe there."

Deena snorted. "After the last few days, I'm not entirely sure it's safe here."

"Good point," Jack nodded. "Okay then, it's a deal."

"Where are you staying over there?" she asked.

"Ah, yeah. I guess I forgot to mention that," Jack said. "I'm going back to Wildwood Lane, to our old house."

Deena looked confused. "You mean just to look at the place? Do you even know who owns it now?"

"No, I mean to stay there. Turns out my mom lied about selling the house all those years ago. She never sold it, if you can believe that. She's owned it the whole time. Kept it up and everything."

"No way," Deena said, walking back and sitting in a chair opposite Jack. "Are you serious? It's just been empty all these years?"

"Apparently. She didn't want to rent it out, so it just sat. She tells me all this right before I left for this trip, and dropped the other news that she's given it to me as an investment. Transferred it through some kind of trust."

"Oh my God," Deena said. "I mean, I guess that's a good thing. It's just weird. Sorry, but after everything that happened, it's just so weird. I haven't even been back there, much less to look at our old house. Mom's condo is going to be strange enough."

"Yeah, caught me completely off guard."

"What are you going to do with the house?"

"Sell it at some point, I guess. I sure as hell would never live there. Holy shit, talk about heavy baggage. I told myself I would never even go back there, and then I find out, out of the blue, that I own the place." He gave a heavy sigh. "I'm not sure how much more chaos I can take."

"I feel you on that," she said. "Does your mom still live in Blowing Rock?"

"Yeah, and maybe I'm a bad son, but I'm not telling her I'm going to be in town. I'm not up for a visit, and I'm sure as hell not telling her about any of what's been going on. She'd have a stroke."

"Good call, I think," Deena said.

Jack looked at his phone. "It's four-fifteen. You going to try to get some more sleep?"

"Are you kidding?" Deena said. "I think that ship sailed. What about you?"

"I was thinking I'd head back to the hotel," Jack said. "I booked two nights, just in case, but I got way more than I was hoping for, so I think I'll do an early check out and hit the road."

Deena grinned and cocked her head. "What do you mean, way more than you hoped for?"

"Ah, well, let's just say, given how things have been going for me lately, my expectations were very low." Jack stood up and stretched. "I wasn't sure I'd find you at all, and I thought if I did, I'd be lucky to have a thirty minute conversation with you, in a public place with your professional body-builder husband scowling at me the whole time, looking at his watch. So, you can see how much better this has been for me." He grinned back at her.

"Well, when you put it like that."

To Jack's surprise, she stood up and hugged him. He hugged her back and felt a rush of emotion.

She stepped back and looked at him. "It's been great, actually. I'm glad you came."

"Yeah, it has been," he said. "It's been good to see you. Will you be okay here, I mean with..."

"Oh yeah," she waved him off. "I'm turning on every light in the house and two TVs while I pack for this trip."

She reached out her hand. "Give me your phone and I'll put in my number. Give me a call sometime tonight. I'll be over there by one or so."

As Jack walked back beneath the glow of the streetlights, through the deserted streets of Black Mountain on his way back to the hotel, he could hear the highway sounds from I-40 in the distance. When he crossed Hawthorn onto Davie, he turned around and looked back up the hill in the direction of Deena's house and grinned. All the neighboring houses were dark, but hers was lit up like a Christmas tree. True to her word, she had apparently turned on every light in the house.

As he turned back toward the hotel, he thought of everything that had happened in the last twenty-four hours and how glad he was that he had come. But he had also begun to feel a growing sense of dread over his imminent return to Benton, and most importantly to The Farm. It had only been an abstract idea up to now, but he knew it was about to get very real.

Going back through it all with Millie, in the comfort of her mid-century-modern sitting room had been one thing, but this was going to take him to the very places where Andy's life had ended and his own life had been torn apart. In every way that mattered, this was going to be returning to his own personal ground-zero, and there was some part of him that wondered if he would survive it.

CHAPTER 8

The drive from Black Mountain took Jack east for nearly an hour on I-40 before he left the interstate and headed north on Highway 201, the winding road that would again carry him high into the mountains, where he would eventually turn onto Highway 29 and drive for another half-hour before arriving on the west end of downtown Benton. Jack had not been back for over a decade, and that had only been passing through on his way to Roan Mountain, Tennessee for a hike on the Appalachian Trail. Even then, driving down King Street had been like seeing an old ghost; one that he did not recognize any more. He could only imagine how the place had changed after another decade.

A grey dawn had finally broken, and a light rain was falling as Jack drove the last few miles into town, and he braced himself for the inevitable wave of mixed emotions that he knew would come from seeing so many landmarks from his past, mingled with or replaced entirely by new development. But the changes became evident well before he even reached the town proper. Highway 29 had become a four-lane, and rather than the wooded ridges he remembered on either side of the long uphill stretch that led into town, Jack was stunned to see a sprawling gravel mine on one side and a "Hillbilly Trading Post" and RV campground on the other. The trees had been clear-cut on that side and a small city of RV campers littered the valley, while blinking signs on portable trailers beside the highway shouted "Mountain Honey," "Coon-skin Caps" and "Handmade Crafts" in yellow plastic letters.

"Jesus Christ," Jack muttered to himself as he peered out between the windshield wipers.

The remaining straightaway leading into Benton that Jack remembered as high-grass fields, was now fully developed on both sides, with everything from car dealerships and a carwash to a Days Inn and a restaurant called "Tucker's Barbecue." He had heard that his old high school, the only one in the county, had been torn down after sixty-five years, so he was less surprised to see an apartment complex on the hill where the school had been, but he still felt an odd pang of loss as he passed.

Much of what was now considered the historic downtown of Benton had not changed, for better or worse, and felt much like it had during his childhood. It had remained a small town, and like so many others in the mountains, the downtown was modest, with many buildings from the 1930s and 40s, and none taller than three stories. The old Granville Cinema was still there, a relic of the 1980s, with gaudy bulbous lights on a traditional marquee. The former Benton landmark was apparently living its second life as a two-dollar theatre, running only classic oldies. They were showing *Alien* and *Caddyshack*, which made Jack smile. The building on the corner that had been home to Benton Hardware since the 1920s had been converted into a Ward & Dean clothing store, which somehow seemed a shame, and he hoped they had kept the original hardwood floors, worn and weathered, that had given the building so much character.

The businesses and other buildings along the roadsides began to thin as Jack left the downtown and traveled east on King Street toward the outskirts of town and his old neighborhood. Some of it seemed familiar, but much of it seemed alien. As he reached the turnoff to Forest Hills Drive and his old neighborhood, Jack felt a powerful melancholy grip him, and he had the distinct feeling that he was trespassing on ground that was not intended to be disturbed. He drove slowly up the long winding road, shocked at how overgrown and claustrophobic it felt compared to his childhood memories of playing along the same streets. *Amazing what twenty years of growth looks like*, he thought, shaking his head. He passed a scattering of houses along the way up the hillside, before arriving at his old street, Wildwood Lane. The highest street in the neighborhood, it ran across the ridge line and bordered what had been in years past, miles of forested land south and east of town.

Now, as he turned and drove past the weathered and partially bent street sign, he could not help but think what a cruel twist of fate it had been that brought his family, *when he had a family*, to that particular street in the first place. A street that just happened to border hundreds of acres of wilderness and empty fields that young boys would love to play in and explore. A wilderness that concealed a strangely lifeless valley where a cloying melancholy seemed to permeate the very air, and even the wind barely stirred. A valley where a long-abandoned farm, with no known origins stood decaying among the weeds and birch trees.

A farm where something evil lives.

There were only three other houses on the street in addition to his old house, now *his* house, number 108, which was at the end of the street on the right. Deena's old place, a red brick rancher with a carport, was one house up, about fifty yards from his. His memory was briefly alive with images of kids playing and riding their bikes in the street; of backyard birthday parties, barbeques and chasing each other with water balloons.

But just as suddenly, darker memories flooded in, washing over the happy ones and erasing them like the rising tide obliterates sandcastles on the beach; police and emergency vehicles and uniforms everywhere, the house awash in a sea of strobing lights, the copper taste of adrenaline in his mouth as their gawking and crying faces hovered over him. His mother screaming in the kitchen as his father's fist snapped her head back and sent her glasses flying, while Jack screamed for him to stop. An empty pill bottle on his bedside table and blurry images of frantic paramedics bustling him onto a stretcher and into an ambulance in the driveway. His mother crying, always crying; about his father, about Andy, about Jack.

"Stop it, goddamn it," Jack chided himself in the muted silence of his car.

He took a few deep breaths to clear his mind and pulled the car into the driveway. As he got out and surveyed the yard and the painfully familiar Colonial-blue and brick split-level house, it was evident that the man and his son who his mom had hired were earning their keep. By all outward appearances, anyone would assume that the house was occupied, and not by just anyone; by someone who gave enough of a shit to mow their grass and trim their hedges.

Maybe someone who had a happy life, where they could think about things like grass and hedges because nobody had accused their thirteen-year-old son of murdering his next-door best-friend and disposing of the body. Maybe somebody who's family had not exploded one night, without warning, like a Halloween jack-o-lantern after you shove a lit M-80 into its gap-toothed grin.

Stop it.

Jack breathed again and headed for the fake rock by the flower bed where he knew he would find the key. At that moment he hated his mother for keeping the place, and even more for giving it to him. He had planned to never come back. Wanted more than anything to never come back. And now this...

Fuck the investment.

Several hours later, across town on Greenway Road, Deena was fighting her own emotional battle as she stood in her mother's empty condo and tried to force her mind to see the mountain of things that lay ahead of her as a series of practical problems to be solved. But as she did, she clutched a wadded tissue in one hand, because as much as she had tried to keep it at bay, pain from some deep place inside her kept clutching at her; drawing her mind toward the darker realities of her mother's life and the circumstances of her death, threatening to derail her focus on the pragmatic, the must-do list. With everything ahead of her, she could not afford to let that happen.

But it was Jack's unexpected visit and shocking revelations about Andy that had preoccupied her thoughts all morning. Her mother's death, tragic as it was, had not been entirely un-expected, at least not to her. She had watched Mel's steady and seemingly unstoppable slide, deeper and deeper into depression and substance abuse as the years had passed, and she had always believed this would be the eventual outcome. In her mind, it was never a question of if, only of when. So, when she had gotten the call from Sergeant Courtney Reed of the Benton PD, telling her that her mother had passed away, the sadness she felt was more for the tragic arc of her mother's life, rather than for a sense of loss. She was ashamed to admit it, but apart from the weight of handling her mother's affairs, Deena felt an odd sense of relief at her passing. And in her heart she knew that after the service was over and the condo sold, her life would go on as if nothing had happened.

That was not the case with Jack however. His visit and the unexpected night they had spent together at her house had left her feeling profoundly changed. Apart from the shock of seeing her childhood friend out of the blue, as a grown and surprisingly attractive man in his mid-thirties, what he had revealed about Andy's disappearance—the dreams, and The Farm—had rattled her to her core. It was true that she had always believed more in the metaphysical than most people, but discovering in one night that some evil thing, not of the living world, had taken her brother and that some part of him was still alive and communicating with both her and Jack, asking for their help even, had almost been too much to grasp. Yet it seemed to confirm what she had always suspected; that there was something vast, dark, and unseen below the surface of day-to-day reality.

As Deena walked to the window and looked out, she felt a ripple of fear as she imagined going with Jack to The Farm, or whatever remained of it. Part of her was genuinely afraid of what they might find there, but mostly because she sensed that by making the trip, she might well be crossing a dangerous line into something she was not prepared for; something she might not fully come back from.

She remembered seeing a motivational poster about "DIS-COVERY" on an office wall somewhere, with the classic above-and-below image of an iceberg. The caption had read, "Once you see what's below the surface, you'll never see what's above it the same way again."

No shit, she thought.

Her phone rang and snapped her out of her thoughts. Despite her malaise, Deena smiled when she saw it was Jack.

"Hi neighbor, how's it going there?"

"Strange doesn't even come close. It probably helps that it's mostly empty, but it's pretty intense and not in a good way. How about you?"

"I haven't been here that long, but I'm with you on the intense part. It's been harder than I thought. The place is pretty much a wreck. And I told myself I wouldn't think about the fact that this is where they found her, but the paramedics left shit all over the living room floor and that was the first thing I saw."

"God, I hadn't thought about that," Jack said. "Must have been rough."

"Hey," she said, changing the subject, "You said your old house was 'mostly' empty. What did you mean?"

"Oh, nothing really. I found a make-shift seating area in the living room; a couple of folding chairs and a plastic table. And there's a bunch of beer in the fridge. I'm guessing the old guy and his son who kept up the place up all these years had a key and they knew it was empty, so they probably set it up for breaks and lunch."

"Weird, but I guess it makes sense. I hope it's at least a good beer."

It was Jack's turn to smile. "Lucky for me, yes; Modello. I'm ashamed to say it but they are a couple of beers down. I didn't feel like running out to the store first thing, so I've been using their break-room to do some research on my laptop. No big surprise unfortunately, but it turns out our Spanish explorer, De Soto was real bastard."

"Do tell," Deena said, walking clear of the living room and sitting at the dining table.

"Well, you know how much has come to light since the inter-net about our history books being white-washed when it comes to all the so-called 'explorer heroes,' right?"

"Yeah, I think so. I know they conveniently left out the parts about how cruel they were to the indigenous people."

"That's putting it mildly. From what I've read, under today's laws all of these guys, Cortez, Pizarro, even mister 'sailed the ocean-blue' himself, Christopher Columbus would be hauled to The Hague and tried for war crimes. I'm talking full-blown genocide in some cases. Anyway, turns out that De Soto was a card-carrying member of the same club. Most of the articles are more white-wash, really casual about his travels through what are now the southern states; almost like he was just bee-bop-ping around and hanging out with the locals. But he actually went through the native American population like a chain-saw; killing, raping, destroying villages, just taking whatever they wanted and using the tribal men as slaves. It's grim reading to say the least."

"Jesus, I guess I didn't realize it was that bad."

"Yeah, unfortunately. But that got me thinking about our chevron beads, and about my nightmare."

"Okay," Deena said, her interest piqued.

"Well, if we're right about De Soto being in the valley near The Farm during that time, and about the Chockowan people living there, then maybe he committed some kind of atrocities there. Sadly, it wouldn't be out of character."

"You mean, like a massacre?"

"Yeah," Jack said. "One of the places De Soto's army stayed, somewhere in what's now Florida, they practically slaughtered the entire village; I'm talking hundreds of men, women, and children. They call it the Napituca Massacre. But it sounds like that was no big deal to them at the time, so what if they did it here?"

"That's an awful thought," she said, trying to keep her mind from going there.

"Try dreaming about it," Jack said. "I don't know why I did, but that's exactly what was happening in my nightmare, only I was on the receiving end."

Deena shuddered. "All of that makes sense, but why would Andy want us to know about it? Wasn't that hundreds of years ago?"

"Nearly five hundred years, actually," Jack mused. "But Andy seemed almost desperate, so it's got to be important. Maybe if there was a massacre, it's related somehow. I think I'm just going to dig some more."

Deena hesitated. "So, you're not going to try and go down there?"

"Oh, God no," Jack frowned. "Not today anyway. I don't know if you remember, but it's a good two-hour hike to get there. Tomorrow would be the earliest, but I'm not even sure about that. It depends on when you're available, right?"

"I did say I wanted to go with you, didn't I?"

"Yeah, you were pretty insistent about it, actually. But lucky for you, I have a very generous cancellation policy. You can cancel up to ten minutes before we walk out the door."

But Deena had not heard his attempt at humor. For a moment, her nightmare had drifted back into her mind and she was back there, panicking in the darkness of the attic, knowing she was trapped and hammering on the walls; desperate to get out. And then the raw terror of realizing she was not alone. Something was moving in the darkness. She shivered and shook herself back to the moment.

"Okay, well, call me crazy, but I'm still in."

"Good," Jack said. But something about her voice had sounded off and Jack wondered if she really was.

"So, are you roughing it there tonight?" Deena asked, wincing at what he might read into her question.

"No way in hell," Jack said. "I don't know who I was kidding. This place feels like a morgue to me now. I'd rather..." he stopped himself abruptly before he could say "take my own life before I'd stay here," instead finishing with, "get a room down at the Sleep Inn."

Close call, dumb-ass, he chided himself.

"Where is it?" she asked, and at that moment, she realized her own cluelessness in thinking she would be okay staying in her mother's condo. *Where she killed herself.*

"Weirdly, they crammed one in at the foot of the neighborhood, right on King Street, overlooking the valley and Harmon Park Elementary. Oh, and in case you haven't seen it, there's a shopping center where that old house and barn used to be. It's nuts."

"You're kidding?" Deena said, remembering walking to school from their neighborhood through the bucolic valley. There were always cows in the field and the iconic white farmhouse there had been nearly two-hundred years old. "That's such a shame."

"It's pretty shocking. How about you? Will you be okay at your mom's place?"

"I came to town thinking that, for some reason," she said. "But when you're walking around picking up pads from the defibrillator they used to try and re-start your mother's heart... Well, let's just say I've been re-thinking my plan."

"Jeez, I don't blame you. Well, listen, I'm sure on a Monday they've got vacancies, but I went on the cheap and got a room with two queens, so you're welcome to crash at mine."

Deena felt a guilty tingle in her stomach even thinking about it.

"It's kind of across town from here," she said, stalling.

"You're right," he said, "A full five minute drive, if I remember."

"Smart-ass," she quipped. "Okay, well, what the hell? You've already stayed at mine."

"Good then. Maybe we can suss out what some of this ancient history means over dinner later? They've apparently got about five times the number of restaurants here they used to have between here and Blowing Rock. And miracle-of-miracles, they serve booze here now."

Deena snorted. "I never thought I'd see the day, but I have to say, it's good timing. I may need a few to get through some of this."

"I heard that," Jack said. "I'm heading over to check in around five. I'm in 328."

"Okay, see you in a bit."

"Good luck," he said.

109

"Thanks, you too."

CHAPTER 9

The music in Nathan's Tavern was louder than Jack would have liked, but otherwise the woman behind the desk at the Sleep Inn had been spot-on; the atmosphere was good, lots of booth-seating and a surprisingly large menu. The hostess had seated Jack by the window which overlooked the parking lot of the small shopping center and a conspicuously out-of-place brick farm silo rising high above the far end of the lot. It sported a colonial green roof and a "Shops at Moore Farm" sign on it.

By Jack's estimation, Nathan's Tavern currently occupied the spot where the Moore farmhouse stood for nearly two-hundred years. It had been the jewel of a serene 160-acre rolling pasture that was divided by a tributary of the New River, and stopped at the foot of Harper's Mountain. When Jack had been in first grade, they had built a new ultra-modern elementary school at the far end of the pasture to replace the old one, and Jack had spent the remainder of grades two through eight there. He could not count the number of times he, Andy, and Deena had walked those fields going to and coming from school over the years. It had been one of his favorite places in town; one of the few he still carried fond memories of.

Then, nearly a decade after Jack moved away, his mother had sent him a newspaper article that had shocked and saddened him. It showed a photo of the Moore farmhouse, fully engulfed in flames and surrounded by firefighters. They were, according to the article, burning it to the ground for "practice" to make way for a new shopping center. After the last of the Moore family had passed away, an investment firm had bought the entire valley and had announced plans for the shopping center and a housing development. And to capitalize on the folksy appeal of the soon-to-be erased town landmark, they would leave the brick silo and name the new shopping center "Shops at Moore Farm."

When the Sleep Inn woman had recommended Nathan's and told him where it was, something about the dark irony of having dinner there had appealed to Jack. But sitting in the window-booth and surveying the scene had proven to be like nearly everything else since he arrived in town; exceedingly strange.

Progress is a bitch.

By the time Deena arrived and sat down, Jack was on his second beer and had made a noticeable dent in the basket of complementary tater-tots the server had delivered to the table.

"I told her to wait and bring these after you got here," Jack grinned. "I knew I wouldn't be able to stay out of them, but she said she'd bring more whenever we like."

"Wow, bottomless tot-basket, that's pretty dangerous," she grinned, sliding into the booth. "And you got me white wine? Perfect."

"Took a chance," he shrugged. "My memory is shit half the time, but I did remember that."

She raised her glass and they toasted.

"Can you believe all this?" Deena said, waving her glass around them and toward the window.

"It's very weird, actually," Jack sighed. "It's like the past is being erased, bit-by-bit. Sometimes I think that would be a good thing, but then seeing it happen just..."

"Takes the wind out of you?" she finished.

"Yep. How did it go at your mom's place?"

Deenah shook her head, "Okay, I guess. But after today, well let's just say I'm going to have to significantly adjust my expectations about getting everything in order and selling the condo."

"So, it's in worse shape than you thought?"

"Worse shape and more of it. I honestly think she packed enough shit in that two-bedroom condo to fill up a house three times that size. And don't get me started on the piles of paperwork. What about you? How did it go at 108? What does my old place look like?"

Hearing her question, Jack's mind drifted back to his old house. Before he had left for Nathan's, he had put away his laptop and been standing in the foyer, unable to push away the terrible memories of that night; of hearing the police officer trying to quell the argument between his parents and Andy's and Deena's parents, in that very spot. He had remembered how profoundly strange it had seemed to him, even as a child, that some kind of monster had just dragged his best friend away screaming into the darkness, and their parents were bickering like children in the foyer where he stood.

Jack had turned in the silence and looked back into the empty house, glancing down the basement steps into the gloom. For reasons he could not explain, he had reached into his pocket and pulled out the cricket.

Click-click. The pop echoed in the foyer around him as he waited.

Click-click. From somewhere in the basement.

Jack had felt a chill flow through him.

"I'm trying, Andy," he had whispered, almost under his breath. "I'm trying."

Deena reached across the table and put her hand on Jack's.

"Hey, are you okay?"

Jack startled, and realized that he had been staring blankly at the partially empty basket of tots like a catatonic in the psych ward. His cheeks flushed.

"Jesus, sorry about that. This has all been a little surreal. What did you ask me?"

"About my old house, and how it went at yours."

Just then their server appeared and took their orders, before Jack continued.

"Your house hasn't changed at all. Apart from all the trees being much bigger, and some privacy hedges between the Wentworth's old house and yours, nothing much on the street has changed. It's like stepping back in time, which makes it even weirder."

"Did you find anything else out about De Soto and the Chockowan?"

"I did," Jack said. "Not only are there references in the tribal writings about their people warring with Spanish soldiers, but a couple of them mention a place they call Nowatek, I think translated to 'Valley of the Moon,' where hundreds of their people were killed, but I couldn't find anything else out about the incident or a more specific location."

Deena blinked, "But that's huge. That could be *our* valley?"

"It very well could be, I just wish there was more information. But I did find one other reference to Nowatek. It's not much, but it's interesting. In 1973, a graduate student at ASU was doing her thesis on the history of the Chockowan in the Blue Ridge Mountains, and she was interviewing some of the oldest living elders in the area. The article had actual transcripts. One of the old women, who now lives in Tennessee, mentions the tragedy at Nowatek."

He took out his phone, pulled up a photo, and handed it to Deena.

"Look at this part."

D. Johnson: Did the Chockowan settle in Nowatek again?

V. Little Creek: After the tragedy of Nowatek, the valley became tsau cha'ta and our people would not go there again. It is considered a tapu place; forbidden among indigenous people.

D. Johnson: What does tsau cha'ta mean?

V. Little Creek: A place of great evil.

Deena finished reading and looked up.

"You mean, evil because their people were killed there?" Deena asked.

"Maybe," Jack said, as he took his phone back. "No idea. But she wouldn't say anything more after that. She clammed up and asked the young woman to stop the interview. I couldn't find any other references to Nowatek on the internet, but I did find a book on Amazon about the Chockowan and their culture. That may be the best place to start."

"No need," Deena said, smiling. "I brought my Kindle. It's in my bag. When we get to the hotel, I'll download it."

Jack smiled and raised his beer. "Even better. Here's to you. At least someone came prepared."

Click-click.

They froze, staring at each other, glasses half raised. Even above the music and the loud voices, they had both heard it, loud and sharp, from somewhere across the dining room.

Deena lowered her glass and looked across the room. "Was that..."

Jack scanned the room. "I don't know. Could have been something from the kitchen, but..." For a moment he was staring again down into the shadows of the basement.

I'm trying, Andy.

Their order arrived a few seconds later, but the mood had changed and neither of them had the appetite to finish, asking instead for to-go boxes.

Out in the parking lot, the security lights were beginning to flicker on as the sun disappeared behind the ridge. Carrying the plastic carry-out bag, Jack walked Deena to her car and after she climbed in, he handed it to her and she put it on the passenger seat. But instead of starting the car, she put both hands on the steering wheel and looked into the shadowed landscape, across the valley toward their old elementary school.

"This thing isn't going to let us go, is it?" she asked, quietly.

Jack was silent for a moment, curious at her choice of words. Had she meant Andy? Or the situation?

"No, I don't think it is. Whatever it is, we're in it now." He replied.

After a heavy pause, Deena shook her head and turned and smiled. "See you back at the hotel."

Walking back to his car, Jack felt uneasy, and he wasn't sure why. Normally he would have chalked it up to indigestion from the greasy tot-bomb swelling in his stomach, but this was something else; a foreboding. A feeling that something was coming, something dark and terrifying. Something much worse than Andy.

Room 328 at the Sleep Inn was basic but surprisingly spacious, with windows that looked out over the Shops at Moore Farm and across the valley to the now silhouetted mountains that flanked the north side of town.

"You take the one by the window," Jack said, throwing his bag on the nearest queen bed. "It's a decent view."

Deena shook her head. "Call me weird, but I've never liked sleeping by the window. I read entirely too much Stephen King in college and it ruined me for life about windows by the bed."

"Afraid you'll see the little Glick boy staring at you in the night?"

She cut her eyes at him and he realized she was serious.

"That's not even funny," she said. "I was terrified by that book. And now with everything..."

"Sorry about that," Jack said. "My bad. You take this one."

They switched beds and she flopped down on hers, spreading her arms out beside her. "I'm so beat. If I give you my Kindle could you find that book? I need to get a shower. Maybe when I'm done we can see if it's got what you're looking for."

"Sounds good," Jack said, setting his bag on the floor by the window and sitting on the edge of the bed.

As Deena gathered some things from her bags and went into the bathroom, Jack occupied himself with the Kindle, searching for the book title he had found earlier. Despite his best efforts to focus, when he heard the shower come on, Jack felt a flush of excitement at the idea of Deena undressing just on the other side of the door, and her light humming only made things worse. Part of him was still trying to process how quickly he had bonded with this woman who, after so many years, might as well be a stranger. But bonded as what? He couldn't decide if their chemistry was friendship or possibly something more. The lingering memory of her as a child had initially caused him to sequester the attraction he felt for her, possibly out of some misplaced sense of parental guilt, but it had taken almost no time with Deena as a fully grown and exceptionally compelling woman, to erase that guilt and push old memories of her to the background. He had no idea if she felt a similar attraction to him, at least not yet, but the last thing he wanted to do was push her away right out of the gate by misreading the situation and overstepping. What they were doing was too important, and whatever he was sure of, he was sure that it would take both of them to get it done.

Jack finally located the title he was looking for, *Chockowan in the Appalachians; Culture & Language.* He downloaded it, opened the search field, and keyed in the word Nowatek.

Several minutes later, Deena emerged from the bathroom amid a curtain of steam, dressed in sweatpants and a t-shirt, drying her hair with a towel.

"That water pressure's great," Deena said from under the towel. "I was surprised."

When Jack did not respond, she stopped drying and lowered the towel. He was sitting on the side of the bed, staring at the Kindle. Even from the side, she could see that his face had gone pale with worry.

"What is it?" She asked as a chill crept over her. "What did you find?"

Jack turned to look at her and the chill grew deeper. He looked frightened.

"I think we've got a problem," he said.

Deena walked over and sat down next to him on the bed.

"I only found one reference to Nowatek in this book," he said, "but if it's talking about our valley, it's not good. In the 'Mythology and Religion' section it says that, according to Chockowan lore, what the Europeans did to their people at Nowatek was so brutal and barbaric that it attracted an evil spirit; some kind of witch monster that lives there, guarding the valley against intruders and feeding on the souls of the dead."

"Jesus," Deena said. "That's awful. But they probably had a lot of myths, right? I mean, from what you said, all of that happened five hundred years ago. And we're not even sure it's the same place."

"Yeah," he said, looking down again at the Kindle, "But this book was published eight years ago. And maybe it's just semantics, but it doesn't say the Chockowan believe a monster *lived* in the valley. It says they believe it *still* lives there."

Deena got up and walked back to the bathroom, turning at the door.

"I don't know, Jack. I know you want to find out what's going on here, but that might be a stretch, don't you think?"

Jack closed the Kindle and rubbed his eyes.

"Maybe you're right," he lied, as the awful image of that night in the old house reared up in his mind; watching in horror as the pale dead thing emerged from the darkness behind Andy.

A stretch? Not if you saw what I saw.

"I think I'm cooked for one day," he said, chasing the image from his mind. "When you're done I think I'll get a shower and turn in."

"Let me grab the hairdryer and it's all yours," she said.

Despite feeling exhausted, Jack lay awake in the semi-darkness of the hotel room, looking at the glow of parking lot security lights through a gap in the black-out curtains, and listening to the droning of the A/C unit and the white noise app on his phone. Deena had fallen asleep almost immediately and lay still in her bed, but there were too many thoughts chasing each other in his mind to sleep; too many unanswered questions and troubling implications. In the middle of his nighttime ruminations, it occurred to him that he would likely have to postpone his session with Millie that week, and he made a reminder on his phone. After another restless hour and a half, Jack found his memory leading him out of the woods, past the old fencepost, cloaked in rusting strands of wire fencing, and through the weeds that surrounded The Farm. The valley fell away below him to the river on his right and the house stood partially obscured by winter birch trees ahead of him. Walking through the weeds there was no sound except the distant cawing of a crow. Only the one lone crow.

Jack felt a stab of panic as he realized he was trapped. He looked around him in the dim light and saw curved walls of dusty stone rising on all sides to a small circle of light overhead. To his horror, he realized that it was an old dry well, and he was at the bottom of it with no way out. He could see clouds and sky through the opening of the well, a good twenty feet above him and he knew he could not climb out. He tried to scream for help but no sound would come because his mouth was sealed shut. His fear exploded as he groped for his mouth and felt the rough lattice of threads across his lips, and he tried to cry out, but the sound only muffled inside his mouth, echoing in his head. Panicked, he looked down and realized there were bones all around him, human bones with shreds of rotten clothing and skulls with gaping eye sockets. All of their mouths were sewn shut. And as Jack gaped in terror, a shadow fell over the light above and he looked up in time to see bony fingers sliding a round piece of wood over the top of the well. He threw his arms skyward as the light became total darkness, and screamed another silent scream.

As Jack's eyes flew open, he heard himself shout and instinctively jerked his hand to his mouth, relieved to find it mercifully open as he gasped for air. As he sat up in the bed in the semi-darkness of the hotel room, trying to shake away his nightmare, he heard a strange groaning voice and a frantic scratching coming from the door. A jolt of fear ran through him as he saw that Deena was not in her bed.

"Deena?" Jack called, but there was no response.

He quickly crawled out of bed and hurried across the room. As he rounded the corner he saw Deena in her nightshirt, facing the hotel room door, clawing slowly at it with both hands and speaking strange words that he couldn't understand. Stunned and unsure what to do, Jack walked slowly toward her and it was then that he saw the smeared streaks of blood on the door.

"Deena, it's Jack," he said, putting a hand gently on her shoulder. "You're dreaming."

Suddenly Deena stopped speaking the strange words and her hands fell limply to her sides. Her head drooped to her chest but she did not reply. Gently, Jack turned her around and put one hand to the side of her face.

"Deena, wake up, it's Jack. You're okay."

She shook her head briefly and looked up at him, her eyes disoriented and confused.

"Jack?" she mumbled, and then started to cry. "Oh my God."

"It was a dream. It was just a dream. You're okay," he said, remembering how jarringly real his own nightmare had been. He led her back to her bed and kept a hand on her arm as she sat on the edge of it, then he reached over and turned on a lamp. In the light, he was shocked to see that several of her fingertips were bloody, but he did his best to remain calm.

"It was so awful," Deena said, and as she raised one hand to wipe the tears from her eyes, she saw the blood. "Oh, God," she cried, holding both hands out in front of her and choking back a sob. "Did I do that?" She gaped at the torn nails on several of her fingers and it was then that Jack realized she had felt no pain.

He took both her hands gently in his, careful to avoid her injured fingers, and lowered them to her lap. "It's not as bad as it looks," he said, partly trying to convince himself. "We'll get that fixed up. I keep some first aid stuff in my bag. Just wait here for a couple of minutes while I get it, then we'll go to the bathroom and get your hands cleaned up.

Deena nodded and folded her bloody hands in her lap, watching as Jack knelt by his bag and rummaged for his first aid kit.

"It was so real," she said quietly. "I was in the attic again, and I was desperate to get out. But I wasn't me. I was someone else. In the dream I had a husband and children, but I knew that it was him who had locked me up in that place and I hated him for it. I hated them all."

As Jack found his kit and stepped back to her bed, Deena's voice was trembling. "Jack, in the dream, whoever I was wanted to hurt him. I think maybe even hurt the children. It was so awful."

"Jesus, it sounds like it," he said, sitting on the bed beside her and putting his arms around her. "I'm so sorry."

She leaned into him and closed her eyes. "I'm so tired," she said.

"I know. This shouldn't take long and then maybe you can still get a little more sleep before morning."

From his high-top table by the window of the Sleep Inn dining area, Jack watched as the pale light of dawn crept slowly across the valley and the Shops at Moore Farm. He was sipping his second cup of dark-roast coffee and staring blankly at the crumbs in his now-empty plate, deep in thought about the events of the night before. The Weather Channel droned on in the background about the upcoming hurricane season while an older couple at a nearby table huddled over an iPad, fawning over photos of their grandchildren, but Jack didn't notice.

He didn't startle out of his trance until his phone dinged, louder than he would have liked. The old couple turned and looked in his direction, but he pretended not to notice. It was Deena.

Where r u? TELL me u didn't leave yet!: (

Jack cringed. He had agreed they would go together, but she had been sleeping so soundly when he'd gotten up and packed his things that she hadn't even stirred. After the shitty night she'd had, he erred on the side of letting her sleep, and slipped out, hoping she would understand. Clearly he had been mistaken. *Good damn thing you stopped for a bagel and coffee*, he thought.

Morning! No, still here. Downstairs getting coffee.

He thought quickly and followed with: *Ready when you are.*

She sent a thumbs-up and c *u in 5*.

When Deena walked into the breakfast area she looked rough, but surprisingly determined. She still wore bandages on several of fingertips and she carried a day-pack on one shoulder. Luckily she had dressed for a hike.

Jack smiled as she put her pack on an empty chair.

"Morning. You're awake."

"If you can call it that," she sighed and held her hands out in front of her. "I feel stupid with all this. I look like a four-year old who tried to use a hot waffle iron."

Jack shrugged, "You can barely notice. At least the Band-aids are flesh colored. Besides, it's the only way those nails will heal." He nodded at an extra cup of coffee on her side of the table. "I got you a fresh cup. Black, I think?"

"Yeah, thanks," she said. "What do they have down here? I'm starving."

"The usual lineup," he said, glancing behind him at the buffet. "Eggs, potatoes, pastries, etcetera."

"I'll be right back. Want anything?" she asked as she started toward the serving area.

"I'm good, but thanks," Jack said.

As he watched her getting her breakfast, he thought again about how frightening it had been to find her clawing at the hotel room door in the middle of the night and speaking strange words that he did not recognize. It had been like something out of a horror movie, only it had been Deena. The whole incident, including his own nightmare, had left him deeply disturbed. It felt like their connection to whatever was pushing its way into their dreams, and even their waking life was getting stronger and more intense by the day, the closer they got to The Farm. But what troubled Jack most was, after what he had seen the previous night, he was no longer certain it was just Andy they were communicating with.

"So, what aren't you telling me about last night?" Deena asked as she put her plate and glass of juice down on the table and slid into a chair.

"What do you mean?"

She lowered her eyes and gave him a look that said, *seriously?*

Jack scratched the stubble on his face and looked at her. "You weren't just scratching at the door. You were talking. But it didn't sound like you at all, and it wasn't English you were speaking. I don't know if was gibberish or some actual language."

"Are you serious?" she said, lowering her voice and glancing around them, as if to see who was within earshot. "What was I saying?"

"It was low and kind of guttural, but you kept saying the same thing, over and over. I tried to remember the best I could and wrote it down." He pulled out his phone and looked at the notes. "I spelled it phonetically, but it sounded like "Dru-akay nee-sha-day."

She chewed a bite of eggs and puzzled over the words. "What the hell? That doesn't sound like anything I've ever heard before."

"That's not all," Jack said. He pulled a folded napkin from his pocket and opened it, showing her a symbol, roughly drawn in ballpoint pen on the inside.

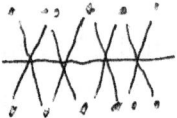

Deena wrinkled her brow. "What is that?"

"I was hoping you could tell me," Jack said. "You drew it on the back of the door last night."

"Drew it with what?"

Jack hesitated and lowered his voice even further. "You drew it in with your finger, in your own blood."

Deena looked stricken as she stopped chewing and put down her fork. After a moment she swallowed and pushed her plate away. "I don't feel so hungry anymore."

"I'm sorry about that," he said.

"No, I asked," she said, sipping her coffee. "It's not your fault. I just don't understand. This is crazy. If Andy's doing this, what is he trying to tell me?"

Jack stared at his coffee cup, considering what to say.

"Last night, what happened to you; I'm not sure it *was* Andy," he said quietly.

"What do you mean?" Deena asked, looking alarmed.

"I don't know," Jack said. "Maybe it's nothing. Maybe I'm wrong. But it just seemed very different, like you really were someone else."

She was quiet for a moment. "You're right about that. It wasn't like the other dreams. Not at all. This was way more intense, more real. I think in my dream, I was the woman who lived in the house; that house, along with my husband and my children. And what scared me was, even after you woke me up I felt like her, or felt her with me, for a good five or ten minutes. In the dream I had memories of things I've never done, thoughts that I could tell were not my own. It was the weirdest sensation."

"No doubt," Jack said. "But, if you're picking up something about the wife of the homesteader who lived there, what was she doing trapped in the attic?"

"I didn't get anything from the dream about why, but Jesus, I hope I don't have any more like that. How about you? What did you dream about?"

Jack shook his head and exhaled, then described as best he could his dream about being trapped at the bottom of the dry well. He almost left out the part about his mouth being sewn shut, but decided to hold nothing back.

When he had finished, Deena looked shaken.

"That's so awful," she said. "It's just like the other dreams, about the mouths being..." she hesitated. "Who do you think they were, the people at the bottom of the well?"

"No clue, except for one thing; two of them were small, like children."

Deena put a hand over her mouth. "Shit, this just keeps getting worse."

Jack leaned over and put his hand on hers. "Last night was rough, especially for you, and you've got piles of other stuff to do. Are you sure you're up for this?"

She took his hand and gently held it, careful of her bandaged fingers. "I'm not sure how to answer that. This started out as trying to come to terms with the past, and unresolved feelings about Andy, and frankly about you, but now it's something entirely different, like it's not even in the past anymore. Like, something has been there the whole time and it's still there. And we're being drawn into it more day by day." She looked at him and shrugged. "I honestly feel like I couldn't turn back now if I wanted to. Whatever this is, it's not waiting for us to come to it. It's coming for us. And if last night was any indication, it means business. We weren't in some old abandoned house, we were in a hotel room in a Sleep Inn, in the middle of town for Christ's sake, and you saw what happened."

"Yeah," Jack said quietly. The feel of her hand in his warmed him and excited him in a way he had not felt for a very long time, and it eased his growing apprehension about what they might find at The Farm.

"What about your mom's stuff?"

"Most of it can wait," she said. "Other than just wanting to get it off my plate, it can sit there until hell freezes over and it wouldn't matter. The funeral home is arranging the memorial service for late next week and other than stopping by to talk to them sometime in the next couple of days, that's all on auto-pilot."

"Okay then," Jack smiled. "Well, we'd better get going. The forecast is cloudy, but supposedly no rain. Since I ruined your breakfast, why don't we grab something for the road. I've got water and energy bars, but not much else, so we'll probably need it. I'm not sure how much you remember, but this is not a short hike."

Deena nodded. "Okay then, let's do it."

CHAPTER 10

The hardwood forest that began just behind the houses on Wildwood Lane sloped downhill for a mile and a half before giving way to weedy brambles and rhododendron groves. Beyond these were open fields that wound along the banks of the New River as it made its way through The Blue Ridge Mountains into Virginia.

It had been on one of their earliest explorations of the forest that Jack and Andy (this time without Deena) had discovered what remained of an old roadbed partway down the hillside. It was barely more than a wide overgrown path, but it was level, and they had followed it, eager to see where it led. What they would later call the Farm Road followed the contours of the ridgeline, twisting and turning for miles, without ever going noticeably up or downhill. They had run out of time that first day and had turned around and gone home. But they had been undeterred, vowing to go back when they had more time and to find out what was at the end of the road.

If only we hadn't, Jack thought, as they pulled into the driveway of his old house.

But you did, a quiet voice in the back of his mind whispered. *And now you've got to go back, because Andy's there, and he's waiting for you.*

After they got out and Deena took a few moments to marvel at the strangeness of being back on their childhood street, they double-checked their packs and crossed between the houses before heading into the woods. There was no path as they made their way down the slope, but thanks to the heavy canopy above them, the forest floor was blanketed in leaves and largely open and clear, apart from sparsely scattered ground shrubs and an occasional rhododendron. Jack led the way, having spent so much time in those woods as a boy that he did not need a map, even after twenty-three years.

As they walked, Jack noticed that Deena kept glancing at him, as if she expected him to say something.

"What is it?" He finally asked.

"Just wondering how you're doing. This must be weird."

"Weird doesn't do it justice. Everything since I drove back into town stirs up another old memory; stuff that I buried a long time ago and now I'm digging it all back up, one corpse at a time."

She cut her eyes at him.

"Sorry, poor choice of words," he said. "But you know what I mean."

"Yeah, I do," she said. "I really do. And unfortunately, in this case it may not be a poor choice of words at all."

Jack felt a sudden shiver and redirected.

"I think the beginning of the road, if there's anything left of it, should be about a hundred yards this way. There used to be a steep bank beside some bushes that dropped into a small flat area, and it went on from there."

"Didn't the road connect with our old neighborhood somewhere; I mean back in the day?"

"Maybe, but we never found any sign of it. It was like the road just started in the middle of nowhere."

Deena was silent as they walked on, and true to Jack's memory, within another few minutes they found what they were looking for. The rhododendron grove was much larger now, but still overhung a steep dirt bank beside the flat spot, exactly as he had described it. Erosion through the years had left it smaller, with less definition, but it was still clearly visible, as was the path that led away from it along the ridge.

"Alright," he said, as they half-walked, half-slid down the dirt bank onto the flat area. "It's still here. Let's hope the rest of it is too."

Deena's hellish dream from the night before still lingered in her mind, and a small part of her hoped that it wouldn't be there. That some wealthy development firm had finally cut a road into the valley from another direction and built a sprawling condo complex and a park where The Farm had stood for so long, erasing whatever dark legacy was harbored there and closing that door forever.

Still, the greater part of her knew what a devastating blow that would be to Jack, possibly to both of them. The last several days had been chaotic and confusing, but one thing had become clear; it was the only place where they could get the answers they needed and hopefully learn what Andy was trying to tell them.

"Let's hope so," she said, "For all our sakes."

The weeds were higher and thicker on the roadbed as they walked, and the steep, root-laced dirt banks on the uphill side had collapsed in places, requiring them to climb over or make their way around, and while it was mostly easy going, their silences grew steadily more uneasy the farther along they went. Occasionally, the trees to their right would thin enough to catch a glimpse of the valley and the river below and Jack kept glancing that way, trying to gauge their progress. He knew that the valley did not parallel the ridge they were on, but came toward it at an angle, bringing the river steadily closer as the ridge gradually fell away and opened up where they converged—at The Farm. There, the river curved in a wide arc around the fields and the remains of the homestead, no more than fifty yards away from it at the peak of the curve. Beyond the river, the sheer face of a high mountain ridge formed an imposing wall that curved around the valley like a portion of a giant bowl, further isolating that strange place from the outside world.

From their proximity to the river, Jack knew that they had another half hour to walk, and as they rounded a curve, he slowed and pointed to the large trunk of a fallen tree by the path.

"Hey, want to take a break, maybe grab a bite? I don't know about you, but I don't think I'm going to feel much like eating when we get there." He tried to sound casual, hoping to mask the apprehension he had been battling for the last half hour in an attempt to keep it from edging into full-blown anxiety.

By the knowing look on her face, he saw that she was not fooled.

"Sure," she said, stopping in front of the log and taking off her pack. "Probably a good idea."

Jack joined her on the log and soon they were busily munching bagels and energy bars, listening to the near-silence of the forest around them and the occasional faint sounds of the river, carried by a breeze. As it had been in childhood, there were no sounds of civilization here. No cars or car horns, no sirens, no voices or dogs barking. Only the stillness of the valley.

"How much do you know about this place?" she asked, in between bites.

"You mean other than the obvious?"

"Yeah, I mean, did you ever research it when we got older; try to find out about the land and who lived there?"

He finished his energy bar and reached for his water.

"I did, or at least I tried to a few times over the years. Randall County has surprisingly good records going back that far, I mean the 1920s and 30s; deeds, registrations, early surveys and land maps, you name it. But not for this place."

She frowned. "What do you mean?"

Jack glanced sideways at her. "I mean, I can't find any official records related to this valley at all, much less who owned the land or built The Farm. I can't even find a survey map that includes the valley, for Christ's sake."

"Well, that's got to be a clerical mistake, right? All land is owned by someone."

"I would have thought so," Jack said. "But that's not the strangest part."

Deena looked up. "Oh yeah?"

"Google Earth shows an aerial photo of the valley. I think the photos are about eight or nine years old. You can see the buildings, but not in much detail. If you click over The Farm, it shows you what the latitude and longitude is for that spot, supposedly a unique number, right?"

She nodded, but felt a pang of unease.

"Well, you can use lat-lon coordinates to pull up property records for the county, but if you put in those coordinates, you get a plot map that ends at the top of the steep mountain ridge just beyond the valley. It's a huge plot, nearly six hundred acres, but it doesn't include the valley or The Farm. The same thing to the north and west. It's like the absolute coordinates of that place don't line up with property records in a half-mile radius in any direction."

Deena furrowed her brow. "That's bizarre. So, as far as public records go…"

"This place doesn't even exist," Jack finished.

She stared at him as she rolled the implications over in her mind.

"That's beyond strange, but why am I not surprised?"

"Sadly, I wasn't either. I never took the time to find out more, or why, probably because it was just more frustration; more unexplained things related to Andy. Seemed like there was nothing but unexplained shit, wherever I looked. Anyway, the bottom line is, I think we're on our own where research is concerned."

"Great," she sighed as she began packing up the trash from her lunch.

As they donned their packs, Jack glanced again in the direction of the river and pushed back the painful memories he had of the last time he had been on the road; running wildly in the dark of night away from the valley, lungs burning and heart pounding, consumed by fear and shame, desperate to get back home—to live.

"We're getting close, aren't we?" she asked.

Jack sighed, "Yeah, maybe twenty more minutes."

"What do you think we'll find?" Deena asked as they started off.

Jack was silent for a moment before he replied. "I think we'll find The Farm. I think this place and whatever evil thing lives there have been undisturbed for God-knows how long, except for whoever built The Farm, and we have no idea who that was or what happened to them, but I'm not getting the feeling it was anything good. I've wondered about it too many times to count, but I keep coming back to the same conclusion; it's still there. Otherwise, I don't think Andy would be trying to take us back."

Deena cleared her throat. "Do you think we're safe in the daytime?"

Jack let out a heavy sigh.

"I don't think I ever felt safe in that house. But I think we'll be okay in the daytime. Just promise me one thing; we stay together, no matter what. Daytime, or no. I don't trust that fucking place."

Deena felt the edge in Jack's voice and it gave her a chill. "No worries, we'll stay together. I promise not to wander off. Besides, you're the one with the flashlight."

Her attempt to lighten the tone fell hollow against Jack's somber resolve.

"Thanks," was all he said. The last time he had seen Andy's face had been in the beam of his flashlight as it shook wildly in his trembling hand, but it had been enough to see the mask of sheer terror his friend's face had become; eyes bulging and mouth stretched wide in scream after piercing scream.

Lot of fucking good that flashlight did last time, eh Jackie?

They walked in silence for the last stretch of road as the trees on their right thinned and the valley began to open up. The river was clearly visible now, winding gently through the open fields. After the road curved through one final bend, it straightened out for fifty more yards before the woods on either side of it ended abruptly at the edge of a weedy hillside and open sky. As if to mark the transition, one lone weathered fence post stood at the edge of the field. It tilted lazily inward and a single bent nail protruded near the top of it, still holding a jagged portion of rusted wire fencing in place.

Jack stopped and stared at it, as his hand drifted unconsciously to his upper arm and he gently massaged his outer bicep through his jacket.

"I've still got it," he said, almost to himself. "The scar."

"What scar?" Deena asked.

"The one from the nail in that fence post. I ran into it that night in the dark; gashed my arm and didn't even know it until I got back home. The paramedic bandaged it up, but it left a pretty nasty scar."

"I'm not sure I ever knew that," she said, but she saw that he wasn't listening. He was deep in thought as he looked past the fence post and out across the open slope. She followed his gaze to a grove of trees in the distance, and her heart sank as she saw portions of an aging metal roof through the foliage.

Jack exhaled slowly. "It's still here."

Deena took his hand and squeezed it. "You'll be okay. I'm here and we'll do this together."

He seemed to come out of his trance and she felt him squeeze her hand in return.

"Thanks, Deena. I appreciate it. More than you know."

Beyond the woods, the hillside overlooking the valley was now mostly weeds and meadow grass, with patches of weather-hardened dirt visible in places. A few tall trees grew in the open space between the woods and The Farm, but most of them were clustered in a grove that surrounded and (more recently) grew up between the crumbling buildings. Just beyond the river, the familiar sheer wall of the ridgeline that surrounded the northeast end of the valley rose hundreds of feet into the sky, like a vast military rampart protecting it from the outside world.

Or maybe it's protecting the outside world from whatever abomination lives here, Jack thought.

As a boy, emerging from these woods to the sight of a complete, yet mysteriously abandoned farm and the picture-postcard valley that surrounded it had felt magical, as if they had come through a time portal and arrived in some strange and mystical place. That's how it had started out anyway. But it had not taken long before the almost palpable sense of emptiness and melancholy that permeated the valley began to extinguish their childish excitement, effectively draining away the happiness they felt at being there. In its place they had begun to feel something akin to somber reverence, like the living often feel when they trespass on graves in a cemetery. And when they had first dared to venture into the house, that reverence had given way to raw fear. Fear of what, they had not known.

Standing at the edge of the woods now, with Deena, Jack felt his long-suppressed childhood emotions emerging fully intact and struggled to keep them at bay. He squeezed her hand again.

"Let's go," he said, stepping into the open and heading across the hill.

The leaves had begun to turn and fall away, leaving gaps in the veil of foliage on the trees surrounding The Farm, and as they made their way across the hill, they could see more clearly what a toll another twenty years had taken on the already dilapidated structures. The rust-covered metal roof of the old slaughterhouse (Jack and Andy had assumed as much from the bleached animal bones they found there) had collapsed completely, exposing to the elements its dust and cobweb-covered insides along with its scattering of bones. The house itself was largely the same; windows empty and dark, doors and pieces of siding scattered in the weeds nearby or missing entirely. Except for a few holdout patches, all the white-wash on the siding had long ago succumbed to time and sun, leaving the old house cloaked in a sad weathered grey. Weeds and a few saplings grew freely up through the many gaps in the ragged flooring of the porch and something, likely a fallen tree branch, had punched a sizeable hole in the rust-streaked metal roof, toward the back of the house where Jack knew the attic was.

He imagined Andy trapped there in that dark place all that time, desperate to get out and unable to call for help because his mouth was sewn shut. Jack quickly chased the thought away and chided himself for going there.

Keep it together, he thought. *You're just getting started*.

"God, it's such a wreck," Deena said. "I don't remember it being anywhere near this bad."

"It wasn't," Jack said. "But it was probably worse than you remember, even back then. If my guess is anywhere near accurate, this place was well over a hundred years old when we were kids. Who knows how long before that it was abandoned."

"I've been wondering what happened to them; the people who lived here," Deena said. "Something about my dreams. I don't know, but I've been having the strongest feeling that something really awful happened to them."

"Like what," Jack said, taking off his pack and pulling out his flashlight.

"I don't know," she replied. "But for some reason I think they never left here."

Jack looked at her and felt a shiver as he remembered her standing in her nightshirt, scratching at the hotel room door with bloody fingers, speaking a phrase that she had no waking knowledge of, and he wondered again if something else—something that was not Andy—was communicating with her; probing its way into her mind. What if it was some lingering trace of one of the original homesteaders? What if it was something darker; something evil?

The thought scared the hell out of Jack.

"I hope you're wrong," he said, turning on the light. "But at this point, I wouldn't put money on it. Are you ready?"

She nodded and followed Jack's lead as he made his way carefully up the remains of the steps and across the porch, testing the boards with one foot as he went. The morning sky was blanketed by a layer of clouds, allowing only a muted grey light to creep through the gaping window and door frames, into the dark and ruined rooms of the house. Except for the march of age and decay, along with the encroaching weeds and vines, it was exactly as he remembered it; main room off the porch, one room at the rear left, a kitchen to the right, stairs to the far left. Jack stopped and shone his light on the open spot in what would likely have been the living room floor, as if seeing something that Deena could not.

"What?" she whispered.

"That's where we laid out our sleeping bags that night," Jack said quietly. "We had a lantern and our packs. They were right there."

"What happened to them?"

Jack continued to stare at the spot on the floor, then his gaze drifted up and around the room.

"I have no idea," he said. "I was sure I was going to get caught in a lie, because I told them we camped by the river. I never said anything about coming in here because I didn't want them to know about..." He paused. "I was sure they would find our things and it would all come out, but time went by and I never heard any more about it. I learned later that when the police searched the house, there was nothing here. No sign that we had been here at all."

Deena did not respond and when he looked at her, he realized she was staring at the ceiling, her eyes focused on something far away.

"Deena?"

She startled, but kept staring. "Are you hearing that?"

"Hearing what?"

She cocked her head slightly. "There. There it was again. It's so faint, but it sounds like someone calling out. Calling a name."

Jack strained and tried to focus but he heard nothing. And it was then that he felt the hair on his neck stiffen.

"What name? I don't hear anything?"

Finally, Deena blinked and looked at him with frightened eyes. "That was weird. It was so faint, but I know I heard it."

"Could it have been from somewhere in the valley?"

She shook her head. "No, it wasn't like that. When I say faint, I don't mean far away, I mean it wasn't solid like a real voice. It was thin, dim somehow, like a bad recording on one of those old vinyl cylinders they used before flat disc records came along."

"Do you still hear it?" Jack asked.

"No, it's gone. But it sounded close, like from right here, somewhere in the house. And it was definitely a woman."

Jack glanced nervously at the stairs, unsure what to make of Deena's story.

"Could you make out what name she was calling?"

"Yeah," Deena said, "It was William."

He shrugged. "That's really strange. I don't know what you were hearing. But let me know if you hear it again. Let's keep going. I don't want to stay here any longer than we have to."

She nodded and moved closer to Jack, looking nervously around them.

"What are we looking for, exactly?"

"I wish I knew," Jack whispered.

He slowly swept the light around the floor and walls as they moved into what was once a kitchen, stopping to inspect a recessed nook in the wall where a wood stove likely sat. Deena pointed to something on the floor and Jack shone his light on it.

"I'll be damned," Deena said. "It's a piece of a plate."

It was dust-covered and partially hidden beneath a small cluster of leaves, but by the light they could clearly see what looked like a large portion of a broken dinner plate. Deena was just stooping to pick it up when a loud thump on the ceiling just above their heads made them both jump, and Deena grabbed Jack's arm with a vicelike grip.

"Shit!" she gasped, staring at the ceiling.

Jack's whole body had gone taught.

"Jesus, I think there's somebody in here," he said, hurriedly pulling off his pack and unzipping it, still scanning the ceiling and listening. Deena watched in shock as he pulled a pistol from inside the pack and stuck it under his belt, behind his back.

"What the hell are you doing with that?"

"Sorry," he whispered. "I probably should have said something."

Normally she would have been angry, but despite her usual convictions to the contrary, in the moment she was glad he had it.

"Let's get out of here," she whispered, clamping harder on his arm.

He nodded and they started back into the living room, but just as they turned toward the front doorway...

Click-click.

The noise echoed through the house and they both startled again, whirling instinctively in the direction of the sound. It had come from the room behind them and even though the room was well lit enough to see, Jack shone his light in a trembling hand.

His breathing was rapid and his heart raced as he tried to fight the urge to flee the house. He reached with his free hand and pulled his cricket out of his pocket. He glanced briefly at Deena and she nodded.

He pressed the button with his thumb.

Click-click.

In the oppressive stillness of the house, it almost sounded like a shot. The reply was almost immediate.

Click-click.

It had come from the room on the northeast corner of the house, through the doorway, barely a dozen feet in front of them and to the left.

Jack exhaled slowly and clenched his jaw as he put the cricket back in his pocket and took Deena's hand. Her palm felt clammy and she was shaking, but she gripped his hand tightly. Together, they walked through the doorway and into the next room, both on edge and looking nervously around the space, half expecting to see Andy standing there staring at them. But they saw nothing. Just like the other rooms, this one was empty.

Even though he could not see his friend, Jack somehow felt that he was there.

"Andy?" he said, very quietly.

Click-click.

They flinched again, but less so this time. The noise came from almost directly in front of them, as if they could both reach out and touch its source. Jack took a couple of tentative steps forward and slowly reached his free hand out in front of him.

Suddenly there was a loud crunch as the floorboard beneath Jack's foot splintered and gave way, dropping his left leg through the gaping hole. Deenah screamed and grabbed him with her other hand, bracing his fall. He wrapped both arms around her and managed to sit on the floor with his lower leg still sticking through the floorboards into the space below.

"Oh my God!" she gasped. "Are you hurt?"

"I don't think so," Jack managed, as he leaned back and gingerly lifted his leg from the hole. Deena helped him to his feet and he quickly checked his leg for injuries but found none.

"All good," he said, deeply relieved.

"Thank God," Deena said. "I can't think of a much worse places to break a leg."

As he stood up and they turned back toward the living room, Jack stopped, suddenly deep in thought.

"Hang on a second," he said, still gazing somewhere far away. "I saw something."

"What do you mean? Where?" she asked.

Jack turned and shone the light down into the hole in the floorboard.

"There," he said, pointing with his other hand. "In the crawl-space. I caught a glimpse of it when I pulled my leg out."

Deena knelt carefully down and looked into the cavity below the floor. There was something that looked like a small, shallow box wrapped in a dirty rag. "What is that?"

"I don't know, but it looks like someone hid it down there." He knelt beside her and started to reach into the hole.

"Wait," Deena said, putting her hand on his arm. "That could be anything, Jack. Just leave it. You got lucky once. Why push it? Let's just get the hell out of here."

He saw the fear in her eyes and for a moment he hesitated. At that instant, another loud thump on the upstairs floor sent a jolt of fear through them. It was followed by another, and then rapidly several more. Something was moving across the floor above them.

A whimper escaped Deena's lips and she pulled at Jack's arm.

Without hesitating further, Jack thrust his arm into the crawlspace and grabbed the object, rag and all, and pulled it out of the hole, even as the heavy footsteps above them seemed to reached the top of the stairs.

"Run," Jack shouted. "Go! And don't look back."

Deena bolted out of the back room and through the living room, with Jack close behind her. Just as they cleared the open front doorway and skirted the gaping holes in the porch, they heard the footsteps coming quickly down the stairs behind them and into the living room.

They both leapt over the porch steps and landed on the ground in front of the house at a flat-out run and sprinted away through the weeds, dodging rotting boards and branches as they went. When they were thirty yards from the house, Jack stopped.

"Hey, hold up!" he gasped, holding up a hand.

Deena stopped and turned to see Jack drop the object in the rag and pull the pistol from his belt. He spun back toward the house and dropped into a firing stance, fully expecting to see an attacker close behind them, but they saw nothing. There was nobody there and they heard only the sound of their own heavy breathing and the rustling of the branches in the breeze. The farmhouse stood empty again, as it always had, with darkened windows that now seemed somehow like malevolent eyes. It was then that Jack noticed how badly the pistol was shaking in his hands, and he knew he would have been lucky to hit the broad side of a barn.

"Holy shit," Deena gasped, as she tried to catch her breath, bending over and bracing her hands on her knees. "What was that?"

"I have no idea," Jack said, between breaths. "But whatever it was, it didn't like us being there."

"Maybe we should call someone, report this," Deena managed..

Jack stuck the pistol back under his belt and put his hands on his hips, breathing deeply and pacing as he tried to calm his nerves.

"Two things," he said. "Check your phone, but I'd be amazed if we have service out here at all, wherever here is, and second, and I say this with all respect, who exactly are we going to call? And what are we going to tell them?"

She considered this and shrugged, waving her hand as if brushing the idea aside. "Okay, I get it. Dumb suggestion."

Jack shook his head and looked at her. "No, not dumb at all. Under normal circumstances that's exactly what we would do, but there's nothing normal about any of this. Nothing."

Deena nodded. "That's putting it mildly."

As their breathing slowed, she walked over and looked at the object he had brought from the house. The rag had fallen partially away and they could see the corner of a book.

"What do you think it is?" she asked.

Jack knelt down, continuing to glance warily in the direction of the house.

"We can take a quick look, but I'd like to get as far away from here as possible before we spend much time on it. I hate this fucking place."

He carefully picked up the book and unwrapped the rag from it. It was obviously very old, badly worn and faded, with a hand-stitched leather binding, but they saw no title printed or embossed on the cover. They both leaned closer as Jack carefully opened the book, revealing dusty and yellowed pages. The first two were blank, but on the third page they saw in written hand, in faded ink:

"Property of William Gregory McNeill."

"Oh, my God," Deena whispered as they looked at each other.

"William," Jack said. "What you heard in the house..."

She nodded. "That was the name, I'm sure of it."

They looked again at the book. Below the first line was written, "Husband of Margaret McNeill; father of Rebecca and Henry McNeill."

On the next line: "Diary of events: April, 1924—..." There was no ending date.

"I don't believe it," Jack said, looking wide-eyed at Deena. "It's got to be from the family who originally lived here. Hell, 1924? They probably built the place."

"Wow," she said, reaching out and running her fingertips slowly over the page. "How has it lasted this long in that crawlspace?"

"Who knows?" Jack said, turning the book over and inspecting it. "Maybe the crawlspace stayed dry enough that it was protected from the elements. And it was wrapped in the cloth. God knows it was hidden well enough. No wonder nobody found it before now."

Suddenly Deena gasped and grabbed Jack's arm, and he saw she was staring toward the house.

"I just saw somebody in the house," she said in a harsh whisper. "They just moved past the upstairs window."

Jack stood up and turned to look at the house. Pale light was showing through the framed openings from the windows on the opposite side of the house. Not much, but enough to silhouette something passing in front of it.

"Could you tell who it was?"

"No. It was just like a shadow passing by the window, but not like from a cloud or a tree. It moved, like someone walking." She looked imploringly at Jack. "Could a ghost do that? Block out the light?"

Jack scanned the house for another moment, considering the question.

"No, I don't think it could, at least not what we think of as a ghost," he said, as he opened his pack and began wrapping the book. Then he looked at her and his expression was grim and hard. "But something real enough to snatch and kill a child could."

Deena looked aghast at the thought and glanced again at the house.

"Anyway," Jack said, "We've done enough for one day, and I don't want to be anywhere near this place when the sun goes down."

"You've got that right," Deena said. "Let's get the hell out of here."

CHAPTER 11

By the time Jack and Deena finished climbing the final quarter-mile stretch of the return trip, up the steep wooded slope behind their old street, they were exhausted, both physically and mentally. Sensing that their harrowing experience at The Farm had pushed them both dangerously close to the limit of what their minds could process, Jack had used the hike back as an opportunity to steer the conversation to more manageable life topics, for both their sakes.

After he had asked Deena about how she ended up in the antique business, she had seemed relieved to tell him the whole story, beginning with how her brief marriage had ended in such a "cliché." She had discovered that her (by all outward appearances) devoted husband was sleeping with his boss, a.k.a. "the Alpha-slut," and that most of the two and three-day business trips he had been taking were actually sexual trysts at mountain cabins outside Asheville. She had played dumb long enough to get a good lawyer and hire a private detective who was good with a camera, and had then hit the bastard simultaneously with a divorce filing and an alienation-of-affection (that was a thing in North Carolina, apparently) lawsuit. Because of her financial dependence on his sizeable income, and his and the Alpha-slut's egregious behavior, Deena's settlement had been enough to allow her to buy the shop outright and pursue her long-time passion for antiques and interesting artifacts. She had been there growing the business ever since.

Jack had also learned more about Deena's strained and distant relationship with her father. She described how Andy's disappearance and their mother's subsequent breakdown had driven a wedge between her parents, and that as a child, she had seen her father moving out as absolute abandonment. While she had eventually come to appreciate how hard it must have been for him to cope with Mel's mental state, and had even developed a modicum of sympathy for him, it had not been enough to warm the chill between them. She had also long suspected that she reminded him too much of Andy and the whole terrible chapter, and that having contact with her was simply too painful. She had confessed that the few times each year they now spoke, always by phone, she found it awkward and felt deeply relieved to end the calls.

As uncomfortable as it had made him, Jack had also shared some of his own struggles, including his estrangement from his father and his complicated history with alcohol. He confessed that he had never understood exactly where the line between dependence and alcoholism was, but that he was certain he had come very close to crossing it at several low points in his life. He also told her a little about Millie Braxton and had found himself smiling as he described her unique manner and style. He admitted that in all the years since they were kids, he had tried desperately and unsuccessfully to wall off the past, and that with Millie's help, he had only recently begun to understand how harmful his stubborn refusal to come to terms with the past actually had been to his psyche.

Deena had congratulated Jack on his willingness to work through it and remarked that Millie sounded like the best kind of people. To Jack's surprise, she had even said that she hoped he would introduce her to Millie one day. Her words had meant more to Jack than she could have known.

An hour later, they sat together on the small sofa in the hotel room, eating Mexican take-out off the coffee table and eyeing what they now knew to be the diary of one William McNeill, founder of The Farm, still wrapped in the dusty cloth they had found it in and sitting on a nearby chair. As eager as they had been to examine it, they had agreed that they would shower and eat something beforehand, as the snacks they had taken on the hike had proven to be a poor substitute for lunch, and they were both ravenous.

When they had finished and bagged up their containers, Jack started to head for the kitchen when Deena put a hand on his forearm and stopped him. He sat back down beside her and saw that she was looking at him and seemed to be gathering her thoughts. He took her hand and set the bags down.

"What is it?" he asked.

She cleared her throat. "Well, before we look at that diary, or whatever it is, there's something that I need to get out of the way."

"Okay," Jack said slowly, a hint of caution creeping into his voice.

To his surprise, Deena reached one hand up and put it gently on the side of his cheek. Jack felt a wave of excitement ripple through him at her touch, and he was further astonished when she leaned toward him and kissed him warmly on the mouth. He hesitated for only a moment, then eagerly returned her kiss, only then fully realizing how strong his attraction to her had grown.

Finally, she pulled back, smiling, her cheeks lightly blushing and her blue eyes shining.

"I Just wanted to tell you how sorry I am for everything you went through back then and how glad I am that you came looking for me."

Jack felt his throat tighten, but he smiled and stroked her still-wet hair with his fingers.

"Me too," he managed. "Thank you for saying that."

Finally, she sighed and nodded in the direction of the book. "Now, want to do a little light reading?"

He laced his fingers in hers and smiled. "Yeah, but I'm not sure we got that other thing fully out of the way yet."

She grinned and leaned in for another kiss.

"Well, then we'll just have to keep working on it."

"Sounds like a plan," he said.

Deena pointed at the book. "Do you want to do the honors? I'll top-up the drinks."

Jack brought the bundle back and set it on the coffee table, carefully unwrapping the cloth and opening the book again. As Deena set the drinks on the table in front of them and sat down next to him, Jack felt an odd mix of excitement and dread as he reached for the cover page and turned past it to William McNeill's first two entries.

For Henry and Rebecca. In the hopes that my rambling notes will one day help you remember.

April 18, 1924:

The well is a success and the water is good. Raymond and I finished the cupboards and put the door on the ice house. I will take the wagon into town tomorrow for the last of the seed and supplies and bring Margaret and the children. Rudy Forrester has agreed to sell three sows and a boar hog next week and the Beverly Brothers will bring the first four Holsteins in two weeks which will give us time to finish fencing the pasture.

Margaret is excited but understandably nervous about our grand endeavor and even if she has not said as much, I believe she has trepidations about trading our life in the city for a new one on a farm. Only time will tell if we have the grit of true homesteaders.

April 30, 1924:

Started planting corn today, later than I had hoped, but most other vegetables already planted. Two days of rain this week will help the new crop. Carl Beverly brought the cows yesterday. They look healthy and are already giving milk. Two are already bred. It will be easier now that the milking shed and stalls are finished. I think the bred sow could birth her litter at any time. Rebecca is excited to see baby pigs and I have told her they are not pets, but I am afraid she will get too attached.

Henry has been a big help but has not taken to farm work as well as I hoped he would. Maybe in time. Rebecca stays close by Margaret as she does the cooking and house work and likes to feed the chickens. Margaret is a determined and hard-working woman and knows how to put a good meal on the table, but sometimes I see her looking out the kitchen window and I know her mind is somewhere else – maybe back in Chicago.

"Wow," Deena said, marveling at the idea that they were reading the century-old hand-written notes of The Farm's original patriarch. "So, they *were* the ones who built it."

"Apparently so," Jack said, skimming back over the two entries. "It was an honest-to-God working farm, and I guess he just decided to keep a journal to have some kind of record of how it all went."

Deena wrinkled her nose. "So, these people moved all the way from Chicago to the middle of nowhere, no offense to us, to try and make a go of farm life? Damn, they had to want it bad."

Jack looked at Deena as the reality of it sank in. "No kidding. And he's talking about 'taking the wagon?' This was years before farm trucks. You saw how far that place is from any kind of civilization. Can you imagine how long and how many trips it would take to get enough materials and supplies down there to build all that from scratch?"

"It's crazy. He's talking about having 'grit,' but I can't even imagine how hard everything would have been for them."

She saw that Jack was no longer looking at the book but somewhere far away, and she could tell by the troubled look in his eyes that his mind had drifted back to their terrifying episode that day at The Farm. She reached over and lightly ruffled his hair, then turned the page.

"Let's keep going."

Jack refocused and they leaned over together and examined the next series of entries.

May 8, 1924

The cows got spooked two nights ago by a coyote and Henry and I had to fix the fence on the south side of the pasture. Shot at the coyote but it was too dark. Maybe, God willing, they will stay away. Sow farrowed a good litter of twelve last week and only lost one. Rebecca stays out at the pig stall in the barn in between chores until Margaret calls her in.

Tomatoes are coming up but it is worrying that other crops have not. Lee Wheeler at the feed store says everything should be up by now. Put extra manure on the fields yesterday and had Henry hoe the rows. Looking out for more rain.

He has caught a few small trout in the river that made good eating. Margaret is learning to cook with less stores than she was used to in the city. We are stocked on bought supplies until the first crop comes in but there is no extra. Savings are low.

May 14, 1924

Finished cutting hay in north field yesterday and will finish putting it up tomorrow. Henry got a bad cut on his leg from the blade and Margaret put iodine on it and bandaged it. She thinks we should take him into town to see a doctor but it will heal.

Smaller Heffer looks like she might be having some kind of trouble – not eating enough. Will wait and see if she needs a vet.

The entries varied in length and there seemed to be no consistent time gap between them; sometimes it was a week, other times ten days or as much as two weeks. There was one more entry in May of that year, three in June, and two in the last ten days of July. They all documented the day-to-day challenges the family faced in getting their farm up and running, as well as greater or lesser events William found notable. He had occasionally included personal observations about the family, but these were rare. As they made their way through the entries for the summer growing season and into the autumn harvest, Jack and Deena continued scanning for signs of anything unusual;

anything that would provide clues as to what eventually happened there and what connection any of it had to Andy. But as fascinated as they were by the details and sometimes harsh realities of farm life, they saw nothing that seemed obviously out-of-the-ordinary. That was, until the one-and-only entry for September of that year.

September 17, 1924

Finding still more black spots on the crops. May be some kind of blight but not like anything I've seen before. Will take some to Ag extension and get them to look at it. Margaret is doing her best to cut around it, but she says we will only put up two-thirds of what we should. It will make things harder for the winter and there will be no extra.

Spotted sow killed another of her litter last week and had to put the rest in a separate pen. She never showed any sign of aggression until two weeks ago.

Henry and Rebecca have started to complain about how hard life here is and Henry asked me yesterday if we could go "home." I whipped him and told him never to ever ask me that again. We are home.

Margaret has been quieter than usual and she looks like she is lost in her own thoughts a lot of the time. I found her standing in the lower field in her apron, with a wooden spoon in her hand the other day. Just staring out across the river. When I asked her what she was doing out there it was like she woke up from a dream. She said she didn't know.

I am growing concerned she may be falling deeper into a melancholia or a depression.

Maybe there is something wrong about this place.

Jack and Deena looked at each other.

"Wow," Jack said, glancing back through the entry. "That's different."

"Yeah, very." Deena said, wrinkling her brow. "You know that life had to be hard on them, and I'm sure it was exhausting. God knows I would probably be dead at that point, but this sounds like something else. And he's getting worried, particularly about her."

"Yeah, that's the most he's said about it so far. And that last part about Margaret is a little creepy." Jack did not say it, but the scene invoked his own memory, yet again, of finding Deena standing at the hotel room door in a trance-like state the previous night.

"Maybe," Deena mused. "But depression is a strange thing. It can manifest in all kinds of ways. My guess is, it wouldn't have been okay for Margaret to tell William if she was having trouble coping. She would have suppressed it and tried to soldier on. And that's what can push people over the edge."

"And that other stuff," Jack remarked. "The crops, the animals, on top of issues with the family. Maybe it was to be expected, but makes you want to know where this is headed." He gave a wry grin and opened the book to the last page. "Why don't we skip the suspense and just cut to the..."

Deena clapped a hand on his and stopped him before he could open the book.

"Don't even think about it!" she scolded, in mock outrage. "Don't tell me you're one of those people."

"What people?"

"The read-the-ending-first kind of people."

Jack rolled his eyes and relented, returning to their original place in the book.

"Whatever you say, dear," he grinned.

Her smile faded. "But in all seriousness, I think we've got to look at this very closely. For some reason I feel like what we're looking for is in there, we just have to be patient and go through everything with a fine-toothed comb."

"Agreed," Jack said. "I'm glad clearer heads prevailed. We definitely don't want to miss anything. Let's see where this goes."

October 8, 1924

Ag office couldn't say what kind of blight is on the crops. They haven't ever seen one like it. Said it could be something in the soil but no idea what. Said it looks like decay on rotting vegetables, but these are still on the vine.

Got the tractor belt fixed and cut down a big poplar out on the hill for winter wood. Even some of the wood was rotten and soft.

Almost all the crop is canned and put up, and will slaughter a hog next week for sausage and salting.

Henry and Rebecca are bickering more and I keep having to separate them. Margaret does not seem to notice it and I keep having to tell her.

She has looked awfully tired and I asked her directly yesterday what had been the matter. She told me she feels empty inside (whatever that means) and she hasn't been sleeping well. She says she has nightmares a lot. When I asked her what they were about, she said it was awful things, but she wouldn't tell me what. I am worried about her.

"There it is," Deena said softly. "The nightmares. She's having them every night."

Jack looked at Deena and the hair stirred on the back of his neck. "What do you mean, every night? He doesn't say that here. Did you read ahead?"

For a moment, Deena seemed far away, then she shook her head. "I don't know why I said that. It's like somehow I know it's true. Not because I read it, but because I see it, almost like I lived it. She's waking up terrified and afraid to say anything to William. She's frustrated and exhausted."

Jack watched her in silence for a moment, his mind racing. Something about her words made him feel afraid, but he wasn't entirely sure why.

"Do you think it's possible you just relate to her because you've been having nightmares yourself? Or maybe it's your mind inferring what's going on from the other things he's written?"

Even as he said it, Jack knew he was reaching. Something in him knew there was more to it than that. It was as if she was developing some kind of psychic connection to Margaret Mc-Neill, or perhaps like Andy, something of Margaret still lingered at The Farm and was somehow reaching out to her. Either way, the ramifications were troubling.

Finally, Deena shrugged. "I don't know. Maybe. But it doesn't feel like that."

Jack nodded. "Okay, well let's see where this goes, but will you let me know if you feel anything else like that, I mean about Margaret?"

"Of course," she said, squeezing his hand.

"Hey," Jack said, glancing at the time on his phone. "It's getting late. I don't know about you, but I'm wiped out from today. Why don't we save some of this for tomorrow morning?"

Deena rubbed her eyes. "You're probably right. We've been so heads-down I haven't even though about how tired I am."

They left the book open on the coffee table and brushed their teeth together in the small hotel bathroom before turning off the lights and heading to bed. As Jack pulled back the covers, he realized that Deena was still standing beside her bed in her nightshirt, watching him.

"Feel like sharing?" she smiled.

Jack felt mildly dizzy. "Absolutely," he smiled in return.

She tiptoed over to his bed and slid in next to him, wrapping one bare leg over his and putting her arm across his chest. Jack stroked her hair and kissed her, and as she let her hand play along his body, they both gave in to the desire that had been building between them for days. Their lovemaking was urgent and intense, and afterwards they both quickly fell asleep.

Sometime in the night, Jack awoke in the darkness to the sound of Deena's angry voice. She was sitting up in the bed beside him and appeared to be scolding someone. She did not sound like herself.

"Rebecca Jean McNeill, you get in here! We saved up for that dress, and you've ruined it."

Jack blinked and put his hand on her back. She paused, but only for a moment.

"Hush your mouth, young lady!" she continued, her voice rising. "You knew better, and we told you no, but you did it anyway."

"Deena," Jack said, "Wake up, you're dreaming."

Deena stopped talking but didn't look at Jack.

"It's okay," he said, sitting up and rubbing her back. "You're dreaming. Go back to sleep."

After a moment she blinked and looked at him, sleepy and confused. "Okay," she mumbled, and lay back down. She was asleep in seconds.

Early morning light was creeping in around the curtains when Deena awoke the next morning. The bed was empty beside her and she did not see a light on in the bathroom or hear any signs of movement.

"Jack," she called. "Are you in here?" There was no response.

She crawled out of bed, went to the bathroom and peed before brushing her teeth and her bed-hair, then found her phone. She was just about to call Jack's number when she heard a clunking sound and the room door open. Instinctively she grabbed a jacket to cover herself, just in case.

The door opened and Jack walked in, holding a cardboard cup carrier in one hand and the room key in the other, while a take-out bag was tucked under his arm.

"Morning," he smiled. "You're up."

She relaxed and tossed the jacket on the bed. "Morning, where'd you go?"

"For coffee and egg biscuits," he said. "Interested?"

"You had me at biscuits," she said, walking over and kissing him briefly before looking in the bag. "I'm starving."

Jack set the cups and the bag on the kitchen counter and put napkins down for the biscuits.

"Yeah, you had a busy night," he said, casting a sideways glance at her.

She looked quizzical.

"What do you mean?"

"You were talking in your sleep, and you were pretty pissed."

"Seriously? Shit, was I sleepwalking again?"

"No, not this time," Jack said as he pushed a biscuit and coffee in her direction. "You were sitting up in bed, but you were chewing Rebecca McNeill out. Something about a dress."

169

Deena looked blank for a moment and then a look of realization slowly crossed her face.

"Yeah, I remember now. I was mad in the dream; so mad. It was a yellow dress with white lace trim. We didn't have the money to buy it, but we wanted her to have something nice to wear when we went into town."

Jack was mesmerized.

"She had wanted to go outside in it and 'twirl' in the grass, and William and I had told her no. Then when she showed up at the door with mud on the front of that dress, I just wanted to..." Deena hesitated. "I was so mad. It was so real."

"Yeah, it was pretty real," Jack said. "I didn't know what was going on. And you don't remember waking up and looking at me?"

Deena took a bite of her biscuit and shook her head.

"My favorite part was, 'Hush your mouth, young lady,'" Jack grinned.

"I said that?" Deena gaped.

"Among other things," Jack replied.

"Sorry about that," she said.

"No worries. I understand, believe me."

"You had one too?"

"Unfortunately," Jack said, his smile fading. "I was in that damned well again. It was pretty awful. And I kept trying, but I couldn't get out."

Jack stopped there, unwilling to tell her more. He was ashamed and angry that his subconscious had conjured it up, but in the dream, he had seen a face leering down at him from above, as bony hands pushed a heavy wooden cover over the well opening, blocking out the light and leaving him to die in the dark, alone with the decaying bodies piled around him. The face had been gaunt and the eyes cloudy and cold, but in his dream there had been no doubt; it was Deena.

CHAPTER 12

"Ready to read some more?" Jack asked as they finished their impromptu breakfast.

Deena hesitated, but then let out a heavy sigh. "I can't, Jack. As much as I want to, I played hooky yesterday and I need to spend today at mom's place." She leaned over and kissed him. "I really want to see where all this is going, but I've got the shop to think about too, which means I've got to wrap up whatever I'm hoping to get done by the end of tomorrow and get back."

Jack shrugged it off, but felt crestfallen. "Oh sure, I completely understand." He lied, as he waved a finger casually in the direction of the book. "We got a lot done yesterday. A hell of a lot more than I expected, and this stuff's not going anywhere. I can just keep it on ice until..."

"Oh, no, don't do that," she interrupted. "You should keep reading, it's important. You can fill me in later, maybe over dinner somewhere?"

"Absolutely," Jack smiled, artfully hiding his disappointment. As he looked at her, he marveled again at the powerful, almost instantaneous connection he had felt with her and how much he had been relishing their time together. So much so, that in some childishly naïve part of his mind, he had imagined their adventure together going on and on, uninterrupted by the day-to-day noise and demands of their adult lives. But that was of course not the real world and he knew it.

"I completely forgot to call Tanya yesterday," she continued, shaking her head. "And she never called me, which is either a very good or a very bad thing."

"No worries," Jack said. "I'll carry the torch and keep digging. We can talk later and figure something out for dinner, and I can always call you if I have a breakthrough."

"Good," she said. "Sounds like a plan. Now, I'm going to grab a shower."

Deena got up from her barstool and walked toward the bathroom, pulling off her nightshirt as she went, revealing her fully naked and wonderfully toned body. Jack grinned in awe amid a dizzy wave of adrenaline.

"Want some company?" he said.

"Sure," she called over her shoulder, "but I warn you, I like it really hot."

"Yes, you do," he said, still smiling as he pulled off his shirt and followed her toward the bathroom.

After wishing Deena luck with her mother's condo and waving her off at the door, Jack found himself alone with the myriad thoughts and emotions crowding his mind; euphoria, intrigue, frustration, and something edging toward fear.

He looked at William McNeill's journal, still lying open on the coffee table and thought again about the troubled tone the entries had begun to take before he and Deena had stopped for the night. Jack had felt a sense of foreboding as he read through them, unable to shake the feeling that something much darker lay ahead for the McNeill family. But whatever clues, if any, the remainder of the book held to Andy's cryptic communications, at least Jack now had names and dates for more research at the County Hall of Records and on the internet. And there was still the open question raised by the chevron beads, of how Hernando De Soto and the Chockowan were connected to any of it.

Jack brewed another cup of coffee at the Keurig in the kitchenette and sat back down on the sofa. Looking at the open book, he thought about how hard it must have been, amid the daily mountain of chores on a farm, for William McNeill to find a rare quiet moment to himself to make entries in a journal. And based on what he had read so far, Jack was certain William would have taken great care to ensure that none of his family saw what he was writing, particularly Margaret.

As Jack turned the page and started to read the entry for October 27th, a jolt of electricity ran through him and he put down his coffee cup. He re-read the entry slowly, scrutinizing each word as he went.

October 27, 1924

Had the first frost last Thursday. Margaret managed to finish putting up what food we have for the winter but I worry it is not enough. We will almost certainly have to use some of what little savings we have to buy supplies, but the road may not be fit to travel much of the winter.

Margaret is struggling with her depression, and her dreams have gotten worse. I kept at her and she finally told me that she is having dark, wicked dreams about killing and death. And she feels angry in the dreams, and there is something with her and it speaks to her, but she cannot see it.

These dreams frighten me, and she does not seem herself.

She slapped Rebecca yesterday over the yellow dress. I've never seen her do that. Margaret saw it in a Sears catalogue in town a few weeks back and wanted Rebecca to have it so she would look nice when we go into town. I finally agreed, so they ordered it.

Rebecca wanted to carve faces in the pumpkins yesterday but we told her no. Then she asked if she could wear her new yellow dress outside to dance in the field but we said no to that too.

She got mad and wore the dress out and did it anyway—got dirt on the front of the dress and all over the white lace trim at the bottom. Margaret slapped her hard and made her take off the dress right there in the kitchen. Rebecca told Margaret she hated her and Margaret slapped her again and made her go to her room without supper.

I am not sure what to do to help Margaret. I may take her into town and ask Preacher Rayburn to talk to her and pray with her.

Jack felt his pulse racing as he hurriedly picked up his phone and called Deena.

She answered one the third ring. "Hi, you. I just left. Did I forget something, or you just miss me that much?"

"No, it's not..." he stammered. "Did you read ahead in the book? I was just curious."

"What book? You mean in McNeill's journal?"

"Yeah, I just wondered if you read ahead a little at some point before bed last night, or maybe during the night."

"Ah, no," she chuckled. "If I recall, you and I were pretty occupied last night and I fell right asleep afterwards." She paused. "What's wrong, Jack? You sound strange. Why are you asking?"

Jack could still hear Deena explaining her strange dream earlier that morning, and why she was yelling at Rebecca McNeill in her sleep. *It was a yellow dress, with white lace trim.* Everything else she had so casually described about her dream matched William's journal entry detail for detail. *Exactly.*

He opened his mouth to tell her, but something held him back.

"It's nothing, no big deal, I just wondered. Thanks, though."

"Jack?" Deena sounded concerned.

"Seriously, I've just had too much caffeine. It's nothing, really."

"Okay, if you're sure."

"But just so you know," he deflected. "I *do* miss you that much already."

He could almost hear her smiling. "Me too. Talk to you soon."

They ended the call and Jack looked first at the phone, then at the book.

"What the hell?" he whispered, as he considered more rational explanations. Was it possible she had gone back to the book last evening when he wasn't looking, or after he went to sleep? No, they had been together every moment before bed and the book had remained in plain sight. Maybe she had gotten back up after he went to sleep, but not likely; she had fallen asleep first and hard. Even when he accidentally bumped her with his elbow while reaching to turn off the lamp, she hadn't stirred.

No, he thought, this was something else. Since the night of Deena's sleepwalking incident, he had feared that something or someone besides Andy was communicating with Deena through her dreams, but this seemed to confirm it. Jack felt strongly that what remained of Andy was somehow trapped; his soul imprisoned in that strange and unnatural place, but what if he wasn't the only one? At The Farm, Deena had said she had the strongest feeling that the people who lived there never left, and Jack had thought at the time she meant they died there. But what if she meant they were *still there*?

In Deena's dream about the yellow dress, she *was* Margaret McNeill. She hadn't just seen through Margaret's eyes; it had been more than that. She had felt Margaret's emotions as if they were her own. And if Margaret McNeill was a sentient presence, like Andy, and she had somehow found a psychic back door into Deena's subconscious mind, there might be no limit to how deeply she could push and how much of Deena's mind she could occupy. The more he considered it, the more unnerved Jack became.

And if Deena's dreams were actually memories, what were his own? He had dreamed about a massacre, and about being trapped at the bottom of a well among a pile of dead bodies with his mouth sewn shut. *Jesus*, he thought. *What if...*

Just then, he remembered something from an earlier entry and turned several pages back, scanning as he went, until he found it under the very first journal entry, dated April 18, 1924.

The well is a success and the water is good.

"Damn," Jack muttered. "They *did* have a well."

He tried to remember if he had seen anything at The Farm that looked like a well cover anywhere near the house, but the weeds had been high, and he and Deena had only been focused on what they would find inside the house. They could have walked right past it and never have known.

Jack stood up and paced across the room, massaging the back of his neck as his mind turned. The idea was almost unthinkable, but it would explain why the authorities had never found Andy's body. The had searched the entire area with a fine-toothed comb back then, but would have had no reason to look for a well, and if the cover was concealed or overgrown it would have been very easy to miss.

In that moment, Jack knew he had to go back. The more he thought about it, the more sense it made, and despite the terrible prospect of finding Andy's remains after all these years, he had to know. Andy was communicating with them for a reason, and even though Jack hadn't said it to Deena, he had always felt that finding Andy was the key to understanding what it was.

But when? And what would he tell Deena? She would want to go with him, but he knew how busy she was with her mother's arrangements and her life in Black Mountain. Even though she was clearly torn, she had been unequivocal about needing to get back to the shop, and he wanted to respect that. No, he would have to go alone. She wouldn't like it, but part of him wondered if it was better that way. Deena was strong, but finding what remained of her older brother might be a bridge too far.

There was also William's journal to finish reading, and he needed to do more research on the chevron beads. They clearly had an important connection to Andy and The Farm, and Jack felt a nagging urgency to know what it was.

Just then his cell phone chimed a calendar reminder and he realized that he had completely forgotten about his Zoom appointment that morning with Millie. He only had fifteen minutes to make himself presentable and get the laptop set up. As he hurriedly brushed his hair and dressed, Jack wondered what he would even talk about with her. So much had happened since they last spoke that it wouldn't be like picking up the conversation where he left off. In one short week he had gone from barely being able to talk about Andy and the past, to wading straight into the darkest (and possibly most dangerous) part of it up to his neck, and falling hard for Andy's younger sister in the process.

No, he thought as he opened the laptop on the kitchen counter and turned it on, definitely not the same conversation. He had considered cancelling or rescheduling, but for some reason, thought better of it. As much as he hated Zoom and the unpleasant feeling of having what should be a 3-D, in-person conversation flattened into a 2-D one that confined everyone's head to a small box, he appreciated the flexibility it provided. And it was increasingly, if somewhat sadly, how the world communicated.

He maximized the participant window, and within fifteen seconds of their appointed time, Millie's face appeared, sporting slightly unkempt wavy grey hair and a pleasant smile. She was wrapped in something resembling the Navaho sarapes Jack had seen on his only trip to the Southwest, and sipping from a ceramic mug.

"Good morning, Jack. Can you see and hear me alright?"

Jack warmed at her voice and remembered what a strong impression her calm, reassuring and supportive manner had made on him, and he knew why he had kept the appointment.

"Good morning, Millie. Yes, I can. How about you?"

"Loud and clear from this end," Millie said, relaxing back into her chair. "Have you done one of these before?"

Jack nodded. "Once or twice. I'll be honest, they're not my favorite."

Millie sipped from her mug. "I know what you mean. It's a little de-personalizing, but so-goes the world. And everything has it's trade-offs. How have you been since we last talked?"

Jack glanced down at his bare feet and wrestled with how to answer and how much of what had happened over the last week to share with her.

"Pretty good, I guess, all things considered."

"What do you mean?" she asked.

Jack paused and imagined himself trying to walk her through a blow-by-blow account of everything that had happened over the previous week, but it felt all wrong. Something in him rejected that idea outright as stilted and unnecessary. There were bigger questions now and he sensed that he didn't have time to waste on the trifle.

"A lot has happened in the last week," Jack began. "Too much to go through, unfortunately. But the reason I needed this one to be remote is, I'm in Benton, just down the road from my old house. I'm here in town with Deena Redmond, Andy's younger sister."

Millie seemed genuinely surprised. "Really? Had you kept in touch with her?"

Jack shook his head. "Ah, not at all. I looked her up on a chance and we connected pretty immediately."

"I hope that's a good thing for you both," Millie said, and he knew that she meant it.

"Seems like it is," Jack replied, unable to suppress a smile and the heat rising in his face.

"What are you doing in Benton?"

Jack did not give himself time to craft a benign response. "Looking for Andy and whatever killed him."

Jack saw the expression on Millie's face change, albeit subtly, to one of concern and curiosity.

"You've come a long way, it sounds like, in a very short time."

"You have no idea," he said.

"How are feeling about being there?" she asked, studying his face more carefully now.

Jack's worry about everything he had seen and experienced in the last week bubbled to the surface and he kept thinking about some of the books he had seen on Millie's bookshelf.

"What would you think about postponing that conversation for a later time? Some things have come up that I really need to ask you about. Things I wouldn't ask just anyone."

Millie considered the question, then nodded. "Okay, I guess that would be fine. What did you want to ask about?"

Jack took a breath. "Do you remember last time we talked, when I said I thought Andy had somehow come back?"

Millie nodded. "Yes."

"Well, things along those lines have gotten more complicated. And whatever these metaphysical connections are to the spirit world, if that's what you call it..." He considered his words. "They're escalating; getting stronger and somehow more real, in a way that's got me very concerned. And it's not just me. Deena is having similar experiences."

"You mean the connection with Andy?" Millie asked.

"That's the part that's got me worried," Jack said. "It's not just Andy anymore."

Millie set down her mug and leaned closer to the camera. "Okay, tell me more."

Jack proceeded to give Millie an abbreviated version of what had transpired over the last week, focusing at first on the connection with Andy through dreams and the cricket-clicker, then on his trip to Black Mountain to find Deena. When he told Millie about their nearly identical dreams, in which Andy had his mouth sewn shut and had (somehow) given them each an actual chevron bead, she seemed keenly interested.

"So, you each have one of these?"

"Yes. They're not identical, but almost."

"Do you think I could have a look?"

Jack reached into his pants pocket, where he had taken to carrying it, along with the cricket, and held it up to the camera. Millie leaned in and studied it, as Jack slowly rotated it to show the intricate patterns of color.

"That's remarkable," Millie said, finally leaning back in her chair. "Thanks for showing me."

Jack put the bead away.

"I've heard of incidents where a spirit caused objects to appear, but I've never seen one before. I have no idea what it means, but in my opinion it's very significant." She paused. "And I think the stitching on Andy's mouth is significant as well. It's possible that it's dream symbolism, but these are clearly not ordinary dreams. Normally, the strange things in our dreams are invented by our subconscious to try and focus our attention on emotional struggles or areas of our life that need work, but the bottom line is, it's normally a closed communication loop; it's us communicating with ourselves. But what you're seeing, well..." She reached for something off camera. "Would you mind if I smoke? I'm trying to cut back, but this is one of those times."

"Not at all," Jack said, quietly grateful that it was a Zoom call. "If I had even the slightest inclination, I'd be having one as we speak."

She lit up and took a drag, exhaling slowly. "I know it's difficult, but I think it's possible what you're seeing in these dreams is not symbolic at all. It's possible, even likely, that what you're seeing are reflections of reality; Andy's reality."

Millie's meaning was clear and Jack felt his stomach tighten.

"You mean, like Andy's..." he pointed to his mouth, but didn't finish the sentence.

Millie nodded.

Jack winced. "That's what I've been afraid of. The more of this I've seen, the more convinced I am that we're seeing snippets of actual memories, his memories, like video clips he wants us to see."

"That sounds about right to me," Millie said, flicking the end of her cigarette in an ashtray just off camera.

"But there's more, and it gets worse," Jack said. "What's happening to Deena is not the same, and I'm almost certain it's not Andy."

Millie studied Jack for a moment. "Who do you think it might be?"

"First let me back up and tell you about what we've learned about The Farm, and what Deena and I found there yesterday..."

She furrowed her brow.

"You went back there, to The Farm?"

He realized how reckless it probably sounded to her, given how much she knew about his deep emotional scars and how closely they were tied to that place. Of all people, she would understand the emotional risks of going back there so early in the process, but at that moment, Jack thought her expression showed concern for something more than that.

He nodded. "We did."

Millie took another drag on her cigarette and looked directly at Jack. "Do you think that was a good idea?"

Jack considered the question.

"Probably not. But I think it's important for us to figure all of this out, and I don't think we have a lot of time."

"Why do you say that?"

"I don't know exactly," he said. "I feel like something is going to happen, or maybe it's already happening; something bad. And I believe the only chance we have to stop it, and help Andy in the process is to unravel whatever he's trying to show us." Jack paused. "It may not make sense, and I know it's a risky thing for me, but I've got to do it."

Millie nodded. "I can appreciate that. And in the end, you have to be the one to decide what makes sense for you. Why don't you tell me a little more about these dreams, yours and Deena's, and about going back to The Farm; what you've learned and what you found there."

Glad to have a sympathetic ear and eager for her thoughts, Jack recounted in as much detail as he could remember, Deena's sleepwalking incident, his own dreams, and their trip to the farm.

Millie interrupted him several times to ask questions, including whether he had a photo of the symbol Deena had drawn on the hotel room door. Jack still had the napkin he had drawn the image on and sent her a photo from his phone. Millie also wrote down Jack's best guess at the strange phrase she was repeating.

When he had reached the part about reading the entries in William McNeill's journal, and about Deena's vivid dream about McNeill's daughter Rebecca and the yellow dress, Millie interrupted again.

"So, you asked her about reading ahead in the book?"

"She said she didn't and I believe her. But the details were all there, and they were identical."

Millie thought about this as she stubbed out her cigarette off camera.

"Let me think some about what you've told me. There's a lot to unpack there, but we've already run a little over, so I'm going to need to get back to you with some impressions when I've got more time. And I mentioned the books on my shelf, because in addition to counseling, I have spent a great deal of time studying the role of metaphysical beliefs and practices in cultures around the world, and it's possible I can shed some light on what you're dealing with. No guarantees, but I'll do a little digging if I can grab a few minutes before we talk again."

"That would be great," Jack said, genuinely surprised by her offer. "Anything would be appreciated."

She coughed and cleared her throat. "Jack, before we go, there's a couple of things I need to say. First, some of this has thrown me a little. Based on what you've told me, this isn't just a question of our working through unresolved issues from the past. This is becoming something else. Something that is happening in real-time and is, quite frankly, a little frightening. Under normal circumstances I would not step this far off the counseling path with a client, but what you're dealing with is highly unusual, and apart from my selfish professional curiosity, I am genuinely concerned about you and Deena."

Jack blinked. "Concerned about what this might do to us psychologically?"

"No, Jack," Millie said, clasping her hands on the table in front of her. "I mean concerned for your safety."

"What do you mean?"

"I'm not sure exactly what you're dealing with, but whatever it is, it's a conscious entity of some kind, whether spirit or something else, and I believe it wants something. I don't know what that is, but until you know, until you're sure, I would only say be very, very careful. Whatever this is has made some kind of powerful psychic connection to both of you, possibly through Andy, and you have no idea what it may be capable of."

Her words chilled Jack, but they rang true.

"I understand," he said. "And we will. I really appreciate your time and your thoughts on this, as well as your patience. I know I've thrown you a bit of a curve ball."

She smiled. "That's not a problem, but thank you for saying so. I'll be in touch."

CHAPTER 13

Jack left the call with Millie with mixed emotions and a re-newed sense of urgency to unravel the dark truths behind The Farm and whatever was happening to them, but particularly Deena. Jack had long felt responsible for what she had gone through after Andy's disappearance, and while he was deeply grateful for her help and their connection, he was determined that he was not going to see her suffer more because of him.

Determined to get as much done as possible before he talked to her again, Jack returned to the book. As he read, Margaret McNeill's deteriorating condition became an increasingly prominent part of William's entries, while the tone of his writing became noticeably more alarmed and frustrated.

November 12, 1924

Henry's chest cold did not turn into pneumonia, thank the Good Lord, and he is coughing less every day. Rebecca has been helping take care of him.

Margaret is doing chores mostly in silence now, and sometimes she stops for no reason and stares at me or the children. She looks like someone else when she does it and I try to talk to her but she rarely responds. There is no letup in her nightmares. I pray for her every day.

Reverend Rayburn came last Thursday and tried to pray with her, but she got mad and tried to spit on him. I thought I would die. I apologized and told the Reverend that she has not been feeling well and has not been herself. She has always been polite and Godly and it breaks me to see her like this...

The entry continued, but Jack was no longer paying attention to the notes about the workings of the farm. Feeling like he was closing in on something important, he began scanning the entries for references to Margaret and her behavior. The closer the timeline got to the end of 1924, the more frequently she was mentioned, and the worse things became.

November 28, 1924

Yesterday was Thanksgiving but it was hard to be thankful. I am angry at God for Margaret's affliction and for not answering my prayers.

The children have been so worried about her and I thought that the holiday meal would be good for her – for all of us. Rebecca went into the kitchen to help her mother and a minute later I heard her scream. Margaret had thrown the turkey out in the yard for the dogs and put a pig's head from the slaughterhouse scrap bucket in the pot instead. She had put the vegetables and herbs in with it, and was about to cook it for us like there was nothing wrong. It was terrible. Both the children started crying and nobody felt like eating. I made Margaret go lie down.

Why is God punishing us?....

"Jesus," Jack said, as he imagined the shocking scene unfolding in the McNeill's kitchen.

December 8, 1924

...The road was bad, but I made a trip into town yesterday to see Reverend Rayburn again and beg for his help. He told me he thinks something has taken hold of Margaret and is twisting her mind...he said the Bible tells about evil spirits possessing people and making them do wicked things that are not human, and the spirits must be cast out by God. He said that he has never seen it before but if evil is at work in her, there may be nothing to do but pray and try to keep her from hurting herself or any of us.

I got angry at the Reverend, God forgive me, and told him he was wrong. Margaret is a loving woman and no matter how afflicted she is, she would never do that...

As he read, Jack grew increasingly alarmed by the idea that Deena was somehow developing a psychic connection with Margaret McNeill, or what remained of her. If Margaret had mentally decompensated so quickly in life, and with such disturbing results, where did that leave Deena?

Jack had always avoided the topic of demonic possession, even the thought of it, not because he was a skeptic, but because the idea was far too close to home. Given what he had seen, it was simply too awful to think about. But as he re-read William's last note and the Reverend's advice, he started to wonder. What if Margaret *had* been under the influence of some external entity at The Farm? Something evil. As he considered the question, he shuddered as his mind drifted back to the farmhouse and whatever had come out of the impenetrable darkness of the attic that night to snatch Andy. He had wondered a thousand times what it was and where it came from, but he had never stopped to consider how long it may have been there. And now he was left wondering if it was tied somehow to Margaret's deteriorating condition.

On the other hand, what if she had simply cracked under the stress of their life on the farm and had some kind of mental or emotional breakdown? Couldn't that explain some of her strange and erratic behavior? Neither option was good for Deena, but while one was bad, the other could be disastrous.

He knew they would be talking soon and he struggled with how much to tell her about what he had read and what it might mean. She had a right to know, but if knowing somehow made her more vulnerable to whatever was on the other end of the psychic bridge, it could be the worst possible thing for her.

When Jack's stomach prompted him to check the time, he saw that it was nearing the lunch hour, and he had an idea. He texted Deena.

Hey, want to meet for lunch?

He went to put his empty coffee cup in the sink, and a moment later his phone dinged.

Hi. Good timing. Not feeling so great. Maybe eating will help. Where?

Jack quickly pulled up his map app and checked restaurants on her end of town.

Sorry to hear that. Looks like Pepper's is still there. Sound okay?

Great. In 30?

He smiled and sent a thumb's up, but felt a pang of guilt as he glanced at the book open on the coffee table. He knew she would be curious, but he had no intention of taking it with him. Despite feeling slightly Machiavellian, Jack had suggested they meet out somewhere because he knew it would be easier to keep her away from the book, at least until he knew more, and he wasn't willing to take the chance.

Pepper's was smaller than Jack remembered it, but apparently just as popular with the lunch crowd. He was lucky to get a booth along the back wall, just as Deena arrived. She squeezed his hand as she slid onto the seat opposite him. Jack did not say so, but thought she looked very tired.

"Good suggestion," she said, looking around the dining room. "I'm surprised this place is still here. I used to come here a lot back in the day."

"I think we all did," he said. "It was a high school hot-spot for sure, but the food was always good. If I remember, my go-to was the spicy chicken and pepper-jack sandwich."

She smiled, but seemed distracted. "I think I remember that sandwich."

"You said you're not feeling so great," Jack said. "What's going on?"

Deena's smile faded and she shook her head. "I don't know, I've been trying to work through Mom's things and make a few phone calls, but all of this stuff keeps swirling around in my head. I can't stop thinking about it. Maybe it's partly lack of sleep but I was so addled I..." she hesitated, "lost track of time."

"I know what you mean," Jack said. "I was heads down and by the time..."

"No," she interrupted, lowering her voice. "I mean seriously lost time. Like, it scared me."

Jack frowned. "What do you mean?"

Just then, the server arrived with their drinks and offered to take their lunch order but Jack asked for a few more minutes and waved her off before turning back to Deena.

She waited until the young woman was out of earshot before continuing.

"I was sitting on a chair with her financial files on the coffee table, sometime between eight-thirty and nine, going through her bank records, and I remember hearing a strange banging noise coming from somewhere far away, but almost like it was in my head. I remember the numbers on the bank statement got fuzzy and everything seemed to slow down." Deena's voice had started to tremble and he saw her eyes watering.

"Hey, it's okay," Jack said, reaching across and taking her hand. "You're okay. What happened?"

"The next second I was standing at the sink with a glass in one hand and a dishtowel in the other, just staring out the window." She took a shaky breath. "I don't remember walking over there or picking those things up, or anything that happened for..."

She hesitated again and lowered her voice to just above a whisper.

"It was an hour later; nearly ten o'clock. A whole fucking hour passed and I have no memory of it. I have no idea what I did for that hour."

"Damn," Jack said, "That had to be weird." Her story alarmed him, but for her sake he tried to conceal it. "You haven't been sleeping well. Do you think it's possible you dozed off in the middle of working on the bank statements and ended up sleep walking again?"

"I thought about that," Deena said, rubbing her eyes, "but it didn't feel like that. When you wake up from sleeping you feel groggy, kind of disoriented, and it takes a few minutes to feel wide awake. I was wide awake looking at the files, and the next instant I was wide awake standing at the sink holding the damn glass. There was literally nothing in between. Like someone flipped a switch."

"I'm sure it felt like that, but you *have* been pretty stressed for weeks now, right? You've said as much a couple of times. If it makes you feel better, I was so sleep deprived one time last year that I graded a whole set of math papers and had no memory of doing it. It was like I woke up and someone else had graded them for me. Kind of freaked me out."

Deena sighed, but somehow looked encouraged. "Seriously?"

"Yeah, when you're exhausted, weird shit like that can happen."

Another possible and more ominous explanation for Deena's incident loomed large in Jack's mind, but he wasn't ready to call it credible yet, and he wasn't about to suggest it to Deena, at least until he had more to go on.

"Listen," Jack continued. "I've been thinking about what you said about your mom's stuff. If cleaning out her place really can wait, why don't you give yourself a break. Lock it up and let it sit for as long as you need. It's not going anywhere. You already had enough to deal with before I showed up and dragged you into all this."

"I'm glad you showed up," she smiled. "And for what it's worth, you didn't drag me into anything. If you remember, it was Andy who showed up first."

Jack smiled darkly and nodded. "Yeah, I'll give you that."

Deena shook her head. "Speaking of that, I'm really sorry. I've been blabbering on about me and I haven't even asked you about the journal. What else did you find?"

Jack's pulse quickened.

"Mostly just more of the same," he lied. "Life on the farm, putting up crops for the winter, problems with the animals, you name it. It is kind of sad about Margaret. From what he says in his notes, she fell into a pretty deep depression and started getting withdrawn and moody. Snapping at the children, stuff like that. I don't think William knew what to do for her."

"God, I can't say that I blame her," Deen said. "All the way out there in that valley trying to slog it out on that farm. It sounds brutal. But nothing that ties to what you're looking for, about Andy?"

"Not yet," Jack said. "But I haven't finished yet. I was also thinking about going by the county Hall of Records and see if they've got census data from those years. If I can't get what happened to the McNeill family from the journal, I might be able to see what years they show up in census data, and when they stopped showing up."

"Good idea," she said, just as the server came back to the table.

They both ordered the chicken and pepper-jack sandwich (still on the menu) for old time's sake and a side of sweet potato fries. When the server left, Jack continued.

"And Millie is actually going to help out with the chevron bead and Chockowan question."

"No kidding?" Deena seemed pleasantly surprised.

"Yeah, I talked to her this morning. Turns out that she's studied a lot of historical and cultural topics beyond counseling, and she's going to do a little research and let me know if she finds anything. It's probably a long shot, but better than nothing."

"I'm so glad, Jack. I know you'll appreciate the help."

"For sure," he nodded. "But, all that said, I've got plenty for now to go on, and I'm fine to keep digging here for a few more days. Why don't you wrap up at your mom's and head back to take care of things at home and get some sleep? You're not going to be any good to you or the shop or anyone else completely burned out."

"You're probably right," she sighed again, looking down at her hands as she began absentmindedly shredding the paper wrapper from her drinking straw. "I've never been good about knowing when to throttle back. Plus, I think Tanya is about to blow a gasket at the shop and Henry's cough has gotten so much worse. I'm worried it might turn into pneumonia."

Jack froze, eyes wide as Deena's words hung in the air.

He looked at her, unable to hide the panic he felt, but she was still looking at the small pile of shredded paper in front of her.

"What did you just say?" he asked quietly and evenly.

She blinked and looked up. "Just that I really do have to get back. Tanya had a difficult customer yesterday and now he's trying to..."

"No, not that part," Jack interrupted, more urgently than he meant to. "The part about Henry having a cough and it turning into...." He trailed off.

"What?" Deena asked. "What are you talking about?"

Jack's nerves pulsed with adrenaline and his mind scrambled for a foothold. He felt like he had just touched a live electrical wire.

"Just now, you said that one of the reasons you had to get back was..." he hesitated and reconsidered as he saw the genuine bewilderment on her face. It was clear that she had no memory of making the comment about Henry. Yet it had confirmed in an instant Jack's fears about the psychic connection between Deena's subconscious mind and Margaret McNeill. It was getting stronger; so much so that the lines between Margaret's reality and Deena's were actually beginning to blur.

You have to get her away from all this.

"Nothing," he said. "Never mind. I just... It was nothing. I'm a little worried about you is all; I'm just glad you'll do it."

Deena pulled his hand up in hers and kissed it.

"Thanks for thinking about me."

Just then their lunch arrived and as they ate, Jack artfully changed the subject back to Deena's progress at her mother's condo. She seemed glad to tell him about what she was finding and how everything for the memorial service was falling into place.

When they were finished, Jack walked her to her car and they stopped for a surprisingly passionate kiss. For a moment Jack wished intensely that he had reconnected with her sooner and under different circumstances.

"Are you sure you don't want me to stay?" Deena asked, her cheeks fully flushed. "I could go in the morning."

Jack's fleeting impulse to say yes was quickly overshadowed by the dark certainty he felt that time had now become a factor. He understood why Millie had said what she did about concern for their safety. The danger was real and it seemed to Jack that the farther away from it Deena was, the better her chances of shaking off whatever was clouding her mind.

"Tempting," he smiled. "Very tempting, but I'm willing to sacrifice and take a rain check on the night until you've gotten some rest." He paused and felt his cheeks burn. "The truth is, I would love for there to be a lot of nights. Who knows, maybe I could even learn something about antiques?"

She grinned and, for a moment she seemed entirely herself.

"I would love that," she said. "I really would."

But as she searched his eyes, her smile faded.

"Please be careful, Jack. I know this is very hard for you and frankly it's pretty frightening. I'm sorry to be abandoning..."

"Don't," Jack said, holding up his hand. "I'm the one who suggested it, remember?"

She nodded and kissed him again before climbing into her car.

"Let me know when you get home, okay?" he said, looking in her window. "And good luck talking Tanya off the ledge."

"Will do," she said, and started her car.

As Jack watched her drive away, he felt a strange mix of hope and fear. He desperately hoped that putting distance between herself and the insidious pull of The Farm would help. But he was far from certain. It was also possible that it might make no difference at all, and that thought chilled him to the bone.

He had also avoided thinking about the other inevitable consequence of her leaving; the one he dreaded most. If he went back to The Farm to search for a well, he would be alone; alone with his past, with his fears, with Andy, and whatever else was still lurking there in the shadows. It would take more courage than he had yet mustered, but he was fully committed. There was far more at stake now than his own mental health and closure on the past.

CHAPTER 14

After leaving Pepper's, Jack drove across town to the Randall County Hall of Records on West King Street. Deena was still heavy on his mind as he pulled into the parking lot, and he made a mental note to check in on her later that afternoon. The older lady behind the Customer Service counter, Eileen by her nametag, informed Jack that while North Carolina census data had been digitized for years, the data was only collected every ten years at the start of each new decade. Unfortunately, this meant that the earliest census after the timeframe of the journal to include the McNeill family should have been May of 1930; however, they were not listed. Eileen had been very helpful in running a search, informing him that there was a Walter McNeill and a Winston McNeill, but no William.

When Jack asked her what this meant, she shook her head and shrugged.

"No way to tell, really. It just means that county census workers did not find anyone by that name in 1930. The family could have relocated or possibly were deceased at that time, or some combination of the two. It's possible that they were missed, but the census is a federal mandate, so the county has always been thorough in tracking down resident households in our rural areas."

Eileen had given Jack the link to search the State Archives for death records, which she said were recorded after 1918, and he had thanked her and left.

On his way back to the hotel, Jack had the strangest sense of Déjà vu as he thought back to his conversation with Deena about the anomalies he had encountered years earlier while searching for land records related to The Farm valley. Her words still echoed in his mind.

So, as far as public records go, this place doesn't exist...

"Apparently, neither did the family," he said under his breath as the roof of the Sleep Inn came into view over the treetops in the distance.

As he was getting out of the car his cell phone rang and he cringed when he saw "Mom" on the display.

"Shit," he muttered. Was it possible she knew he was in town? *Yeah, too much of a coincidence,* he thought. Something told him that between local gossips and the unexplainable sixth-sense that mothers seem to have, she knew. He thought about taking it, but he didn't feel like making something up and he damn sure wasn't going to tell her what was really going on. There would be a time for that, but it was not now. He let the call roll to voicemail.

When he was back in the hotel room, Jack opened a beer before getting on his laptop and navigating the State Archives website. Despite finding what appeared to be detailed death listings for Randall County for each year leading up to the 1930 census, there were no records for William, Henry, or Rebecca McNeill, and the only listing for a Margaret McNeill showed the surviving spouse as Boyd McNeill, with an address on the opposite side of the county.

"What the hell happened to them?" Jack asked aloud. But then he remembered Deena making the other strange and haunting comment when they were at The Farm, in front of the house.

For some reason, I think they never left here.

It had disturbed Jack at the time, but now he wondered if it could be literally true. Margaret's rapidly deteriorating mental state and the increasingly dire circumstances on The Farm could easily have forced them to abandon the homestead before the 1930 census, which would explain the absence of county records, but their escalating troubles could also have led to a darker and more tragic scenario. Either way, it meant that William McNeill's journal might well be his only hope of discovering what really happened there and how it all related to Andy.

Jack glanced anxiously at the coffee table where the book still lay open to December of 1924, and despite his trepidation about what he might find, he took his coffee and went back to the couch, determined now to finish it.

By the time Jack read the next few entries, it was obvious that by early December of that year, William's concern for Margaret had become all-consuming and it was the only thing he cared about documenting in his journal. His notes conveyed an increasing sense of desperation and worry, along with anger and frustration at being helpless in relieving her condition. And Jack began to sense something else—concern for the safety of their children, Henry and Rebecca.

But it was the entry for December 18th that stopped him mid-sentence and sent a jolt of fear through him.

December 18, 1924

Hard frost last night. Margaret was up in the night again. I heard Henry calling me and I found Margaret standing in the corner of their bedroom barefoot in her gown, scratching something on the wall with the end of her finger. She was writing strange words with her own blood. She had made cuts in her forearm that looked like a symbol of some kind. A row of three Xs with a line through it. It made me sick to my stomach.

I did not know what the words were or what they meant. DRU AKEY NE SHADAY. Maybe it was gibberish or maybe some other language, but Margaret doesn't know another language so maybe she got it from a book...

"Oh, my God," Jack whispered, unable to believe what he was reading. The spelling was different than what he had written down after hearing Deena speaking the strange words in her sleep, but there was little doubt that it was the same phrase. And William's description of the symbol perfectly matched the figure Jack copied on a napkin. Jack took a breath and read on.

I spoke to her and shook her but she would not wake up so I had to slap her. She woke enough for me to clean her and bandage her arm. The children were scared so I sent them to our bedroom to sleep and I put Margaret in their bed. It frightened me to find her in their room. I worry she might hurt them in her sleep and not even know she is doing it. I hate the idea of locking her in our bedroom at night, but it may be necessary. I'm not sure what else I can do to protect them.

Jack's mind was reeling. He had been concerned enough when he thought that Deena's mind was picking up random bits of Margaret McNeill's memories through whatever metaphysical connection had formed between them. But this meant that her subconscious mind was not only replaying dark episodes from Margaret's life; it was compelling her body to act them out during sleep.

He got up and went to the kitchen where he splashed some water on his face and fixed himself a strong drink, downing half of it in one gulp.

Jesus, what have we gotten into? He thought.

207

Then, as he tried to make sense of it, he arrived at an even more troubling question: if Deena's mind was being clouded and her actions were somehow controlled by Margaret McNeill, what the hell had been controlling Margaret McNeill in the winter of 1924?

Jack downed the other half of the drink and briefly considered calling Deena, but he thought better of it and returned to the book instead. He was close to the end and he had to know. He would call her afterwards.

December 22, 1924

Margaret is no longer herself. She paces the house mumbling strange words and stares at me and the children in a hateful way that chills my blood. I have hidden the guns but I worry she will find them. She threw the medicine in the floor when I tried to give it to her and swore at me. She gnashed her teeth like a dog. It was unholy and I believe now it is the work of the devil.

I keep her locked in the bedroom at night but I cannot sleep and I am mostly exhausted.

Yesterday I found her walking toward the children's room with a knife in her hand and when I asked her what she was doing, she said she didn't know. After that I hid all the knives and any other blades in the house.

God help us.

A bead of sweat trickled down Jack's temple as he read, and when he reached up to wipe it away, he realized his hands were shaking. When he turned the page, he was shocked to see that it was the last one in the book. There was one more journal entry.

December 24, 1924

The worst has happened. Henry is gone. I was trying to fix something for the children to eat. Rebecca was helping me and I thought Henry was in the next room, but when I called him he did not answer. I ran upstairs and found Margaret in their room. Her hands were bloody and she was holding a large sewing needle threaded with cat-gut...

Jack gritted his teeth and felt like he would faint, holding onto the edge of the coffee table for support. He tried to slow his breathing but could not shake the image from his mind; Andy's face, eyes wide with terror and his mouth sewn shut. A low groan escaped Jack's lips but he forced himself to finish reading the entry.

I shook her and demanded to know where Henry was but she would not say. I slapped her and thought I would die. I kept asking her but all she would say is – he is quiet now. But she would not say anything more. God help me, I hit her hard enough to knock her out and tied her to the bed. I made Rebecca lock herself in her bedroom and I turned the house inside out looking but I could not find any trace of Henry. I even looked in the barn and the slaughterhouse. I called for him as loud as I could but only heard echoes in the valley. There were no tracks in the snow down in the field by the river but I looked along the river anyway and found nothing. It is as if he has vanished. She has done something to him

I know it. Damn whatever has hold of her. Please, God let my Henry be okay.

Horrified by what he had just read and dumbfounded that the book had no more entries, Jack felt a wave of frustration rising in him and was about to hurl the book across the room when he noticed a small faded note at the bottom of the last page.

End Book 1.

"Holy shit," he said, leaning closer and re-reading the text to be sure. "There were more journals."

But how many more? Where were they, and how would he find them?

Just then Jack's phone rang and he jumped to his feet, knocking over his empty drink glass in the process. He looked at the display, expecting to see Deena's name, but saw "Millie" instead.

"Millie, hi," he said, slightly winded as he picked up the call. "I'm glad you called. I really need to talk to you."

"You sound out of breath, Jack. Are you okay?"

"Yeah, mostly, I've been reading more in the book we found, William McNeill's journal. And well," Jack hesitated. "It looks like what's happening here may be worse than I thought."

On the other end of the call, Millie was silent for a moment.

"Yes, I think it is too, Jack. That's what I was calling to talk to you about. Do you have a few minutes?"

"Yeah, I do, of course."

Jack eyed the half-empty vodka bottle on the kitchen counter and headed that way.

"Good, I'm glad," she said. "First, I found out something about the symbol you sent me, the one on the napkin. I talked to a good friend of mine, Dan Langstall, who is a professor of Native American Studies in the Anthropology Department at Duke, and he was very helpful. He said that almost all of the Native American tribes of the southeast held strong beliefs of mythical creatures, monsters, witches, you name it, and the Chockowan were no exception. These were not vaguely defined, generalized evil spirits. These creatures had names, and the various tribes documented descriptions of their appearance and behavior. And even though unexplained deaths and disappearances were attributed to them for hundreds of years, they have always been considered by European and American academia as purely cultural mythology. Generally speaking, no one who values their reputation has suggested anything to the contrary."

"Sounds about right," Jack frowned, as he poured a shot of vodka into his glass and came back to the couch.

"That said," Mille paused and Jack heard her dragging on a cigarette, "in a few cases, there were symbols associated with these creatures, either based on their appearance or what they reportedly did to their victims. And it turns out, the symbol you sent to me *is* one of those."

"Okay," Jack said, as he felt the goose flesh rising on his arms. "Go on."

"According to Dan, a creature they called Cruxhen (she spelled it out) was a particularly nasty character; a witch monster who roamed the hollows and dark places in the Blue Ridge Mountains and fed on fear and pain. The legends say it was drawn to places where acts of cruelty or great tragedy had happened. It was said to be a tall thin skeleton covered in grey decaying flesh that came at night to take people; sometimes from the roads or the fields, sometimes from their beds. It killed them and imprisoned their souls so it could feed on their pain forever." She hesitated. "Are you okay with this? I know it's difficult."

"Yeah," Jack lied, exhaling sharply, dreading what he was certain was coming next.

"This Cruxhen supposedly sewed the mouths of her victims shut so they couldn't scream. That's what the symbol signifies; it's supposed to be stitches over a closed mouth. The Chockowan used it as a warning to others that Cruxhen was nearby."

"Christ almighty," Jack said through gritted teeth as he clenched his eyes tightly shut. He was shaking again and had braced his forehead in the palm of one hand. Yet as surreal and twisted as it had sounded when Millie said it out loud, something about it resonated with Jack in a way that nothing else had. For the first time in over twenty years, he felt several pieces of the terrible puzzle slipping into place.

"I'm sorry, Jack. I know that's a lot to take in, but I think it's important you know. If I'm right, you're dealing with something evil and very dangerous."

Jack was surprised.

"So, you're not in the 'it's all just old legends' camp?"

Millie snorted. "I'm not in a camp, thank you very much. But I think modern society has a long history of spinning and dismissing anything they couldn't easily explain, anything that made them uncomfortable or frightened; chalking anything in that category up to the superstitions of the ignorant. But legends are almost always based on something real, and the Chockowan may not have had iPhones and Snapchat, but they weren't stupid either. And from where I'm sitting, they knew a hell of a lot more about the spiritual world than we do."

Jack got up and paced again, his mind turning.

"Did your friend say anything about how the Chockowan protected themselves against these things?"

"No, not specifically," Millie said. "But there's someone in your area that he strongly recommended you talk to."

Jack heard her rustling her phone.

"Here it is. A man by the name of Josiah Red Wolf is a Tribal Elder of the Eastern Chockowan, who lives just outside of Banner Elk. He is what the Chockowan call a "Wisdom Giver;" someone who preserves the history and the customs of the tribe and passes them on to the younger generations. I'll text you his contact information, but Dan thinks it's important you speak to him. Mr. Red Wolf consults with Dan and other faculty from time to time, and Dan says he's one of the few people who might be able to help you."

"That's amazing," Jack said. "I didn't know they still had, well, I mean in modern times," he stammered, "Well, anyway, I really appreciate it. That's hugely helpful."

"It's okay, Jack. Most people don't know shit about Native American culture unless they've gone out of their way to study it."

"I guess that's true," Jack said. "Thanks."

"I'd better run. I've got a client coming in twenty minutes," Millie said. "But, Jack, when you talk to this gentleman, and I believe you should, try to put science and so-called rational thinking aside for a little while. For the sake of that conversation, suspend any disbelief you have long enough to take in whatever he says. It might end up being critically important."

"I will," Jack said, rubbing his tired eyes. "And for what it's worth, I don't think that'll be a stretch at this point. I left rational behind a week ago."

"That's a fair point," Millie said. "Before I go, how is Deena doing?"

Jack wanted to confess how desperately worried he was about her and whatever it was that was happening to her, but he knew it was not the time.

"Okay I think," he replied. "She had a lot to do at her work, so she's gone back to Black Mountain. Frankly, I'm hoping it will take her mind off some of this and maybe she'll be able to sleep better."

"Good. I hope so too."

He thanked her again for her help and signed off.

In the silence of the hotel room, dazed and overwhelmed by everything he had learned in the last twenty-four hours, Jack tried to collect his thoughts and make himself think about practical next steps. *You have to keep moving, for Andy's sake and for her.*

CHAPTER 15

Jack picked up his phone and called Deena. She answered on the third ring.

"Hi, Jack."

"Hi yourself," he said, smiling despite his weariness. "Did you make it home okay?"

"Yeah, it was fine. Tanya is on her last nerve with some issues at the shop so it's good I came back when I did, but nothing too bad. I do have a backlog of emails and some new inventory waiting so there will be no shortage of things to do. How's it going there? Tell me what you found in the rest of the journal."

Jack cringed. He had known she would ask, but had been so glad to hear her sounding like herself that he had not been prepared.

"You're not going to believe it, but the journal just ended, right in the middle of everything."

"Oh, no, you're kidding," Deena groaned.

"Yeah, I was pretty pissed. Margaret was not doing well and William was worried about her mental state and concerned for the children. He was still trying to pray her condition away, but nothing was helping. Then it just ended. No clue what happened after that."

"That really sucks. Especially after all that work. I'm really sorry."

"I know," Jack said. He felt a surge of guilt for leaving out so much, as it if were an outright lie, but he reminded himself again that it was only to try and keep her safe. If a few white lies would keep her from being subjected to whatever hell Margaret McNeill had gone through, it was a trade-off he was more than willing to make. "But on the upside," he continued. "Millie called and a professor friend of hers at Duke knows an actual Tribal Elder of the Chockowan tribe, up near Banner Elk."

"Seriously?"

"Yeah, the professor thinks this guy can give me a lot of good information about the beads and maybe whatever that symbol is. Anyway, I'm going to arrange to meet him."

"That's good, at least. So, that drawing isn't just something I made up in my dream?"

Jack hesitated. "Ah, well I'm not sure yet. It looks a little like a symbol the Chockowan used, but I'm hoping to find out for sure when I talk to him. I'll let you know one way or the other."

"I wish you could let me know in person," she said, lowering her voice.

"Me too," he said. "Maybe soon. I need to stay on the trail of this a little while longer."

"I know. I feel bad that I'm not there helping you."

"Thanks, but I think you're doing the right thing. The smart thing. And speaking of that, can you let me know in the morning how your night goes? I'm hoping you sleep better in your own bed."

"Oh God, me too," she sighed. "I'm running on fumes at this point. Fingers crossed. I'll give you a shout in the a.m. and let you know."

"Talk to you then," he said.

Deena was quiet for a moment and Jack wished more than anything that he could be there with her.

"Night, Jack," she said.

Jack stood in darkness at the bottom of the well, his chest heaving in fear as he tried to catch his breath amid the heavy stench of death. He could barely see the rough sides of the well rising around him to a small crescent of light high above. Something was blocking most of the well opening. *Got to get out,* his mind screamed, as he stepped forward reaching for the walls to check for hand-holds, anything he could climb; but he stumbled over something and looked down into the decayed face of a dead child, eyes closed and mouth sewn shut with large, crude stitches. Even in the dim light of the well the face looked familiar, and just as Jack leaned closer to look, terror gripped him. Andy's eyelids snapped open and Jack saw the cricket in his hand.

Click-click. Jack screamed.

He awoke on a soaked, freezing pillow with his heart pounding and realized someone in the next room was banging on the wall.

"Fuck," he groaned. *Must have cried out.*

Jack sat up and rubbed his face, trying to chase away the terrible images from the dream. It was the well again, the damned well. His phone said 3:18 a.m. He crawled out of bed and only then realized that he had pissed himself. For the first time in thirty years, he had pissed himself in his sleep. "Great," he grumbled as he headed for the shower. "Housekeeping will love that."

When he had showered and dressed, Jack made a strong cup of coffee by the dim light from the stove hood lamp and sat at the tiny counter in his kitchenette to drink it. It had hit him in the shower and he knew what he had to do. With or without Deena's help, he had to go and look for the well as soon as it was light. He knew it was there somewhere, and as much as he dreaded the thought of it, he had no doubt that he would find Andy there.

Andy wants to be found. And he wants you to find him.

The coffee was good, but as it started to bring him awake, all the events of the last few days came back into focus, along with all the unanswered questions they raised. He was certain that all of it was connected, but he had to find out how and do it quickly. Time was growing short. He couldn't say exactly how he knew it, but he felt it as surely as you feel the static on your skin when an electrical storm is dangerously close.

And something else had occurred to Jack under the hot water, as he wondered about where William McNeill might have kept another journal; in all his life he had never seen what was actually in the attic, in the dark place behind the shattered wall upstairs in the farmhouse. Whether by a trick of the light or something else, their flashlights had never illuminated the space well enough for them to see, and as kids they had been too scared to risk it. But now it seemed important, and he had made up his mind that he would find out what was in there, even if he had to take an industrial grade spotlight for the job.

Worst of all was what Millie had learned from her professor friend. While it suggested a possible explanation for what had happened that awful night at The Farm, the implications were terrifying. On its face, the idea that a monster from old Native American horror stories had somehow found its way into the real world would seem utterly preposterous to most people. But Jack was not most people. Given what he had seen and heard, he was not so quick to dismiss the idea. No, far from it.

In fact, as he finished his coffee in the quiet of his hotel room, Jack realized that it had resonated so strongly with him that it felt oddly familiar; like putting on an old glove again or clocking the face of someone he used to know on a busy street. This notion, however outrageous, was the first thing that had ever come close to explaining what he had seen that night, and what had happened to Andy.

"Try to suspend your disbelief," Millie had said. He smiled at the dark irony of it. *Suspend?* He had *abandoned* disbelief entirely at age thirteen, in the upstairs of that decaying farmhouse, when he had come face to face with something straight out of Hell.

By some stroke of luck, the Walmart in Benton was one of the few that was still open twenty-four hours, and apart from a few third-shifters and hard-core insomniacs, Jack largely had the sprawling store to himself. He had to scour the aisles of several departments but was eventually able to find everything he was looking for; a compact fire-escape rope ladder along with some tent stakes and a hand axe to secure it, some extra nylon rope, carabiners, a survival knife, a powerful portable LED spotlight and an LED head-lamp. He also picked up some energy bars, nuts, and water for the trip.

A youngish employee (nametag Devon) with heavy black glasses and a particularly harsh mullet eyed him as he scanned the contents of his cart through the self-check-out, but mercifully did not engage him in conversation. Back at his car, under the garish fluorescent glow from the parking lot lights, Jack stood by his open trunk, loading everything into his pack and searching the eastern sky for the first signs of light. By his estimation, if he started the hike at five-thirty, while it was still dark, he would have natural light a half-hour later and full daylight well before he reached The Farm. It was not ideal, but he needed as much time as possible. There was a lot of ground to cover, and he had no idea whether he would be able to find what he was looking for, much less how he would handle it if he did.

Whether it was the early morning chill or the thought of the well and the hellish Cracker Jack surprise it might contain, he shivered as he climbed into the car and immediately cranked the heater up. Dreading what he was about to do, but firmly resolved, Jack drove slowly out of the parking lot and turned in the direction of Wildwood Lane.

Fifteen minutes later, as he pulled into the driveway of his old house and the headlights of the car played across its darkened windows and faded siding, it felt to Jack like the shell of his childhood. It sat empty now, like the lifeless exoskeleton husk a cicada larva leaves behind after it emerges from the ground and hatches into an adult. Jack's mother had deeded it to him with the best intentions and some dim hope that he would want to keep it as a vacation getaway spot, but he had found the idea abhorrent. He would grit his teeth when the time came, fix what needed fixing, and put the place on the market. And when it sold, as he knew it would, he would close that door and never look back.

But that time wasn't now. Now he had bigger fish to fry; much bigger.

An ethereal blue glow had begun to bleed into the night sky, just above the rolling ridges southeast of town as Jack slung on his pack and locked the car. He glanced at his phone as he started across the side-yard and into the woods.

Right on time.

Jack didn't bother taking out a flashlight. From years spent playing in the woods at night, he knew that once his eyes adjusted, the ambient light from the setting moon and the early dawn sky would allow him to see everything around him surprisingly well. He walked quickly and quietly, mentally reviewing the supplies he had brought, thinking of Deena and trying to keep his mind from dwelling too long on any of the myriad dreadful revelations of the last several days. As he did, he found himself oddly comforted by the weight of the pistol in his jacket pocket.

The rising light of dawn had begun to chase the shadows away and brightened the forest around him as he made his way along the familiar roadbed that skirted the ridgeline above the river valley. Jack had begun checking the time, thinking of calling Deena before he got too far into the valley for cell service. He wanted very much to talk to her before the day started. Even though he felt some better about her being home and away from Benton, he was still uneasy and wanted to make sure she was okay. Selfishly, he also wanted the comfort of hearing her voice, particularly now.

His phone said six-forty-five, but he decided to risk waking her. As busy as a shop-owner would have to be, he guessed she would be up most days by then. Four rings later she picked up and he was surprised by how alert she sounded.

"Morning, Jack. How are you?"

"Morning, good," he said, smiling as he walked. "How was your night? Get any sleep?"

"Yes," she said with a luxurious sigh. "It was very good. Best night I've had in a while."

"Damn, that's good to hear. So, no nightmares?"

"No, it's all better," she said. "She's with me now."

Jack stopped on the path, goosebumps rising on his arms. Something about Deena's voice sounded off, and what the hell did she mean?

"What did you say?" he asked.

"What?" Deena ask.

"Who did you mean? Who's with you?"

There was a pause and Deena chuckled. "Oh, Tanya. I was talking about Tanya, my wing-woman. She's the best."

Jack felt his heart slow, but he still felt rattled and uneasy.

"Okay, glad to hear that."

"How are things going there?" Deen asked. "Did you find out anything more?"

"Some more, but mostly more questions," Jack said, staying intentionally vague. "Some of this is pointing to old Native American lore and legends. I'm heading back to see if I can find the other part of William McNeill's journal."

"So, you're coming to see me?"

She sounded strange again.

"What? No, did you not hear what I said? I'm heading back to The Farm to look for…" Jack bit his lip. A warning light was flashing in his mind but he made himself continue. "To look for the rest of the journal."

"Oh, sorry," she said. "I didn't hear you. I guess reception is bad. That makes sense. I hope you find it."

Jack scuffed his feet and tried to calm his thoughts.

"Are you sure you're okay?" he asked. "You were in pretty rough shape yesterday."

"Yes, Jack. You can stop worrying. I'm fine."

He wiped a hand slowly over his face and took a long breath. Maybe he was over-reacting; jumping at shadows, as it were.

"Good," he said. "I'm glad."

"How are you holding up?"

"I'm hanging in there," he said. "Best I can, but you know how it is."

"I know it's hard," she said. "I'm looking forward to seeing you again soon."

"Me too. Do you have a busy day?"

"Oh yeah, we're unpacking crates and checking stuff from the warehouse into inventory and getting some of it out on the floor."

"Sounds like a thrill," Jack mused.

"Hey, smart-ass, I happen to enjoy it," she quipped. "It's not as exciting as doing battle with a bunch of obnoxious teenagers in a classroom, but it has its perks."

"I'm sure it does," he said. "It actually sounds very, very appealing about now."

"Hey, the help-wanted sign is always out. Tanya and I could use a hand."

"Let me think about it," Jack said, looking at the time on his phone. "But I should probably go. I'm halfway there and it's going to be a long one."

"Be careful," Deena said. "And tell everyone I said hello."

Jack's stomach tightened. There it was again.

"Tell who?" he asked.

"Oh, sorry," she laughed. "I don't know why I said that. I was distracted looking at an email and it just popped out. Just something you say, I guess."

His mind was turning again.

"Okay, no worries," he said. "Good luck with your day and I'll talk to you later."

"Talk to you later."

Jack walked on, but could not get the strange call out of his mind. It had been early and she really could have been distracted, but it bothered him never-the-less. Still, running on four hours of sleep and struggling with what was quickly becoming his terrifying new reality, Jack was no longer sure he was thinking entirely rationally. He made a deal with himself that he would call her as soon as he got back to the hotel. Once he had arranged a meeting with Josiah Red Wolf in Banner Elk, he could go on to Black Mountain from there. It would be much better to see Deena in person.

Three quarters of an hour later, as Jack emerged from the wooded road onto the hillside that flanked The Farm, the painfully familiar palpable gloom and melancholy settled over him as he looked across the abandoned, crumbling structures down the slope to the fields and river below. The sky was overcast and the valley was deathly still and quiet, except for the babbling of the river.

But Jack didn't trust the quiet here. He never had. There was always something sinister about it and he was beginning to understand why.

As he eyed the house again, Jack's nerves were on edge.

"I'll start there," he told himself as he hitched his pack higher on his shoulders and started out.

He scanned the weeds and patches of bare ground as he walked, looking for any sign of something that might be concealing the opening to a well, but after so many years, he knew it could be completely overgrown and virtually invisible. The larger the house loomed in front of him as he approached, the more his attention was drawn to the darkened window openings. Reflexively he scanned them for any sign of movement as he imagined some dark presence watching him, waiting for him there. In his mind it had a face, but some primal self-defense mechanism stopped him from seeing it. *Or perhaps remembering it.*

Jack stopped at the crumbling front porch and took several slow breaths as he felt the simmering panic in his chest, coiled like a spring and ready to explode. He couldn't let it. He had to stay in control and get this done. It was too important.

Even though the sun had not yet crested the high ridge that surrounded the valley, morning light was glowing through the gaping window holes and other cracks in the old house and he could see portions of the rooms inside. Despite that, Jack took his spotlight out of the pack and the pistol from his jacket pocket and gripped them both tightly before climbing up what remained of the front steps.

It had occurred to him the previous night, that when he had fallen through the floor of the back room and found the cloth bundle under the floorboards, he and Deena had both been in a blind panic. There had been no time to look for anything else. If there was another journal, that would be the logical first place to look.

But as he stood in the dusty front room surrounded by peeling walls and the stale smell of time and decay, he shone his light up the wrecked steps and knew that the journal would have to wait. The longer he stayed in this God-forsaken place, the more the courage he had mustered to come here would evaporate, so he had to get the worst over with first.

After re-tracing the tenuous route up the shattered staircase, Jack emerged in the open space that faced the attic, his heart in his throat. The lone window here was on the side of the house that faced the river, and while it allowed enough light in to see the dust covered shards of wood strewn on the floor and the ragged hole in the wall that served as the doorway to the attic, it did not light up the interior of that wretched place. A lone beam of light shone through a hole in the roof somewhere inside the attic, but rather than illuminating it, the beam seemed to be smothered by the darkness.

Jack gritted his teeth and fought the rising urge to flee. It had been on this exact spot where he had seen Andy for the last time alive. Where he had seen him taken. He swallowed hard and raised his light, approaching the hole in the wall slowly. It was then that he noticed, for the first time, how different the shattered wall looked than the others in the room where he stood. Rather than being neatly surfaced and wallpapered, this wall was bare and appeared hastily built by someone who hadn't bothered to measure and properly align the boards. It was an improvised wall, built out of some unexpected necessity.

The utility light had three settings, and while the highest would drain the batteries more quickly, he had intentionally picked one with enough lumens for nighttime road work or other industrial functions. As he flipped it to the high setting, Jack saw the inside of the attic for the first time and he reflexively drew in a sharp breath.

The space looked like a nightmarish cross between a prehistoric shaman's cave and the solitary confinement chamber of a third-world prison. What remained of a broken wood and canvas cot lay in a heap against the back wall beside an overturned partially crushed bucket. The walls and floor were stained in faded dark patches and streaks, and every wall was nearly entirely covered in angry faded writings, symbols, and crudely drawn illustrations; some scrawled in what looked like faded paint, and others gouged into the walls with a sharp implement. The language was alien to Jack and none of the symbols and illustrations meant anything to him; all except one. The symbol he had sent to Millie, the one Deena had drawn on their hotel room door was everywhere, peppered among other writings and sometimes on top of them. It was even scratched in the floor. As he quickly scanned the walls, Jack also recognized the phrase William McNeill had mentioned in his journal, the one Deena had spoken in her sleep; *DRU AKEY NE SHADAY.* It appeared several times around the room.

Most disturbing of all were what appeared to be claw marks in several places, some deeper than others, like a wild animal had tried to claw its way out of the room.

"Jesus," Jack whispered, as he carefully set the spotlight down so that it continued lighting the room. He used his free hand to take out his phone and open the camera app. He snapped a few photos before looking closely at the phone, but when he did, he gasped and jumped back, nearly dropping it in the process. A whimper escaped his lips as he looked back and forth between the room and the view through his phone. In the phone view, a waif-thin female figure stood facing the left wall, scratching on it with a sharp piece of wood. Her clothes were ragged and filthy and her long dark hair was matted and frayed.

"What the fuck?" he hissed, blinking hard and looking repeatedly between the two views, unable to grasp what he was seeing. His hands shook as he fumbled with the phone, trying to snap a photo of the figure, but just then she stopped writing. For a moment she was stock still, then her head rotated slowly to look at Jack with milky-white dead eyes that made him groan audibly.

He quickly lowered the phone and grabbed the spotlight from the floor, hurrying back through the opening in the wall. He turned and raised the phone again and when he looked through it, he saw that the figure had moved toward him and was now halfway between the back of the room and where he stood. With his naked eye he still saw nothing.

Jack stuffed his phone in his pocket and ran as quickly as he could down the steps, ducking without slowing into the back room of the downstairs. Not caring where he stepped, he ran straight to the hole in the floorboard, knelt, and thrust his arm into the shallow crawlspace, frantically patting the dry ground beneath it in a wide circle as far as he could reach. With his other hand, Jack wrestled his phone out and held it up, terrified that he would see the dark figure with the dead eyes standing in the doorway, but he saw nothing and this time he heard no footsteps. Suddenly his hand bumped something solid and as he ran his fingers back over it, he was certain it was another book.

As he grabbed it and pulled it out of the opening, Jack felt the hair on his head and neck stiffen and the air around him grow icy cold. He started to raise his phone again to look, but his mind screamed at him to stop, certain of what he would see looking back at him. And as the panic he had been fighting finally erupted, he spun around and, still holding the book and his phone, flung himself through the open window frame.

Jack landed hard on his shoulder and side in the weeds and cried out in pain as he rolled across a shallow pile of boards onto his back. He whipped his head to look back at the gaping window and struggled to his feet, still unwilling to look through his phone, and backed another twenty feet away from the house, not taking his eyes off of it. His breath was coming in shallow gasps and a surge of bitter rage welled up inside him.

"Fuck you," he spat, glaring at the house.

As his anger and fear boil over, he felt something in him snap.

"Fuck you!" Jack screamed, this time at the top of his lungs.

His voice echoed back at him across the valley and he turned, trembling all over, and limped away from the house, toward the river. His shoulder was throbbing as he found a clear spot in the grass and sat down, stunned by what had just happened and terrified by what he had seen. Thinking of the phone, he opened the photos and quickly scrolled through them.

"Holy shit," he whispered.

The shots of the attic were not great, and even with the spotlight he could only make out some of the writing and symbols on the walls, but in every photo, a large dark smudge appeared beside the wall where he had seen the female figure standing. The shape was blurry and he could not make out any details, but he was shocked to see anything at all. Had it been a ghost? If so, whose? He tried to get his head around the idea but his mind felt strangely numb, and for the first time he looked closely at the book he had pulled from the crawlspace. It was nearly identical to the first one, but the cover was in much worse shape, having not been protected by the bundle of fabric. The color had leached out and it had been chewed partially away in several places, no doubt by rats or racoons, but the pages appeared to be intact.

Jack pulled a bottle of water from his pack and took a long drink, then opened the book.

CHAPTER 16

Right away, Jack noticed a difference in the writing. The entries in the first book had been made with a steady hand and the writing was neat and consistent. Even the cover page of this book, the one that proclaimed to the reader, "*Property of William Gregory McNeill*" was written hastily, with a noticeably unsteady hand. As he turned to the first page of journal entries, the uneven writing continued, even getting worse, with some lines almost scribbled.

December 31, 1924

Still no sign of Henry. I have searched everywhere, but I cannot find him, and cursed Margaret will only say she does not remember. God damn whatever has taken hold of her. It has been too long and the ground is frozen. I know our boy is dead but I cannot accept it.

Rebecca is barely eating and she has started wetting her bed again. I have tried to reassure her but she keeps saying she is afraid her mother will kill her in her sleep like she did Henry. What in God's name can I tell her? I have started locking Margaret in our bedroom unless I can stay with her every minute. I cannot take the chance of leaving her alone with Rebecca. She cries and begs me to let her out and it destroys me, but I will not. I am getting little sleep on the couch.

I showed the words that Margaret wrote on the wall to the old Indian woman at the market and she said they were bad words. I pressed her and when she told me I thought I would be sick. She said in her language it means 'kill them all.'

Jack's mouth fell open as the image of Deena writing those same words in her own blood rose up in his mind.

"No, no, no," he said under his breath, quickly moving to the next entry.

January 3, 1925

Margaret tried to attack Rebecca right in front of me. I had to punch her and restrain her again and I locked her in the bedroom. Rebecca was not hurt but she is hysterical and is threatening to run away. Margaret is no longer herself. She speaks in a strange tongue and keeps picking at her skin and clawing at her own face hard enough to draw blood, and she growls like an animal. It is unbearable.

I must protect Rebecca but I cannot bring myself to have Margaret put away in the asylum. My only choice is to keep her locked away here until I find a cure for what is poisoning her. I have started building a wall to partition off a room upstairs where I can put her, so we will all be safe. It is the only way.

"Oh, my God," Jack said. "The attic was for her."

He looked back toward the house, certain now that what he had seen was some remnant of Margaret McNeill. *Or something that looked like her*, he thought.

When Jack turned the page, he was alarmed to see that there were only two more brief entries, hastily made, much rougher and more uneven that the others, and the page opposite had nothing but a partial handprint in what appeared to be blood. The rest of the pages in the book were blank.

January 8, 1925

I finished the wall yesterday, such as it is. I bound Margaret and dragged her kicking and screaming into the room. For a moment before I locked her in, she returned to herself and begged me not to put her in that place. I cried like a baby, and almost untied her, but then something evil passed into her eyes and my Margaret was gone . She snarled and tried to bite me. I do not know how to get through this, but it is done. She is locked away now.

Rebecca fled the house and I had to chase her down in the snow and carry her back. God help us.

Jack was barely breathing as he read the final entry.

January 12, 1925

Something evil is locked up in that room, and it is not my Margaret.

I can no longer sleep. The winter wind howls through the valley at night and rattles the trees against the roof but I can still hear it in there scratching and clawing, always scratching, trying to find a way out. It makes horrible noises, sometimes screaming like a wild animal, and throws itself repeatedly against the wall.

I pray God it will hold.

"Holy crap," Jack said, letting out a long uneven breath as he thought of the shattered wood on the upstairs floor of the house, outside the gaping hole in the attic wall. It confirmed the grim but inescapable conclusion.

"It didn't hold," he said under his breath, glancing back at the house and at the bloody handprint on the last page of the book. And as he thought of William McNeill and their young daughter Rebecca, he shuddered at the thought of what might have followed.

"What in God's name happened here?" he asked aloud, as he looked across the weathered bones of what, by all rights, should have been a prosperous farm back in its day. Instead, it had apparently descended into a nightmare of madness and death.

But why? He wondered. *What was behind it? And why did Andy want so badly for him to know?*

So much of what had happened tied back to the Chock-owan; the native language translation the "old Indian woman" (no doubt Chockowan) had provided for William McNeill, the chevron beads that dated back hundreds of years, and the strange symbol which by all evidence, represented Cruxhen, one of their most feared mythical monsters. Jack felt certain that the odd writing on the attic walls was Chockowan as well, and if he could only show some of the photos to Josiah Red Wolf, he would confirm it beyond a shadow of doubt. But according to William McNeill, Margaret did not know the language, which had to mean that an entity of some kind was working through her, inhabiting her.

Possessing her.

It was the only thing that would explain her increasingly bizarre and violent behavior toward her family.

Then, as he thought of Deena, Jack felt almost physically sick with dread. She had gone back to Black Mountain, but if she had retained any trace of a psychic connection to Margaret McNeill or the horrors that happened here, she would be in grave danger. She had sounded okay the previous day, but it was the nights that had been worst for her. The valley had no cell service and he needed to get back and call her; make sure she was okay and tell her some of what he had found, whatever he could risk telling her.

But Jack was torn. Andy kept showing him the dry well; putting him in it even, and he had come here to find it and learn what it contained. He had the gear he needed and plenty of daylight to search, as long as Deena was okay. It was a gamble, but one he would have to make. It was too important.

Jack put the book in his pack and painfully got to his feet, favoring his bruised shoulder as he hoisted the pack onto his back. Then, continuing to glance warily back toward the house, he began to travel a slow, wide circular path around it, roughly thirty yards out, scanning the ground for any sign of a concealed well cap. He paid particular attention to the heavily weeded areas between the haphazard clusters of trees and the patches of ground partially covered by scraps of decaying wood or rusty metal. His plan was to tighten the circle by a few feet each time he went around until he had combed every inch of ground. Based on what he had read about traditional wells, it should be somewhere within that area.

A faint breeze moved across the valley as he walked, rustling the weeds and lightly raking the branches of the birches across the rusted metal roofs of the farm buildings. The sounds it made seemed eerily like someone moaning and scratching...*trying to get out*, he thought, and shuddered again. Since they were children, Jack had always imagined that the empty house, or whatever lived behind its darkened windows, was watching him. But as he made his way slowly around to the north of the house, toward what remained of a tool shed, he felt eerily certain of it.

The weeds were particularly high on the northeast side of the shed, growing through and around a small pile of rotting wood scraps, and a lone fence post stood there with a twisted strand of rusted wire trailing down and disappearing into the grass. On a whim, Jack made his way around the woodpile for a quick look at the ground beyond it, almost behind the shed, but he only saw more weeds. The ground was partially visible, but he saw nothing that looked like a well cover and nothing pushing up through the thatch that might indicate one.

But as he turned to go back the way he had come, Jack heard a muffled but distinct sound and stopped mid-stride.

Click-click.

He set his foot down and stood there, listening. Had it been the breeze or perhaps his imagination?

Click-click.

He heard it again and felt his pulse jump. But it was so faint, muted; like it was coming from...Jack turned around and scanned the area behind the shed again, walking forward slowly, still listening. As he reached the area directly behind the shed, he heard it again, and it was much closer—beneath his feet somewhere.

Jack began stamping the ground as he walked, moving back and forth across the sixty square foot overgrown patch of ground behind the tool shed.

Click-click.

He was getting closer.

Suddenly he stamped with his right foot onto something hard under the grass and heard a hollow thump and an echo. Jack's stomach tightened at the sound and he looked down, scanning for any sign of a board, but whatever was under the mat of weeds was well and truly hidden.

He stamped his foot again and heard the boom and the echo. He had found it.

"I'll be damned," he said. "Thanks, Andy."

He set his pack down and pulled out the hunting knife he had stowed in a side pocket and began cutting away the dead thatch and live weeds that covered what sounded like a heavy board. After he pulled away several inches of thatch in the spot where he had been standing, he saw the dirty, but unmistakable surface of a board. He began hacking in earnest at the surrounding grass as his pulse pounded, and several minutes later, had exposed the entire wooden well cover. It was several feet across, roughly octagonal, and easily two inches thick.

Jack was breathing hard as he stood up and stepped back, studying the well cover as he put the hunting knife back in his pack.

You don't have to do this, a small voice in his mind whispered. But he knew that he did.

The unresolved guilt and unanswered questions about Andy's disappearance, *Andy's murder*, had followed him, tormented him nearly every day since the night it happened, pushing into every facet of his life. He had made up his mind that he would do whatever it took to find Andy and learn what happened to him, no matter the cost. He was grimly certain that there would be no peace for him until he did.

And then, it occurred to Jack for the first time that helping Andy find peace might be the *only* thing that mattered. He had been wracking his brain for weeks about what Andy wanted and maybe it was just that; maybe he wanted to be released from whatever hellish limbo he had been imprisoned in all those years ago.

Jack took the spotlight out of his pack and tried to move the well cover, but years of rain and seeping dirt had created a dried mud seal. He stood up and kicked it several times until it finally broke free, sliding a few inches to the side. Seeing the darkness of the well and hearing the echo of the wood scraping against its brick sides brought on a powerful surge of fear that caught Jack off guard. He felt dizzy and briefly thought he would pass out. He took several uneven steps back and sat down hard in the grass, gritting his teeth and clenching his eyes shut; willing his mind to calm down and slowing his breathing. In and out.

He couldn't believe it had come to this and that he was going to face it alone. Yet, somehow it had the ring of cosmic justice; his penance for the unforgivable crime he had perpetrated against his friend. Fair was fair and he had it coming.

Jack took a few more slow breaths, looked warily at the house again, and turned on the spotlight. He got on his knees and used both hands to push the well cover aside, into the grass. A stale and vaguely fetid odor wafted across his face as he leaned over the well opening and he reflexively gagged, turning his head sharply to the side, but he resisted the urge to vomit.

He pulled in a couple of breaths of fresh air and pushed the wooden disc clear of the well opening, seeing inside it for the first time. The sides were old-style brick, chipped and faded, and the well was deep enough that the daylight did not penetrate to the bottom. Jack gazed into the darkness and, on impulse reached into his pocket and pulled out the cricket. He held it over the black maw of the well and pressed the button.

Click-click. The sound echoed down the well and back.

Click-click. The response came from the bottom of the well, and Jack flinched, closing his eyes against the ache in his chest. The idea of Andy abandoned to die in the darkness at the bottom of a well was nearly too much to bear.

"I'm coming, Andy," he whispered.

Doing his best to steel himself for what he might see, Jack shone the spotlight down the well. Something was piled at the bottom, maybe thirty feet down at the edge of the beam of light. He squinted and leaned further over the opening, adjusting the beam. And then he saw it.

Bones. And what looked like crumpled clothing. A skeleton hand clearly visible. Part of what might be a femur and the unmistakable profile of a shoe. As his eyes adjusted to the light and he scanned the spotlight across the irregular mounds of material, Jack felt the panic again as he took a quick visual inventory and realized that there was more than one body at the bottom of the well. There were several.

"Jesus, Christ," he said, standing and walking several paces away, glancing back at the well and grimacing as the awful truth of Deena's words sank in.

"I think they never left here..."

If that were literally true, then it had to be some members of the McNeill family; but which ones? Jack exhaled sharply as he thought again of William McNeill's final journal entry and the bloody handprint, and as his mind traveled back to the shattered hole in the attic wall, he felt certain that the family had come to a horrific end. Margaret, or whatever she had become, had probably broken out of the attic enclosure and killed William and young Rebecca, having already killed Henry, and had dumped them all in the well. It was a grisly scenario.

And Andy's been down there with them for twenty-three years.

Jack tried to shake the terrible thought from his mind, but it stubbornly refused to go.

He walked back to the well and knelt by his pack, and as he pulled out the rope ladder and metal stakes, it occurred to him that he had no idea exactly how deep the well was and whether the ladder was long enough.

He had guessed the well to be around thirty feet deep. He was five feet, ten inches tall with a reach of at least three more feet. The ladder was twenty-five feet, so as long as the well wasn't deeper than thirty-three feet, he could reach the bottom and safely get back on the bottom rungs. He could not afford to push it beyond that depth or he would risk getting trapped, and after his series of ghastly nightmares, it was not a chance he was willing to take.

Jack pulled the camping hatchet from the pack and used the flat back of it to hammer three of the heavy metal tent stakes into the hard ground beside the well opening, hooking the curved tops of them over the anchoring loops of the rope ladder. Then he rolled out the ladder, extending it over the well opening and across the grass, before picking up the end of it and putting as much weight as possible on it to test the anchors. Fortunately, it did not budge.

"Okay, here goes," he told himself, beating back the increasingly urgent objections of his rational mind. He bunched up the full length of the rope ladder and carefully dropped it down the well. The wooden rungs clattered and scraped against the worn brick sides as it fell, extending to its full length before jerking to a stop, but he could tell from its subtle bobbing and swaying that the ladder had not reached the bottom.

Damn, but how close?

He leaned over and peered down the well, squinting as he tried to train the spotlight on the bottom of the ladder. It was impossible to tell how close it came to the base of the well, but from his vantage point, it looked close enough. Despite the chill in the air and the light breeze, droplets of sweat had begun to form on Jack's forehead and had run down his lower back. He wiped his forehead with the back of his hand and took the head-lamp and the hunting knife from the pack, donning the lamp and clipping the knife sheath to his belt. He double checked that the pistol was in his jacket pocket with the safety on, then turned at the edge of the well and dropped one leg down so he could stand on an upper rung of the rope-ladder. He gradually put his whole weight on it, watching the tent stakes carefully for any signs of slippage, but they appeared rock solid.

As he started to drop his other leg into the well and begin descending the ladder, doubt seized Jack like a vice and he wavered.

What the fuck are you doing? His mind screamed at him. *You're alone. There's nobody here to help you. There's no cell service. If something goes wrong, if ANYTHING goes wrong, you would die down there without anyone even knowing where you are. What the fuck good would that do for you or Andy? Just step out of the well, call the police, and report it. You found him, that's enough.*

Sweat ran freely down Jack's back now and as he peered down the well with the aid of his head-lamp and thought about his best friend lying down there among the dead, waiting to die, something clapped back at his own doubt.

"Fuck that," he growled. "It's not enough."

You did this, because you were too chicken-shit. Well, not this time. If it goes tits-up, then so be it. If that's what happens, maybe you've got that coming too.

Jack had briefly debated reporting the bodies to the police, but he knew there was something else Andy still wanted him to know; something Andy still needed. And Jack had seen enough true-crime shows to know that the minute the authorities got wind of what he'd found, they would cordon off the entire farm and he wouldn't be allowed anywhere near it. He knew that the only way he could help Andy was to keep going. He would take pictures and report it to the police, but in his own time.

After all, he thought darkly. *They've been down there for years. What difference will a few more days make?*

Jack forced himself to move, climbing very slowly at first, hesitating again just before his head dropped below the top of the well, reflexively taking in one last breath of fresh air. Then he pushed on. The sense of claustrophobia was immediate once he was fully into the well. The curved rough brick wall was practically pressed against his face on the ladder as he descended, while the stale air seemed heavier, and the odor of death stronger with each breath. Jack's hands had begun to shake, but he willed himself to focus on his grip and his footing on the ladder. A slip could be fatal.

As he continued climbing down, the natural light began to disappear entirely and the well was lit only by his headlamp. Several times he glanced up and was alarmed at how rapidly the circle of sky above him was shrinking and how much narrower the well seemed from inside it.

After another minute moving down the ladder Jack looked down and flinched, gripping the ropes and steadying himself against the shock of what lay below him. He was standing three rungs from the bottom of the ladder, and a mere few feet below that, in the bobbing circle of light from his lamp, a jumbled pile of bodies was clearly visible. Skeletons amid rumpled remnants of the clothes they had worn. And then...

A groan escaped Jack's lips and he felt angry tears well up in his eyes as he recognized Andy's yellow hooded sweatshirt. It was faded and tattered, but there was no mistaking it. He had been wearing it that night; the last time he had seen Andy alive. Jack averted his eyes and refocused on getting safely off the ladder so he could stand on solid ground. When he reached the bottom rung, he scanned the base of the well for an open spot to stand, then stepped off.

When Jack looked down again, willing himself to train his light on Andy's body, he recoiled in horror, as he saw what remained of his friend's face. It was virtually unrecognizable. Decades in the dry atmosphere of the well had effectively mummified the body, reducing it to a tanned and stretched covering on a skeleton, still draped in the clothes he had died in.

He had seen it in his nightmares and had tried to prepare himself in case it was more than just a bad dream, but when Jack's lamp light fell on Andy's mouth and he saw the rough cording that had been used to stitch it shut, an agonizing sob escaped his throat, and when he glanced farther down and saw the cricket still clutched in one skeletal hand, Jack covered his face with his hands and wept.

"I'm sorry, Andy," Jack cried quietly, between breaths. "I'm so sorry."

Just then Jack heard a noise echo down the well that froze his blood and stopped the breath in his chest. A scraping noise...*like wood on brick.*

CHAPTER 17

Jack whipped his head to look straight up at the well opening, and what he saw made his heart leap into his throat. He was certain that he had pushed the wooden well cover completely off to one side, leaving a perfect circle of sky visible as he descended the ladder, but now the well cover protruded, barely, but noticeably in from one side, eating into the circle of light the way the earth's shadow gradually eats the moon in the night sky—one bite at a time.

Jack quickly pulled his phone from his pocket and opened the photo app, then held it directly over his head. As he did, on the phone he saw a shadow pass across the top of the well and a whimper escaped him.

"Oh, Jesus," he whispered, as his mind exploded with fear.

With the camera app still open, he frantically pointed it at the bodies at his feet and took a half-dozen shots, then stuffed the phone back in his pocket as he practically jumped back onto the rope ladder, praying that nothing would happen to it.

The scraping noise again.

Jack snapped his head up and saw that the well cover now obscured a full quarter of the opening; and, as raw panic sent adrenaline surging through his body he attacked the ladder, climbing two rungs at a time. To his horror, he saw the shadow again, only this time it was not through the phone. He was two thirds of the way up the ladder when he *saw* the cover begin to slide, slowly and jerkily, blocking out the light as it went.

"No, goddamn it!" Jack shouted as his legs pumped faster on the ladder.

The circle of light was almost gone, leaving the well in darkness as Jack reached the top of the ladder. Without slowing, he tucked his head and slammed his shoulder into the large wooden disc, rocking it upwards and to one side and sliding it halfway off the well opening. Terrified that something outside the well would grab him, he thrust one arm through the opening and pushed his head and torso out of the well, whipping his head around to look for whatever had tried to trap him, but he saw nothing.

As he pushed the cover clear again and climbed the rest of the way out of the well on all fours, his breath coming in great gasps, Jack was horrified to see that two of the three tent stakes holding the ladder had been pulled partially out of the ground. The third had been removed completely.

He thought of his nightmare and nearly choked. In the terrible dream someone had tried to trap him in the well, and when he had looked up, it had been some version of Deena's face he had seen. He had no idea why he would have dreamed it, but he was certain that someone or *something* had just tried to kill him.

Jack hurriedly pulled up the tent stakes with his hatchet and pulled the ladder back out of the well, glancing up frequently and scanning around him for any sign of movement in the buildings or among the trees. Then he pushed the heavy wooden disk back over the well opening, sealing its terrible contents in darkness again. He had started to leave everything and get the hell out of there but somehow, even through the fog of fear, he reminded himself that the well was both a crime scene and a tomb, and it needed to be protected from the elements.

The hike back was as close to double-time as Jack could manage, stopping only twice for a few gulps of water and a short rest. Still reeling from what he had seen and from his close call in the well, he was barely able to quiet the tempest in his mind. The boundary that separated the supernatural from the real everyday world, the world of reason and science and natural laws, had begun to blur several weeks earlier when Andy had begun appearing and Jack's nightmares had worsened. That had been hard enough. But now he felt like the boundary had disappeared completely.

As he walked, Jack took out his phone and forced himself to look at the photos he had so frantically taken at the bottom of the well. He was afraid they would be blurred, and two of them were, but the others were quite clear and devastating to look at. Jack felt the ache in his chest again, but tried to focus on the details and what clues they might hold. He used his fingers to zoom in for a better look, struggling to hold the phone level as he walked, and was immediately struck by how similar the crude stitching over Andy's mouth was to the symbol that both Deena and Margaret McNeill had drawn on the walls. The images made it brutally clear that the symbol was not abstract or arbitrary; it was a crude but literal depiction of what this vile creature did to her victims.

Jack stopped walking as he noticed something behind and beneath Andy's body in the photo.

"Shit, I don't believe it," he said quietly.

It was a partially visible skull, a small one turned sideways among some shreds of fabric. But remnants of the same crude stitching were clearly visible on the mouth and jaw; the same rough thread, albeit mostly decayed and broken in places. Jack scrolled around the rest of the photo and seconds later spotted another skull, or what remained of one, and this one was even smaller than the first. The jawbone was separated from the skull. But even then, when he zoomed as tightly as the app would allow, he saw faint threads radiating from the teeth of the skull and from the jaw.

Jack had no doubt that these were the bodies of Henry and Rebecca McNeill. They had apparently suffered the same fate weeks apart, at the hand of their deranged mother, who by all evidence was possessed and fully inhabited by a monster. He shuddered as he remembered the line from William's journal on the day Henry disappeared.

"I found Margaret in their room. Her hands were bloody and she was holding a large sewing needle threaded with cat-gut..."

But despite the shock of finding their grisly remains, what frightened Jack the most as he studied the photos was their similarity to Andy's. The McNeill children had been murdered eighty years before Andy, yet his wounds were identical to theirs and his body had been disposed of in the same manner and in the same place. Despite the impossible gap in time and circumstances, all of the victims bore the same uniquely horrific signature of the witch-monster, Cruxhen.

But how? Jack wondered as he turned off his phone and started walking again, now with even greater urgency.

If this Cruxhen had driven Margaret McNeill to kill her children and likely her husband, what had killed Andy? How could it be the same thing? Jack knew that memory could sometimes play tricks on people, but the image of what he had seen that night had been burned into his memory like nothing else ever had, and of one thing he was certain: what had taken Andy that night was not human. At least not entirely human. No way it could have been Margaret McNeill.

When Jack checked his phone, he saw two bars and quickly called Deena's number as he walked.

"Pick up," he said, willing her to answer. But after five rings it rolled to voicemail.

He warmed at her smiling voice during the greeting, but it only heightened the urgency he felt.

"Hey, it's Jack. A lot has happened here and I have news, I mean, big news. I hope you're doing okay, just please give me a call as soon as you get this. It's important." He hesitated then closed with, "I miss you."

It was nearly one-thirty when Jack emerged from the woods that bordered Wildwood Lane, tired, hungry, and troubled; mostly by what he had seen and learned at the farm, but partly that Deena had not yet returned his call, even after a second message. He cut across the side yard of his old house and went straight to his car, where he threw his pack in the passenger seat and climbed behind the wheel. As he backed the car out of the driveway and started down the street, he glanced at the front yard of the house and it occurred to him that something was different, but he couldn't place what and he didn't have time to go back. He knew that the son of the man his mother had hired was still keeping up the place, so it could have been anything.

Too ravenous to wait, Jack picked up a deli sandwich at the grocery store and devoured it before he got back to the hotel parking lot, chasing it with a bottle of water. He stopped by the front desk to tell them he needed an extra day, then headed to his room where he got a quick shower and changed before making himself a drink and pulling up the contact information Millie had given him for Josiah Red Wolf.

Over the last several days, Jack had experienced a sense of imminent danger that he couldn't explain, and the incidents at The Farm that morning had only heightened the feeling. Now his nerves were raw and on-edge. Everything he had uncovered had brought him closer to knowing the terrible truth behind Andy's death, but it had also revealed a legacy of horrors that was much darker than even *he* had imagined. The closer he had gotten to the source of that darkness, the louder the warning had become.

All signs now pointed to the Chockowan, and Jack knew his best and possibly only chance to find the missing pieces of the puzzle lay with Josiah Red Wolf. He had to find and talk to this man as quickly as possible. Something evil was coming. He could feel it.

Before he made the call, Jack tried Deena one more time. She didn't answer, and he got a message that her voice mailbox was full.

"Shit," he muttered as he stared at the phone. Something was wrong; it had to be. She had said she was busy with inventory, but it didn't make sense that she would be away from her phone for so long without checking it. On the other hand, it had been less than a day. Maybe he was overreacting. He decided to call

Red Wolf and if he still hadn't heard from Deena, he would try the shop.

Jack had no idea what to expect, but suddenly regretted his near total ignorance of Chockowan culture and history. He hoped it wouldn't work against him. As it turned out, Josiah Red Wolf was expecting Jack's call.

"Hello, this is Josiah."

The man's voice sounded kind.

"Hi. My name is Jack Crawford. Your name was given to me by..."

"Oh yes, Jack, I'm glad to hear from you. Professor Langstall emailed me about you and let me know that you'd be reaching out. What can I do for you?"

Jack was surprised and relieved.

"Oh, okay. That's great. Well..." he hesitated as his old fear of sounding crazy kicked in and he had to remind himself that this man might be one of the few people alive who wouldn't think so.

"I need to know whatever you can tell me about a particular creature from Chockowan mythology. I probably need to give you some background so..."

"You need to know about Cruxhen," he interrupted, leaving Jack mildly stunned.

"Ah, yeah. Yes, Mr. Red Wolf. Anything you can tell me. How did you know?"

"Don't worry, I'm not clairvoyant. And please call me Josiah. Dan emailed the drawing your friend sent him, so I had an idea."

"Good, I'm glad. Can you help me?"

"Maybe, I'm not sure yet, but I would prefer if we talk in-person, if that's possible. It will help me to know more about what you're looking for and why. And if this is what I think it is, it's not an appropriate phone conversation. Does that work for you?"

"Absolutely," Jack said. "Just tell me when you're free and I'll be there."

"How about tomorrow morning, say around ten?"

Jack was impatient, but he knew that it was less than short notice on his part. The following morning would have to do.

"Sure. That works for me," Jack said.

"I'm just outside of Banner Elk. Do you have my address?"

Jack checked his note and confirmed the address.

"I look forward to meeting you in person," Josiah said.

"Thanks, me too," Jack replied and ended the call.

The man's patient manner and soothing tone had reminded him somehow of Millie, but whether he had the answers Jack so badly needed was yet to be seen.

Thinking again of Deena, Jack retrieved his wallet from the bedroom and got the shop number from the business card Tanya had given him in Black Mountain. He downed the remainder of his drink and sat in a chair at the small round table by the kitchen to make the call.

After five rings he heard a click and a recorded greeting came on: "Hello, thanks for calling Stella's Antiques. We are temporarily closed due to an illness in the family, but please leave a message with any inquiries and someone will get back to you at the earliest possible convenience. If you are a dealer rep, please leave your DID in the message. Thanks for your patience and we apologize for any inconvenience."

The skin on Jack's neck and arms suddenly prickled with fear.

"What the fuck?" he said, ending the call without leaving a message. "Temporarily closed?"

He wracked his brain and paced the hotel room.

"Damn it," he muttered, convinced that something was very wrong and kicking himself for not trying harder to reach her earlier.

Then he remembered Tanya's business card. She had given it to him when she gave him Deena's. Luckily it was still in his wallet, and it had her cell number on it. Jack hastily called it, but Tanya did not pick up. Instead, it rolled to voicemail. Jack swore but left a message.

"Tanya, this is Jack Crawford. I'm the friend of Deena's who stopped by looking for her the other day. I've been trying to reach her since early this morning but I can't get her and it's really important. After she went back to Black Mountain yesterday morning, she said the two of you were working on inventory so I thought you might..." He trailed off. "I just tried the shop and heard that it's closed? So, I'm confused and a little

259

concerned about her. Anyway, please call me. I need to get in touch with her."

Jack's mind was churning as he tried to understand what the hell was happening. Whatever it was, it was not good, and he knew that his conversation with Josiah Red Wolf could not wait until the next morning. He had to go now; decorum be-damned. He grabbed his backpack and put both of William McNeill's journals in it before picking up his jacket and heading out the door. He would call Josiah from the road.

Traffic on Highway 29 was picking up and the sun was sinking low in the western sky as Jack headed out of town, winding slowly upward toward the base of Flat Rock Mountain and the turnoff to Banner Elk. His GPS told him the drive would take thirty-eight minutes but that was at the posted speed limit.

"Screw that," he told himself and pressed the gas pedal harder.

Barely two minutes later his phone rang and he saw it was a Black Mountain area code so he picked up.

"This is Jack."

"Jack, it's Tanya. I'm so glad you called. I'm worried sick about Deena and about the shop and I really don't know what to do."

"Slow down," Jack said. "What's going on? Has something happened with Deena?"

"I have no idea," Tanya said, her voice rising in panic and frustration. "I haven't seen her since she left for Benton three days ago."

Her words sent a shock wave through Jack and he quickly slowed and pulled the car off onto a wide portion of the shoulder.

"What did you say?" he stammered. "What do you mean you haven't seen her? I talked to her just this morning and she sounded fine, maybe a little stressed, but fine. She said she had gotten back home and was working through some new inventory at the shop with you."

"She said what? Are you sure?"

"Yeah, that's what she told me."

"Oh, my God," Tanya said. "What the hell is going on? She was supposed to be back two days ago but she never showed up. I can't get her on her cell and her house is still all locked up. No lights on and no sign that anyone's home. I've been by there a half-dozen times."

Jack's heart was pounding and he had a death grip on the wheel as he tried to sort out what Tanya was saying, but a ringing had started in his ears and her voice began fading into white noise.

Christ, he thought. *If she hasn't been in Black Mountain, where the hell is she?*

"I agreed to full time while she was out of town.. supposed to be at my other job two days a week...going to fire me if I didn't... tried to find someone to fill in but... I put up a closed sign...worried about her..."

Jack shook his head to try and clear it.

"Tanya, you did the right thing," he interrupted. "I don't know what's going on but I'm going to find out. She was at her mother's condo. Maybe she got wrapped up in cleaning up the place and decided to stay longer. Maybe her phone battery died. I don't know what to tell you."

"That just doesn't sound like her," Tanya said. "She's never done anything like this since I've been at the shop."

"I know it doesn't make sense. I'm worried too. I'm going to see what I can find out and I'll call you on your cell when I know something."

"Okay, I really appreciate it."

As he was ending the call, Jack was scrambling for any rational explanation. Even if he had believed the flimsy theory he had just offered Tanya, it wouldn't explain the conversation they'd had and her complete fabrication about what she had been doing for the last twenty-four hours. There was no scenario that did not point to the darker possibility; the one he could barely bring himself to think about.

Jack considered turning the car around. He could go by her mother's condo just to rule that out, but then what? No, Josiah Red Wolf was his best chance to understand what was happening to Deena and to help Andy. There was no more time to debate.

Hoping he was making the right call, Jack threw the car into drive and slammed the pedal down, throwing gravel as he drove back onto the roadway, and sped off in the direction of Banner Elk. The sun had already begun sinking below the western mountains as Jack took out his phone with one hand and called Josiah.

CHAPTER 18

It was nearly dark when Jack passed through the small town of Banner Elk and turned west on Summit Road, which snaked its way several more miles into the mountains before taking him past Willow Trail, where he made a left and soon pulled up to house number 312.

The voice on his GPS was the only sound that broke the silence as he looked at the lights glowing in the windows of a cedar sided house, partially buried in a rhododendron grove.

"You have arrived at your destination."

He closed the map app and climbed out of the car and into the loud chorus of night sounds that filled the woods around him. The porch light came on as Jack approached the steps, and a man emerged from the front door to meet him. He had shoulder length grey hair, wore glasses and was dressed casually in a plaid flannel shirt and khakis, with leather slip-on shoes. Jack was no good judge of age, but he was easily in his sixties.

"Jack?" the man said.

"Yes," he said, climbing the steps and extending his hand.

"Josiah," the man said, shaking Jack's hand. His eyes were compassionate and he looked at Jack with genuine concern.

"I'm very sorry for barging in on you like this," Jack said. "I know we talked about tomorrow but something's happened and I think my friend is in real danger. I don't think there's much time and I'm not sure who else to talk to."

"It's okay," Josiah said and motioned to the door. "Come inside. It's getting cold out here."

Jack caught the welcoming smell of wood smoke wafting through the front door as he stepped inside and saw a fire burning in a large stone fireplace to his left. The room had a comfortable and lived-in feeling with dark-stained wood floors, cedar walls, and leather armchairs and sofa. Apart from several Native American art pieces on the walls and a few cultural objects around the room, there was nothing that immediately struck Jack as Chockowan, much less Tribal Elder, but he reminded himself that stereotypes die hard and he had best check his at the door.

"Take a seat," Josiah said. "Tell me what's going on and why you're needing so urgently to know about tribal mythology and Cruxhen."

Jack sat on the edge of a green leather chair facing the fire and Josiah sat on one end of the sofa. And as he looked at the older man's weathered face and probing eyes, he had no idea where to start.

"There's a lot to tell," Jack said, lacing his fingers and shaking his head. "And some of it is going to sound pretty crazy, but it's the truth."

Josiah nodded. "Okay."

Jack looked around at the kitchen and a doorway to the hall. "I'll try to keep it as short as I can. I appreciate you seeing me and I don't want to disturb your family."

"Not a problem. It's just me," he said. "I lost my wife to cancer five years ago and both my daughters are grown and out in the world."

"I'm sorry to hear about your wife," Jack said.

"Thank you."

Jack cleared his throat and did his best to summarize what had happened at The Farm with Andy when they were thirteen. Josiah stopped him at one point to ask for more clarification on where The Farm was located, then he asked for Jack to give him a minute and disappeared into another room. He emerged with a large worn book and a rolled up piece of paper.

"Don't mind me," he said as he set the book down and opened it. "Keep going. I'm following you, but I want to check something."

When Jack got to the part where he saw Andy grabbed and dragged away into the attic, Josiah looked up from the book and stared at him.

"You saw this thing? I mean, got a good look at it?"

Jack nodded. "Yeah, a good enough look that I'll never get it out of my head."

"What did it look like?"

"It looked like death," Jack said, looking away at the fire. "That's the best way I can describe it. It was tall and thin; bony, almost like a skeleton, but it was covered in thin slimy grey skin that looked partly transparent like a fish's belly. It's face looked like a skull with skin pulled tight over it and it had milky dead eyes and a gaping mouth with broken teeth."

Josiah Red Wolf wore a look of intense interest and genuine amazement as Jack continued.

"When it grabbed Andy, I could see its long bony arms and fingers. It was strong and took him so fast, he didn't stand a chance."

For a moment Josiah didn't speak. He appeared to be lost in thought.

"Does that sound like this Cruxhen?"

"Maybe," Josiah replied. "There were numerous accounts of killings and disappearances in tribal history and oral legends that were attributed to Cruxhen, but only a handful of those accounts actually include a physical description. Generally, it was believed that if you saw Cruxhen, you would not live to tell about it."

Josiah stood up and walked to the fire, and as he did, he pulled a paper from his pocket and unfolded it.

"Tell me about the symbol Dan Langstall sent me," he said, turning and holding it up so Jack could see it. "I assume that's how you linked this all back to the Chockowan and Cruxhen?"

"Partly. That's where this gets really complicated, and it's how my friend is involved."

Jack proceeded to give Josiah an abbreviated description of Andy's recent re-appearance and the dreams, as well as Jack's re-union with Deena, and when he described how Andy's mouth had appeared sewn shut in both their dreams, Josiah seemed noticeably shaken.

"Is that where you got this?" He held up the paper again.

"No, I'm getting to that," Jack said and continued. "But the first thing was the chevron beads. I don't know how, but Andy left these for us, one for each of us." He pulled a crumpled envelope from his pocket and produced the bead and held it out for Josiah to look at. He picked it up and examined it.

"Amazing," he said. "This is authentic. Original handmade glasswork from fourteenth century Italy. You can only find these in museums. And you say your friend Andy gave them to you?"

"Yes, he was desperate for us to have them, like there was something important he wanted us to know about them. Look, I know how that sounds but..."

Josiah held up his hand and fixed his eyes on Jack. "We're past that now."

Jack blinked. "I'm sorry?"

Josiah walked back to the sofa and sat down.

"It's been my experience that modern cultures don't allow the spiritual world into their system of beliefs because it's too threatening. But it has always been a rich part of Chockowan culture. It's a living thread that runs through the history of our people, our ceremonies, and our art. It may be a cliché to the Anglos, but it has been very real to Native American cultures for thousands of years. All to say, don't worry about how any of this sounds. Remember who you're talking to."

"Thanks," Jack said, and he meant it.

"The reason I got the book and the map was something you said about the valley where this farm is located." He rolled out the map, which looked like a photocopy of an old hand-drawn map of the southeastern United States, but the state boundaries were not part of the original drawing. They appeared to have been superimposed from a computer map at a later time, and there were various areas and spots highlighted with markers in a swath from northwestern Florida, through the Blue Ridge Mountains and what was now northern Georgia, western North Carolina, and eastern Tennessee.

"What is all that?" Jack asked.

"It's part of the research that one of our tribal historians did about ten years back on when and where the Chockowan interacted with Spanish explorers. Those interactions dramatically changed the trajectory of our people and some of them were outright atrocities that more closely resembled genocide. My role as a Wisdom Giver is to preserve the culture and history of our people and help educate young people and those outside our tribe so these things are not lost. A big part of that is helping to ensure that what is printed in the history books is complete and accurate. As I'm sure you can imagine, much of the past has been altered and heavily sanitized to preserve the romantic aura of the early explorers."

"Sounds about right," Jack said.

Josiah moved his finger on the map to what would be western North Carolina.

"These marks show where the Spaniards encountered the Chockowan, either camped and traded with them or fought with them. This dotted circle is roughly where one of the largest scale massacres of our people is said to have happened, but there has been disagreement about the specific location."

"I read something about that," Jack said. "Nowatek? But there wasn't much information. What happened there?"

"Yes, that's it. It is a truly sad story, I'm afraid. The Spaniards routinely took the food stores and other supplies of the indigenous tribes when they encountered them, and would often enslave men and women as well, for labor and their own gratification. Many of these villages suffered starvation afterwards. There was a large village, roughly here, and when the chief refused to give in to De Soto's demands they murdered him in front of the village, then systematically tortured and executed every man, woman, and child in the village and burned it to the ground. We estimate it was over three hundred people."

"Jesus," Jack said. "That's so awful."

"Yes it is. And tragically, not an isolated incident. But the reason I'm telling you this," he paused and held the book in front of him, pointing to a section midway down the page. "Is because according to legend, there was a shaman among the women of the village who cursed the valley before she died. Evil spirits are drawn to hatred and violence like a moth to a flame, and the evil that happened there was so great that it drew a terrible demon to the valley and it was said that the witch's curse bound it there forever, along with the souls of any who die there."

"Oh, my God. Andy," Jack whispered.

"Maybe," Josiah said. "We're not there yet. The valley of Nowatek was considered tsau cha'ta by the Chockowan after that."

"A place of great evil," Jack said and Josiah's eyebrows raised in surprise.

Jack shook his head. "It was something I remember from an article I read."

"Yes, that's right. And word spread among the other tribes. None of the indigenous people would even travel through the valley, much less camp or settle there. It was considered a dead place. But the exact location of the massacre has never been formally documented and the demon was never identified. The symbol you asked about, the one my people used to signify Cruxhen. You were going to tell me where you saw it."

"First I need to tell you about the McNeill family. They built The Farm and settled there, and what happened to them was..." Jack stopped to chase away the image in his mind of the bodies in the well. "It was bad. But it's the first place this symbol shows up. And from what you're telling me, it may be where the demon shows up."

Jack proceeded to tell Josiah about the journals they had found and what they told of Margaret McNeill's increasingly bizarre and disturbing behavior. When he described William's entry about the symbol cut in her forearm and the writing on the wall, *DRU AKEY NE SHADAY,* Josiah looked deeply concerned.

"Do you know what that means?" he asked.

Jack nodded.

"Go on with your story," Josiah said, standing up to go and put more wood on the fire.

Jack described how Henry had gone missing, and out of fear and desperation, William had built the attic and locked her away in it. When he described William's final entry, Josiah frowned.

"That was the last he wrote?"

"Yes," Jack said. "I think soon after he wrote that she broke out and killed him and their daughter. She put the bodies in a dry well."

"How do you know this?" Josiah asked.

"Because I found them all," Jack said, fighting the emotion he felt. "And I found my friend Andy there too."

"Good Lord," Josiah said. "You're serious?"

Jack pulled out his phone and opened the photos, scrolling to those he'd taken in the well. He handed the phone to Josiah. "Look at their mouths."

He could tell by the expression on the older man's face that he was stricken and struggling with what he was seeing.

"This is Cruxhen," Josiah said, barely above a whisper. "There is no doubt. The accounts of her victims all describe the same wounds. It is her signature. The Chockowan used the symbol depicting this to warn others that Cruxhen was nearby and had taken someone from the village." He shook his head and stared. "I've never seen anything like this. I never imagined I would."

"So, this demon, Cruxhen was making Margaret McNeill do what she did?"

"I'm not a shaman, but that would be my guess. A demon poisons the mind and worms its way in until it takes over someone entirely, until they almost *become* the demon. It sounds like that's what happened to this poor McNeill woman."

"But that was a hundred years ago," Jack said. "What about my friend Andy? He has exactly the same injuries but he died eighty years after Margaret killed her family. Are you saying what I saw that night was Margaret McNeill? How is that possible?"

Josiah Red Wolf was silent for a moment as he laid Jack's phone on the table and pushed it toward him.

"Not exactly. I don't believe there would have been any part of Margaret left by that time. What you saw may have been what she became after being inhabited by Cruxhen for so many years. It's a terrible thought, how that might have twisted and altered her physical body."

Jack felt light-headed again and asked if he could get a glass of water.

Josiah went and brought him one from the kitchen.

"Sorry, I know this is difficult."

Jack took a long drink and wiped his mouth with the back of his hand.

"I need to tell you about Deena and the other place I saw the symbol," he said, chewing on his lip at the thought of it. Jack told Josiah about Deena's nightmares and about the incident in the hotel room, and when he'd finished Josiah stared at him with wide eyes.

"This is very bad," Jack. "Your friend is in danger; imminent danger."

Jack's heart leapt into his throat and he slid to the edge of his chair. "What? Why?"

Josiah's expression was grim. "Because Cruxhen has her. Of that, I am certain."

"I don't understand how that can be," Jack said, his voice rising. "I talked to her this morning and..." He remembered his conversation with Tanya and the sickening realization that Deena had been lying to him about being home.

"What is it?"

"She told me she was home, in Black Mountain, and everything was fine, but just a couple of hours ago I found out she never went home at all. The woman in her shop hasn't even seen her."

"Jack, I'm not sure what's happening there, but know this; Cruxhen is a liar and deceiver. It's how she lures people into her control."

"But how? Deena hasn't even been to The Farm except once."

"You say she is Andy's sister?"

"Yes, younger sister."

"If Andy's soul is trapped there, as you say it might be, there may be a spiritual connection between them that served as a bridge or a gateway of sorts for the demon to get to Deena. That's the only thing that makes sense."

Jack was up pacing now.

"What did you mean, 'has her'?"

"I'm sorry to say it, but once the demon has a way in, it begins burrowing into the mind and poisoning it from the inside. But from what I've read it's not a fast process. It doesn't happen overnight like they show it in the movies. It happens over weeks or months, like in the case of the McNeill woman."

"Shit," Jack muttered, and suddenly all of the strange things Deena had been saying rushed back to his mind. He had assumed she had said them because she related to Margaret's plight and had been dreaming about her, but now he knew he had missed the obvious; she wasn't relating to Margaret Mc-Neill, she was *becoming* her. The implications took his breath away.

Then like a bolt, he remembered the last thing she said before she left early the previous morning.

"I have to get back home...Henry's cough has gotten so much worse. I'm worried it might turn into pneumonia."

"Oh, no," Jack groaned. "When she said she had to go home..."

He stood gaping in silence for a moment and Josiah Red Wolf stood up and put a hand on his arm.

"What is it son?"

"I know where she is," Jack said. "I have to go."

"Hold on," Josiah said, raising a hand to keep Jack from walking to the door. "I know you're scared for your friend and you want to help her, but you need to take a breath and think about what you're doing. If this is what it appears to be, and that's saying a hell of a lot, you're completely unprepared."

Jack's mind was still humming from the adrenaline in his veins but he hesitated, looking back and forth between Josiah and the front door for a moment before finally relenting. He nodded and let Josiah lead him back to the chair.

Josiah watched Jack sit back down, then sat on the edge of the sofa.

"You know what this thing can do; you've read a firsthand account of someone who's family was destroyed by it. Hell, you've seen it with your own eyes. Cruxhen is pure evil. But by all accounts she is clever and ruthless. If your friend is in her grip, she can use that against you. She *will* use it against you, hoping that your love for her will make you do something reckless, and then she'll have both of you. That's not going to help anyone and it's not going to make the past right."

Jack grimaced and ran his hand through his hair, frustrated by the undeniable logic of Josiah's words.

"So, what the hell am I supposed to do?" He said, almost at wits-end. "I'll be damned if I'm going to let this thing have her, *especially* after Andy. This is not like back then; I don't give a damn about what happens to me. You need to understand that."

"I do," Josiah said. "Believe me, I do."

He looked away again, clearly conflicted about something.

"I can see that you are determined to try and save your friend, so I will tell you what I can, but know this; what you are dealing with has not been seen by the Chockowan for centuries. What we know about facing these monsters we know through the stories of our ancestors, so if you do what I tell you, you will have to do it on faith. As far as I know, it has never been tried."

Jack swallowed hard and locked eyes with Josiah.

"I understand. Just tell me what I have to do."

CHAPTER 19

Night driving on the winding mountain roads of western North Carolina could be treacherous for someone at their best, but Jack was far from his best as he made the white-knuckle trip back toward Benton, surviving two very close calls along the way before he reached the four-lane that brought him into town. His tried to keep the things Josiah had told him straight while pushing back the fear and the hellish montage of images that played in his mind, of things he had seen and those he now imagined.

It was nearly midnight when he finally turned down Wildwood Lane, and the windows of all the houses were dark, including his own. As the headlights of his car fell on the driveway and swept across the front yard, he looked closely for the fake rock, but as he suspected, it was not there. It had finally come to him what it was that had seemed off earlier that day about his yard; the fake rock that his mother had used for years to hide the house key had been missing. And it was then that he had realized what Deena had done.

He stopped in front of the garage door and climbed out, leaving the car running and the headlights on as he lifted the door. Her car was there, as he knew it would be, with the driver's door standing wide open.

"Damn," Jack said, before reaching for the garage light.

The pieces had fallen together quickly after he talked to Tanya and realized that Deena had not gone back to Black Mountain at all. Given the strange things she had said about "going home," what Josiah had explained, and the missing rock, he knew now that she had gone straight to his house after their lunch together the previous day. And whether from a childhood memory or a stray comment he had made about where they kept the extra key, she had gotten into the house and hidden her car in the garage before hiking to The Farm.

Jack's blood had run cold as he imagined her there that morning, watching him the whole time he was exploring the farmhouse and reading William's second journal. But what had nearly made him sick was the memory of his close call in the well and the shadow he had seen move across the opening above him, and of the partially removed stakes that secured the rope ladder. The thought that it could have been her, knotted his stomach into a painful ball, but only then had it fully dawned on him that his nightmares had actually been a foreshadowing; a warning.

Josiah's words echoed in his mind; *Cruxhen has her...of that I am certain.*

Although he was confident Deena was not inside, Jack was cautious as he opened the door into the house, turning on the light in the mud room. The glow illuminated part of the kitchen and he saw nothing out of the ordinary.

"Hello," he called softly into the muted stillness.

No response.

"Deena? Are you here?"

Only silence.

He walked slowly through the mud room and reached around the corner to turn on the kitchen lights. The room was suddenly bathed in bright light that carried over into the living room, and what Jack saw made him freeze. On one partially lit living room wall, he saw writing and symbols that looked exactly like the ones he had seen at The Farm, including the stitch-mouth symbol that he now knew was the mark of the demon.

"Deena," he called again, barely able to muster the breath to speak.

Nothing.

He felt for the pistol in his jacket pocket, but then stopped.

What the fuck are you doing? It's still Deena.

Jack walked very softly through the kitchen to the entrance to the hall and turned on the overhead light. When he turned around, he gaped at the carnage that had once been his living room. Now it looked more like a terrifying recreation of the inside of the attic.

The small seating area that the maintenance men had set up had been smashed to pieces and scattered around the room, and the empty walls were nearly completely covered with writing (he guessed Chockowan) and symbols, in what appeared to be paint from the garage. There were deep scratches and gashes in the sheetrock at random places around the room and even several large holes where something had punched through. Most frightening of all were the blood drops on the carpet and spattering on the walls. It was *her* blood; it had to be.

"God damn it," he whispered. "It's hurting her and she doesn't even know it."

The moment crystalized his resolve for what he had to do and confirmed that he was nearly out of time. He had to find her, even though it meant doing the thing he had dreaded most since he was thirteen, the thing he had vowed he would never do...return to The Farm at night.

Without searching the remainder of the house, Jack quickly went back out to his car, closed the garage door and donned his pack, making sure that the items Josiah had put together for him were wrapped securely inside. There was no night moon this time to guide his way through the woods, so he took out the Maglite and headed across the side yard and into the tree line.

As Jack hurried down the ridge, angling toward the point where he knew he would meet the beginning of the remnant roadbed, all he could think about was the host of scenarios, all bad, in which he would be confronted by something that looked like Deena but would not be her, at least not entirely her. The thought was unimaginable.

His chest ached as he remembered Josiah Red Wolf's warning: "The demon infects the mind like a virus and spreads quickly, attacking and replacing memories, thoughts, feelings and most of all, free-will, until there is nothing left. If you can stop the process before the change is complete, there is a good chance her mind will heal itself over time. But you must be prepared because if you cannot, there will soon be nothing left of your friend to save. She will be gone forever."

But how much of her was left, and how long did he have before she disappeared completely?

He kicked himself for not paying more attention to the warning signs; her strange comments and behavior over the last couple of days. Maybe he could have bought her more time.

Still, what could he have done?

Josiah had explained that what gave Cruxhen power and allowed it to remain in the physical world was what the Chockowan called "Tey Wica-nah" or The Evil Relic, the physical remains of the demon's original human host, cleverly hidden and ferociously guarded for centuries. He had made it clear that unless the Evil Relic was found and destroyed, Deena would be lost and Andy would never be free. But The Farm was a big place and the valley even bigger, and it could be hidden nearly anywhere. Even with the means to destroy it, how did he stand a chance of finding it, especially before the clock ran out for Deena?

Yet as Jack made his way through the darkened woods he felt a grim conviction that gave him some measure of strength; he had said it to Josiah and had meant it. This time he did not care what happened to him. This time he would not run. He would get it done or die trying.

Cracks were beginning to appear in the wall of clouds that darkened the night sky as Jack finally reached the end of the wooded road and emerged into the field that flanked The Farm. Patches of stars were visible and moonlight bathed parts of the valley in a pale glow. The babbling of the river sounded cold and indifferent, and Jack zipped his jacket against the deep chill that was settling in over the fields.

"Okay, Andy," Jack whispered, fixing his gaze on the hollow black window-eyes of the distant farmhouse. "I'm ready."

As he made his way across the hillside, Jack scanned the field and the thin groves of trees around him, shining his light into the deep shadows, out of caution. Even though he knew she could be waiting for him anywhere, one dreadful scenario had planted itself in his mind like a poison seed and had taken root. It was the cruelest one, the one he had dreaded above all others, yet as the ultimate twist of karma it would be darkly appropriate; she would be waiting in the attic and he would have to face her there. The very spot where his life had been torn apart twenty-three years ago.

He knew that his only hope was to find this "evil relic" and destroy it, but the closer he got to the dilapidated cluster of buildings the more impossible the task seemed. The only clue that Josiah had given him was that the place would almost certainly be marked, but even that was so vague as to be almost useless. *Marked how?* His already racing heart sped up as he got closer to the house and his light passed across numerous scraps of decaying wood, large stones, and rusting metal objects from The Farm's brief heyday. Briefly he questioned whether something so random could be a marker, but he quickly dismissed the idea. This "relic" would be important to the demon above all else, and even in the realm of evil, he felt certain it would be treated with reverence and marked accordingly.

Jack froze mid-step as he heard something that sounded like a voice; faint but it had been there. He had heard owls many times at night and had sometimes mistaken their strange calls for a voice, but something about this had been different. He stood as still as a stone and closed his eyes. Several seconds went by and he heard it again, and this time there was no doubt.

A hard chill shot up his spine as he realized it was a voice calling for help. He spun around, shining the light in all directions, straining to see by the spotlight, but there was no sign of anyone and he couldn't be certain which direction it was coming from. For a moment the voice went silent, then it called out again, faint and muted. Had it been Deena? He couldn't tell. Jack started walking, still scanning with his light and as his desperation grew, he threw caution aside, cupped one hand to the side of his mouth and called out.

"Deena, is that you? It's Jack!"

For another second there was silence and then he heard the voice scream his name, but still muted and far away. Far away or...

His thought of the well. *The fucking well.*

Without waiting, Jack sprinted in the direction of the tool shed, his light bobbing wildly across the faded wooden structure as he started around the south side where he knew the well cover was.

"Deena!" he called again. "Can you hear me?"

"Oh my God, Jack!" Her voice was louder now but still muffled. She was crying hysterically and the pain and fear in her voice was like a hot dagger through his heart.

"Help me, please! Get me out of here, I'm trapped. My ankle is broken and I can't stand up."

"I'm here, Deena!" Jack called loudly, his voice shaking. "I'm going to get you out. Just hang on."

The thought of Deena at the bottom of that horrible place in the dark, among the bodies of the dead was nearly unbearable. And she had no way to know that one of them was her brother, Andy. Jack had not yet told her about finding him there.

"Jack, I'm so glad you're here," she cried. "Please hurry. I'm scared."

He knelt beside the well cover and threw off his pack, propping his light up against it to free up both of his hands.

Wait, a voice said in the back of his mind.

He braced his feet and prepared to push against the heavy wooden well cover.

Stop! The voice screamed at him and he hesitated, hands resting on the edges of the wooden disc, as the stark reality of what he was about to do hit him like a fist. He was mortified by his own recklessness.

He had been so overwrought at hearing her cries for help that he had momentarily lost all perspective and thrown caution aside. She sounded like herself, painfully so, but how could he be sure? She had sounded perfectly normal on the phone the day before, when she told him she was home in Black Mountain working on inventory at the shop, but it had all been a lie. He knew now that she had been under the demon's influence. Why should this be any different?

She's already tried to kill you once, for Christ's sake.

Jack's mind wrestled with the idea as he began shivering in the cold night air, looking around him and trying to think what he should do. He could play along, stall and try to be sure. What if the demon *had* released her for some reason, maybe to get to him? He couldn't just leave her down there in agony while he figured it out.

She won't die from a broken ankle, but open that well and you might.

Jack's mouth had gone dry.

"I'm working on it," he called out, desperate to buy time. "I think something's blocking the cover. It's okay, it'll just take a minute."

He heard a choked cry rise up from the bottom of the well.

"Pleeeaase hurry! I can't stand this much longer."

"Deena, try to stay calm," Jack called, scanning the area behind the tool shed with his light for something heavy. It had suddenly dawned on him that if he was wrong, and she was trying to lure him into the well, he might be able to trap her in there if he could block the opening with something heavy enough, or at least be ready to do so if this went sideways. It was a flimsy plan at best, given that by all evidence, Margaret McNeill had smashed through a wooden wall like it was made of matchsticks, but he did not believe Deena was fully under Cruxhen's control, at least not yet.

"Almost there," he said, just as he spotted part of a rusted, but clearly formidable wrought iron rack sticking out of the weeds. It looked like something that might have held shelves or bins in the toolshed at one time. Leaving his things, he hurried over to it with the light and pulled on one of the bars. It was heavily anchored in the overgrown grass and barely budged at first, but he kept pulling it in a rocking motion and after a few seconds it pulled free and he dragged it toward the well. He was certain it weighed eighty pounds or more.

"Jack, what's taking so long? Please hurry!" Her muted cry carried across the still night air and Jack thought he detected an edge to it.

His arms were trembling and sweat was running down his face when he finally laid the iron rack down beside the well cover, ensuring it was within easy reach, and got back on his knees.

"I think I've got it," he shouted, trying to quell the tremor in his voice.

"Thank God!" she called back. "I'm so glad you found me."

Jack put on the headlamp from his pack and turned it on, then, with his heart racing and a light ringing in his ears, he leaned over and pushed the well cover partially off the opening. At first it was hard to make anything out at the bottom of the well, but then he saw the top of Deena's head and he realized she was sitting among the awful pile of bones and decayed clothing, looking down at her feet. Oddly, she did not look up when he shone the light down, and a terrible feeling crept over him.

"What happened, Deena? How did you get down there?" he asked, feigning calm.

She did not respond, but he could see her hand moving and something in it; something white.

"Deena?" he called, as the muscles in his chest drew taught.

"I had to see them again," she said, in an oddly sing-song tone, all trace of fear and pain gone.

Jack could barely breath to speak.

"See who?" he asked.

"The children," she said, still looking down at the object in her hand.

Without taking the headlamp beam away from her, Jack eased slowly back and reached one hand for the iron rack; his muscles coiled like a spring.

"I had almost forgotten they were down here, until you reminded me."

The voice no longer sounded like Deena at all, and as she looked up at Jack, he gasped at her milky white eyes and dirty, bruised face.

"They've all been so good," she grinned. "So very quiet like little children should be." At this she held up a child's skull so Jack could see what remained of the stitching over the mouth and he thought he would faint.

Instantly her grin morphed into a snarl and to Jack's horror, she leapt onto the side of the well and crawled up it like a spider climbing a wall. A cry escaped his lips as he scrambled to pull the well cover over the opening, knowing he had only seconds. The demon growled and hissed as he jerked the heavy wooden disk into place and threw himself onto it, standing in the middle of it as he grabbed the iron rack and pulled with all his might. A heavy blow from beneath him sent Jack several inches into the air and he landed hard on his knees. A voice that was not Deena's bellowed from beneath the well cover and another blow rocked him, but he held his position and continued pulling the rack until he had it squarely over the cover.

Alternating blows and clawing sounds continued as Jack took great gulps of air, trying to catch his breath. Hot tears of rage spilled down his cheeks as he imagined the carnage the demon was inflicting on Deena. But just as he thought the storm of emotions would overwhelm him, Jack looked at the darkened silhouette of the farmhouse behind him and it triggered a memory; something that had not made sense at the time, but as he thought about it now he realized what he had missed.

It's there, he thought, as adrenaline coursed through his veins. *It was right there all along.*

In an instant he knew what he had to do. Praying that the iron rack would hold the well cover down long enough to buy him time, Jack lunged off of it, grabbed his pack and sprinted hard through the darkness toward the house.

CHAPTER 20

The headlamp bobbed wildly as he ran, lighting the way as Jack zigzagged through the weeds and between discarded junk, but he paid little attention to the booming of the well cover and the horrible bellowing noises receding behind him. He was seeing the photographs again in his mind and desperately hoping he was correct, but it made perfect sense. In the photograph, the apparition of Margaret McNeill had not just been facing the wall of the attic, she had been staring at something specific, and in the series of photos that followed, he had seen it; the symbol of the demon.

He had been convinced she would be waiting for him in the attic, and by all rights she should have been, but she had been in the well instead and it hadn't made sense until now.

She was never going to meet me in the attic, he thought, as he leaped over the shattered porch steps and charged into the house. *That's why she chose the well. She was trying to keep me as far away from the attic as possible.*

She was protecting The Relic.

The faint banging from the well told Jack that the rack was still holding as he threaded his way up the dark and treacherous stairs, trying to focus on what he had to do. Trying to make the hardest decision of his life. He knew that the fastest and surest way to stop Cruxhen was to find the remains and burn them with the kerosene Josiah had given him, but that was only if he could find them. He didn't know exactly where in the wall they were hidden, and how many times he would have to punch through it. And what if he never found it like that?

The other option was to punch a single hole in the wall where the symbol appeared and pour in the kerosene; to burn the wall from the inside out, along with the attic and possibly the entire evil house. The Relic would surely burn that way, but only when the fire reached it, and he had no way of knowing how long that would take. Which was the better move? He knew that the iron rack would not hold much longer and he was terrified by what would happen when she escaped.

Even as Jack reached the top step and hurried across the open room, dropping his pack at the jagged opening to the attic, he had made up his mind. It might be slower, but the only way to be sure this would end was to burn it all.

Burn it to the fucking ground.

He knew that would likely mean facing the demon, and it might cost him his life, but it had to be done. It was the last chance he would have to save Deena and free Andy.

Jack hurriedly pulled out the Mason jar that Josiah had filled with kerosene, along with the lighter and starter rag, and pulled the camping axe from its holder on the side of his pack, thankful for the hands-free light on his headlamp. Bracing himself against the wave of fear that he knew stepping into the attic would bring, he forced himself ahead, crossing the threshold and heading straight to the far left corner of the room. Despite his best efforts not to look, his eyes were drawn to the angry carnage that had played out on the canvas of the attic's walls as Margaret McNeill had descended into madness and demonic possession, eventually becoming Cruxhen. The walls were thick with countless words and phrases scrawled at crazy angles in some kind of chalk and what might have been blood, some in English, but most in what must have been Chockowan. There were gruesome drawings of killing and torture and symbols that looked deeply sinister, even though Jack was unsure what they meant.

As his light scanned the far corner and the adjacent left wall, he spotted the one symbol that he recognized; the mark of the demon. He hated that symbol for what it represented, but he desperately hoped it had been put there for a reason.

Without waiting, Jack set down the jar and the rag and smashed the pointed end of his hand-axe into the wooden wall, directly over the evil mark, punching a small hole and sending plaster dust flying into the stale air around him. Much of the plaster that covered the wooden lath walls had been worn off by time or scratched off by the creature that had been imprisoned there, and the wood itself had grown weak enough that it barely slowed the axe down.

Jack reared his arm for another blow and stopped, listening intently, but he heard nothing. His heart skipped as he realized that he no longer heard the banging of the well cover.

"Oh, shit," he whispered as terror spurred his hand and he gave the wall another two swift chops in rapid succession, widening the hole to the size of his fist. It would have to do.

He glanced nervously back toward the ragged entrance to the attic, but saw only darkness in the outer room. With unsteady hands, he unscrewed the top on the Mason jar, turning his head to one side to avoid the noxious smell, and carefully poured the kerosene into the hole. He heard it splashing on the floor behind the wall and hoped that he had soaked The Relic, or at least come close.

Jack took the lighter out of his pocket and was about to light the starter rag when a voice spoke behind him in the darkness. *Her voice.*

"Jack, please stop."

Nearly paralyzed by fear, he spun his light to shine on the attic entrance and saw her standing there; Deena, looking frightened and exhausted, barefoot in the cold with arms hanging limply by her sides. The sleeves of her shirt were shredded below the elbow and he was shocked to see blood dripping from deep lacerations on her forearms. Her eyes were a garish, milky white in his light, but otherwise it was her, and the pain of seeing her like that seared him like a flame.

Jack trembled as he held the lighter and the rag, watching her, and suddenly time seemed to stand still. The darkness around him faded and he saw his life before it all happened. He saw Andy smiling and laughing under a summer sky, running with a red water balloon in his parents' back yard. He saw his and Andy's parents sitting in lawn chairs with beers in their hands watching Deena and her friends as they ran giggling through the sprinkler. And for a brief moment, he saw what their lives might have been.

And then the darkness rushed back in and he saw the terror in Andy's face and felt the white-hot pain and the unbearable shame that had hollowed out his sole that night and left him a shell of the person he could have been. But finding Deena again had been like seeing a light in darkness, and being with her had given him his first glimmer of hope that he could still find and become that person.

But for this, he thought, looking at her pitiful condition and sensing her terrible suffering.

"But for you," he said, speaking directly to the demon now, as he felt rage swelling in him like a wave, rising upward through his body.

Deena's empty eyes had been studying Jack and she took a step toward him.

"I love you, Jack. Don't."

Jack was no longer afraid. His muscles had stopped shaking and he felt a profound sense of peace. He knew that the moment had come and he was ready for the end.

"I love you too, Deena. And if you're still in there, you know that's why I have to."

He took a breath and flicked the lighter. The rag burst into flame and the placid face that had been Deena's instantly turned to pure rage as the demon lunged toward him with a deafening shriek. In one swift motion, Jack stuffed the burning rag through the hole in the wall and spun around, launching himself directly at the charging figure and slamming into her. As they crashed to the floor Jack felt stabbing pain and the crushing strength of her grip, squeezing him so tightly that he smelled the sick odor of sweat, blood, and urine, even as he felt his ribs crack.

They rolled across the floor and he tried to hold on to her, to keep her from pulling away and getting to the hole in the wall, but she managed to get one arm free and smash a clawed hand across his face, snapping his head sideways and sending a searing pain across his cheek. Drops of blood spattered into his eyes, but over her shoulder he caught a glimpse of flames breaking through the wall and climbing up it, bathing the room in an angry orange light and filling the air with smoke. The demon looked at the fire and bellowed in protest, thrashing harder and kicking Jack away as she stood and tried to get to the wall.

Through his pain, Jack managed to lunge at her legs, tripping her and sending her to her knees. With a sinister snarl, she whirled and attacked Jack, rolling him onto his back and biting at his face. He screamed in pain as she sat on his chest, and pulled back, her mouth dripping with the blood from his wounded face, and raised an arm to its full height, ready to strike. But as she did, there was a tremendous whooshing noise behind her as the entire attic wall exploded in flame, bathing them in a wave of heat as Jack coughed and gasped for air beneath her weight.

For a moment she sat frozen, her arm raised and her milky eyes staring toward the wall of flames. Suddenly her mouth stretched wide and her head tilted backward as she let out an ungodly deafening shriek. Then her body shuddered violently and went completely limp, as she tipped sideways off of Jack and hit the floor beside him.

"Deena!" Jack groaned, "Deena, can you hear me?"

Her eyes were closed and she did not respond. Jack felt his skin beginning to burn as the flames rapidly spread across the ceiling above them, filling the upper part of the room entirely with smoke. The roar was deafening and he knew that they had no time.

Coughing and gagging against the terrible pain in his side, Jack crawled to his knees and, bending low, shouted Deena's name and slapped her hard across the face. When she did not respond, he slapped her again.

This time she stirred and lifted her head slightly and started coughing. Her eyes partially opened and he silently gave thanks; they were bloodshot and glassy, but they were *her* eyes.

Without waiting, Jack grabbed her wrists and started dragging her toward the attic opening, crying out from the pain as he pulled. After a few feet she twisted and pulled one hand free, propping herself partially up and trying to crawl with him.

"Good," he shouted, over the noise, then coughed a wracking cough. "That's it. Keep going!"

Together they crawled out of the burning attic as the flames consumed two more walls and began spreading across the floor, turning the entire room into a fiery furnace, and as Jack looked back, he knew that another sixty seconds would have seen them both perish.

Deena cried out and groaned as her arm buckled and she collapsed. Jack maneuvered sideways and put an arm behind her, lifting her partially back up.

"We've got to keep going," he shouted. "I know it hurts, but you can do it."

He felt her struggling and finally they started moving again. He knew that getting her down the stairs would be the worst part. She seemed to be coming more awake and he heard her say his name.

"Don't try to talk, just focus on moving," he said. "We've got to get the hell out of here."

"Okay," she croaked, gripping him tightly as he pulled her to a standing position at the top of the stairs. The air was foul here, but not yet entirely choked with smoke.

"Can you see where you're walking?" Jack said. "I'll hold on to you, but you've got to be careful where you step."

She nodded and they started down, slowly and unevenly, keeping next to the wall in single-file as far away as possible from the gaping holes in several of the steps. As they reached the halfway point, there was a deafening boom as part of the attic roof collapsed, sending a wide jet of fire into the rest of the upstairs. Deena screamed and tried to duck but tipped sideways and started to fall. Instinctively Jacked grabbed for her arm but his hand slipped in the blood on her wrist and when he thrust one foot out to break his fall, it found only air where a step should have been. He toppled forward off the staircase, gasping in disbelief at the falling sensation as he heard her scream, then the world went dark.

He heard his name. He felt pain shooting up his side and through to his back.

Jack opened his eyes and Deena was hovering over him, coughing and trying to wipe the dirt and smoke from his eyes.

"Jack! Thank God!" she cried. "I thought you were dead."

Jack growled in pain as he tried to raise himself up. The fire was raging in the upstairs now and sparks and burning embers were raining down all around them. The heat was nearly unbearable.

"I think I can move," he said through gritted teeth as he eased himself to a sitting position then stood slowly up.

Leaning on each other for support and ducking low to stay clear of the smoke, they limped as fast they could out the front door and carefully across the porch. Jack held onto a post as Deena climbed awkwardly down the steps and helped him down. Above them, flames were licked high into the night air through several gaping holes in the roof and jetting out the upstairs windows as the fire rapidly engulfed the rest of the house. It was going up like a tinder box.

Still coughing and gasping for air, they stumbled another hundred feet away before collapsing in the grass, awash in the orange glow and radiating heat from the blaze.

"It's going to burn to the ground," Deena said, looking with wild eyes at the spreading inferno.

Jack stared at the flames and wiped the blood from his face.

"Let it burn," he said.

Deena was still losing blood and shaking all over and as he watched her fighting to keep her eyes open, Jack knew that she was rapidly slipping into shock. Trying to think through his own pain and exhaustion, he felt for his pocket knife and silently gave thanks that it was still there. He pulled it out, then took off his jacket and his shirt, exposing his bare torso, and began to cut strips from his shirt. Deena looked quizzically at him but didn't speak and then suddenly almost fell over. She was slipping quickly toward unconsciousness and he had to hurry.

Angry that he had nothing to clean her wounds with, Jack did his best to brush the dirt and debris from the cuts on her arms and feet, then wrapped them tightly with improvised bandages, grimacing against the pain. Every move felt like a dagger to his ribs.

"Stay with me, Deena," Jack said over the roaring inferno behind him. His teeth chattered despite the warmth of the fire.

"You've been so strong. Just stay with me."

"I'll try," she managed, but her voice was barely above a whisper.

When he had finished bandaging her wounds, Jack took off his shoes and his hiking socks and put the socks on Deena's bare feet before putting the shoes back on his own. Then he put what remained of his shirt and jacket back on and wrapped his arms around Deena, pulling her down beside him on the grass, which had mercifully been warmed by the fire's heat.

She groaned softly and then was silent.

It was only then, as Jack tried to stay awake and think what to do, that the grim reality of their plight came crashing down on him. They had somehow survived the demon and miraculously escaped the fire alive, only to face what now seemed like an utterly hopeless situation.

They were both badly hurt, it was the middle of the night and they were miles from town, with no cell phone coverage and no passable roads to their location. Their only real first aid supplies had burned up in the fire, along with everything else in Jack's pack, including their only drinkable water, leaving them with nothing but the clothes on their backs and a pocket knife. Deena was not even wearing shoes and the temperature was barely ten degrees above freezing.

He knew that shock and hypothermia were a deadly combination, and even if they somehow found the strength to try and hike back to civilization, they would almost certainly succumb to exposure along the way. All of which brought him back to the cruelest irony of all; rather than fleeing that cursed place, their best chance now to stay alive was to stay in the warmth of the fire. Maybe it would at least buy them time.

But what would happen then? Jack did not allow his mind to go there, but he thought he knew. Maybe they could at least put it off for a little while; just a little while.

Almost too weak to keep his eyes open, Jack propped his arm behind his head and watched as the house that had been the site of so much suffering and death, the house that had taken his best friend and haunted his dreams since childhood, met its tortured end. The fire spread rapidly to the downstairs as glowing embers and collapsing sections of burning ceiling set the bone dry floorboards and walls alight, and soon the inside of the house was a swirling maelstrom of flame and embers that looked like the inside of a fiery furnace and roared like a jet engine.

Neither of them stirred as the outer walls were engulfed and portions of the house began to collapse. The heat grew so intense that, had they not been lying on the ground, they would have had to pull back. Jack held his other hand in front of his face to shield him but continued to watch. The blaze was so large that it lit the entire valley, bathing everything down to the river in an eerie red glow that reminded him of hell, and as he watched Jack felt like he was in a dream.

No longer able to keep his eyes open, Jack leaned into Deena, wrapped his arm across her and drifted in and out of consciousness as the sounds of the fire and the collapsing structure turned into a kind of white noise. Waves of heat continued to wash over them, and even as Jack began to sweat beneath his clothes he was barely aware. The smell of smoke was heavy and in his dreamlike state, Jack felt briefly like he was resting at a college bonfire on the practice field, or camping out with Andy. Then the feeling passed and he was neither of those places.

Then, through the thickening fog in his mind, Jack noticed something different; faintly at first but it was a new sound, a rhythmic sound that blended strangely with the cacophony of the fire. And just before Jack fell into darkness, he wondered...

Jack was in a frightening dream. There were voices and strange noises and terrible pain, then none. Faces and hands jostling him and tugging on him, hurting him, then darkness.

Someone calling his name, but he couldn't speak. He was moving, but he did not know how. The rhythmic sound was back and it was much louder, along with a chemical smell, and he no longer heard the fire. Deena. He thought of Deena, but could not feel her beside him. Then darkness.

He was being jostled and tugged again by hands and voices. New pain in his arm and something bright. He heard the clanking of metal and he was moving again.

Then darkness.

CHAPTER 21

Jack slowly opened his eyes. He was in a bed in a room but everything was blurry and he felt thick. He heard a steady beeping and clicking and his head hurt. He tried to think but his mind was moving in slow motion and he felt removed from his thoughts, as if they were on the other side of a curtain. Gradually his mind and his vision began to clear and he recognized the familiar trappings of a hospital room, but he had no idea where he was and how he had ended up there. Cords ran from his chest and arms to a rack of beeping monitors and displays beside his bed and a rolling cart stood beside the bed with a cup of water and a sick tray.

Hazy memories from their terrible ordeal at The Farm came back, slowly at first, then like a flood. And as he thought of Deena and what she had endured, he heard the heart monitor behind him speeding up. He had to know where she was and whether she was okay. An alarm on the monitor went off and a moment later the door opened and a heavy-set woman in a nurse's uniform came bustling in, barely glancing at him as she crossed the room to turn off the alarm.

"Good, you're awake, but you need to try and relax and let's see if you can't bring that heart rate down a bit. I'm Nurse Ronda. You're safe now, and you're being looked after by good people. So is your friend."

"Where is she," Jack said and tried to sit up, but pain exploded in his side and he cried out, just as the heart monitor alarm went off again.

"No, no, you can't do that," Nurse Ronda said as she put one hand on his shoulder and gently pushed him back toward the mattress, reaching to turn off the alarm again with her other hand. "Those ribs need to heal. You've got several fractures and..."

Jack cut her off. "Where's Deena? How is she?"

"She's in the ICU recovery room. She was in pretty rough shape when they brought you in last night. You both were. She needed some surgery on her arms and I believe she was pretty badly dehydrated. But she did very well in surgery."

"Is she awake?"

"She's resting, and they don't allow visitors in the ICU. If the doctor clears her, they'll move her to a room in a few hours and you might be able to see her then. Now, your meds have been through IV, but since you're awake I'm going to give them to you orally." She glanced at a computer screen and squinted through her glasses. "You're due pain medication and an anti-inflammatory in a half-hour. Besides the ribs, you also had a concussion and some pretty deep facial lacerations, but they've been sutured up and you'll need to wear that bandage for a few days. I'll give you some anti-biotic cream."

Jack reached his right hand up to his face and only then realized that there was a large rectangular bandage taped to his cheek.

"I didn't even feel it," Jack said, feeling confused again.

"Yeah, they're really good pain meds," Nurse Ronda smiled. "But they'll wear off, and then you'll need the Tylenol. One other thing; your concussion was minor, so you should recover fully. You may have some headaches and dizziness for a few days and possibly a little confusion for the first twenty-four hours, but those things are normal and they'll pass. Unfortunately, they can't put a hard splint on rib injuries, so you'll have a soft wrap for support and you can use ice packs to help keep swelling down to improve the healing, but it will mostly take rest and time. No strenuous activity of any kind; no lifting and no exercising for at least six weeks."

"Jesus," Jack mumbled and shook his head. He laid back down on the pillow and closed his eyes, massaging his forehead gently with one hand.

Nurse Ronda was busy explaining about the nurse call button and the plastic urinal and about trying to walk to the bathroom with the IV still in, but her voice sounded far away, and behind his closed eyes, all Jack could see was fire; a blazing inferno. He had watched it for...how long? He had no idea, but at that moment it felt like he would see it raging in his mind forever.

"...would you like me to get it for you?" Ronda was asking as the fog in Jack's mind lifted again.

"I'm sorry, get what?" he managed.

"Your cell phone," she repeated.

"Sure, thank you."

"Your clothes were in bad shape so we bagged those up for the laundry but, well, the police officer asked us to hold onto them. We'll get you something to wear though, don't you worry."

Jack tensed and the beeping on the monitor accelerated. How had he not seen this coming?

"What police officer?" he asked, already knowing the answer.

"An officer from the Benton Police Department showed up a couple of hours ago and he's been waiting to talk to you." Ronda glanced at the racing heart monitor and gave Jack a conspiratorial look. "I could tell him you need a few more minutes, you know, to wake up and whatnot."

"I'd appreciate that," Jack sighed. "Thanks. And thanks for everything."

"Your most welcome," she said, turning to leave. "I go off shift at noon but Brianna will take care of you. Let me know if you need anything."

"Thanks, I will," Jack said, as something occurred to him. "One more thing, I forgot to ask what hospital this is. You said 'their department,' like he was from somewhere else."

"Lord, I'm sorry, I should have told you that right off," she said. "You're in Saint Marry's Regional, in Winston-Salem. They brought you and your friend in early this morning in an air ambulance helicopter from up in the mountains, in Randall County."

"Oh, wow," Jack said, still shocked and baffled by the circumstances of their rescue.

"I'll give you a few minutes before I send him in," she winked and left the room.

Jack stared blankly at the closed door, trying to kick-start his brain.

"Out of the frying pan and into the fire," he whispered, remembering one of his mother's old sayings. Only this was in reverse.

He had justified not reporting finding Andy's remains to the authorities because he knew that they would cordon off the scene and keep him and Deena out. He had promised himself that he would report it when they had found the answers they needed. He had assured himself naively that the police would be none the wiser. But what had played out had been so much worse than anything he had imagined, and now he had landed both of them fully in it up to their necks, with no rational or reasonable explanation for any of it.

Still, he reminded himself that whatever they might face, he had succeeded against all odds in freeing her; in saving her, and that was something.

He had already decided that he would take the blame for whatever was deemed to be wrongdoing, and despite the pain it would cause him, he would assist the authorities in any way if they decided to re-open the investigation into Andy's murder. Given everything that had happened, it was the least he could do. But what if they weren't willing to dismiss her part in it? What if, after everything she had been through, she ended up being charged with a crime?

Then, just before the knock came on his hospital room door, Jack had an idea. It was a long shot, and it would hinge entirely on him being able to talk to Deena before the police did. If he didn't pull it off he knew it would land him in even deeper trouble, but, given what was at stake, he was willing to take that chance.

The officer who knocked did not wait for a response before stepping into the room. He was a young man, Jack guessed no older than mid-twenties, with tight-cropped brown hair and a stocky, muscular build. He wore a uniform and carried a notepad.

"Mr. Crawford?" the officer said, stepping across the room toward Jack's bed. "I'm Officer Brent Nolan, with the Benton Police Department."

"Hi," Jack said, extending his hand and doing his best to appear relieved to see the officer. "I'm really glad you're here."

Officer Nolan shook Jack's hand and briefly looked him over, as if assessing his condition, as Jack continued.

"Things were looking really bad last night and we had about given up. There's no cell service out there and we were in no shape to hike out."

"You were very lucky, as it turns out," Nolan nodded. "We got a call from the Forest Service early this morning about the fire. One of their spotters had seen it and called it in and they sent an NCFS chopper out from Shelby to get eyes on it. They were the ones who spotted you and Miss Redmond and contacted us."

"I'll be damned," Jack said, "What were the odds?"

"If it weren't for the fire, probably zero," he replied. "But with that location being so remote, our local fire and EMS had no quick way to respond so we coordinated with Saint Marry's to send their Life Flight crew to evac you. They can pretty much get anywhere."

"Thank God for that," Jack said, genuinely amazed at the sequence of events that led to their rescue but also trying to not overplay his part.

"Anyway, I'd like to ask you a few questions about what went on out there last night if you're feeling up to it." The officer looked at the empty chair against the wall behind him. "Mind if I pull up a chair?"

311

"No, I'm fine with it, please do." Jack reached for his water as he felt his mouth going dry and took a sip as Nolan pulled the chair close to the bed, sat down and opened his notepad.

The officer started by getting Jack's and as much of Deena's personal information as he could provide, then cut to the chase.

"Okay, I've got a number of questions, but can you start by telling me what you and Miss Redmond were doing way out there in the first place?"

Jack swallowed and looked directly at Officer Nolan.

"We were looking for the body of my dead best friend," he began, "and we got attacked in that damn house by a crazy woman."

The young officer stared at Jack while his writing hand hovered above the notepad, as if suspended by a string.

"Excuse me?" he said. "You were doing what?"

Jack sighed. "Let me explain. But first, how long have you been with the Department?"

The young man frowned. "Two and a half years. Why?"

"Because your department was involved in investigating my friend's disappearance, but it was twenty-three years ago."

It was like a light came on in the recesses of the deputy's mind.

"Oh, yeah, I thought your name sounded familiar. One of the senior officers in our department was talking about that case a few months back. She said it was never solved. I had forgotten about it until just now."

"I don't suppose it was a woman named Sharon Nance was it?"

The stunned expression on the officer's face confirmed Jack's hunch. "How the hell did you know that?"

"Because I spent a half an hour staring at her nametag when I was thirteen years old, the night my friend went missing. She was the officer who interviewed me and I, well, I couldn't look her in the eye so I stared at her nametag while I was answering her questions. I've never forgotten her name."

"That's a hell of a thing. She's a captain now. Been with the department twenty five years. She's retiring next spring. Anyway, I remember a little about what she told us, but if you don't mind giving me the key points that would help. And of course, walk me through what happened last night?"

"Sure," Jack said, "I'll do my best."

Per Jack's hastily improvised plan, the version of the background story he told the officer was partly accurate; just enough to ring true with anyone who knew the details of the case or could research them. And as he transitioned to his more recent past, he leaned heavily on the lasting damage the lengthy childhood trauma had inflicted on him and Deena, both to garner sympathy, and to provide a credible motive for their expedition to The Farm. He very deliberately omitted any mention of spirits, demons, chevron beads or Chockowan Tribal Elders. Jack knew that the lite version of the narrative was more fit for human consumption, but as he watched the young man furiously taking notes, he couldn't help thinking of his favorite Jack Nicholson quote, from that military movie; "You can't *handle* the truth!" Old Jack had it about right; most people wonder what it is that lurks in the closet at night, or hides under our beds, waiting for us to fall asleep. They wonder, but they don't *really* want to know, he thought. They really don't.

"I guess it's just eaten at me all these years that Andy's body was never found. I always felt like it was there somewhere. And not long after I reconnected with Deena, I started having these dreams about a well. Now, I'm not a big believer in the metaphysical stuff," he said, with a slightly contemptuous shrug, "But these were so realistic that the idea stuck with me. I had never seen a well there when we were kids, but the more I thought about, the more it made sense. It's exactly the kind of place someone disposes of a body, at least that's how it is in the movies."

Officer Nolan grunted softly at that, but continued scribbling in his pad.

"We got our supplies together and hiked down there, thinking we would easily be back before dark, but the time got away from us and we realized it was late afternoon. We were just about to pack up and head back when we found it; the well."

The officer looked up, clearly caught off guard. "So, there really was a well?"

"Oh yeah," Jack said, his face genuinely solemn now. "And Andy was in it, along with the remains of at least two other children."

"Good Lord, are you serious? How do you, I mean, are you sure?"

As terrible as Jack felt about doing it, he knew that the photos he had taken in the well would give instant credibility to his story. He also knew that if this almost-rookie cop was like most, he would salivate over something other than a low-level B and E or a domestic dispute. Most small-town cops dream of working a murder case.

Jack reached for his phone and opened the photos, pulling up the closeup in which the juvenile skulls were clearly visible. When he held up his phone for Nolan, the officer's mouth dropped open.

"Jesus," he managed, but said nothing else for several seconds as he studied the image.

Wait for it..., Jack thought.

"Holy hell," the officer said, visibly recoiling from the phone. "On their mouths; is that?"

Jack nodded turned away, caught off guard by the sudden knot in his throat. "Somebody sewed their fucking mouths shut. I'm guessing it was that psycho hag in the house who attacked us. She looked older than God; wild grey hair and rotten teeth, but she was as strong as a demon." *Go easy, Jack thought. You're walking a wire here.*

315

"And you're certain one of these bodies is your friend?"

"No doubt. The one on top of the others. I still remember what he was wearing and his shoes. And there was one other thing." Jack pointed to the plastic bag on the chair. "Would you mind handing me that?"

The officer retrieved the plastic bag and handed it to Jack. He fished around until he found his pants and in the pocket, where he knew it would be, he found the cricket. He pulled it out and handed it to Officer Nolan, who rolled it over in one hand and seemed to recognize it immediately.

"Yeah, I've seen these before, but this one is vintage. They still use a modern version of these to train dogs, I think."

"When we were kids we saw soldiers using them in movies to signal each other, so we bought a couple of them at an Army Surplus and used the hell out of them. I've still got mine." Jack pointed to the phone in the officer's hand. "If you'll swipe a couple of shots over, you'll see that Andy is still holding his."

Nolan eagerly swiped and stopped, leaning closer and using his fingers to zoom in.

"I'll be damned," he whispered. "He sure is. This is unbelievable."

"Yeah, and it was pretty awful," Jack said, reaching for his phone before the officer had a chance to scroll through any more photos.

"How did you get down there?"

"I took a rope ladder and stakes to anchor it, just in case we found anything."

"That's pretty risky. Wells are damned dangerous. Why didn't you contact us?"

Jack raised his eyebrows in disbelief. "And say what? 'Ah, I know your department already combed every inch of that old farm and didn't find Andy Redmond's body, but I had this dream, see, so maybe suit up a half-dozen officers and come help me look?'"

Nolan shrugged. "Well, when you put it like that..."

"And no, offense, but I'm pretty sure most of the police and half the town thought at the time that I killed him and they just couldn't prove it. So, not so big on the trust thing where the police are concerned. I had decided that if I found him, I'd report it then, so I guess that's what I'm doing now."

"Well, I know you've been through a lot, and I appreciate your cooperation. Sorry, this is taking so long."

"It's okay," Jack said. "I've got no place to be."

The officer turned the page in his pad.

"Ah, Mr. Crawford..."

"Just Jack, thanks."

"Right. Jack, did you handle or disturb any of the remains in the well?"

"Hell no," Jack lied, shaking his head. "It was all I could do to stay down there long enough to take those shots." The horrible image reared up in his mind of Deena grinning up at him from the bottom of the well and holding up one of the children's skulls. God only knew what she did down there, but nothing to be gained by telling him about that. The remains would be what they would be. They would have to cross that bridge when the time came.

"So where was this woman you say attacked you?"

This part of Jack's story was still taking shape in his mind, but he knew that any hesitation would be obvious, so he plunged ahead.

"By the time we finished at the well and packed up our things, we knew we would be stuck hiking back in the dark, but we were okay with it because we found what we were looking for. And I'm thinking that I might, you know, get some closure on this after all the years. Well, anyway we were just starting to head back home when Deena saw a light in the upstairs window of the house. Not like an electric light from a bulb. This looked dim and yellow-orange, like a candle or a lamp flame. It scared the shit out of both of us that someone was in there and we were thinking they had probably been watching us the whole time."

"So, you went back to the house?" The young man was clearly rivetted, but agape at the idea of it.

"Yeah, probably not the best choice, but I'll be honest. I was pretty pissed at that point. We figured that it was probably a squatter, just living in the abandoned house. I guess homeless people do that, but this place is just so far out in the middle of nowhere, something about it didn't seem right. I knew in my rational mind that there was probably no chance whoever was in there had anything to do with the murders, and Deena tried to talk me out of it, but part of me just couldn't let it go. I had to know, so I talked her into going back." Jack paused. "I should tell you that I had a pistol with me at the time."

"You were armed?" Nolan had stopped writing.

"Don't worry, it's registered and I've got a concealed carry. I don't normally carry it, but I took it along for protection."

"Did you use it?" The young man's sympathetic expression had hardened.

"No," Jack said emphatically. "I didn't even get the chance to take it out of my jacket pocket. It all happened too fast."

"Okay, please continue." He was scribbling again.

"We went back to the house and thought about trying to sneak in, but the place is falling to pieces and there's no way someone wouldn't have heard us, so I just called out and said we were hikers and we were coming in and coming upstairs. I figure better not to surprise someone, just in case *they're* packing."

The officer shook his head, clearly dismayed at their recklessness, but waited for Jack to continue.

"Anyway, there was no answer, so we made our way upstairs, you know, being careful, and there was this weird wall in the middle of the room, not like the other walls; like it was an add-on or something. There was a huge hole in it and inside we saw an oil lamp on the floor, but it was makeshift, not like a fancy antique glass lamp, but made out of a Mason jar. It had wick in it. That was the light we had seen, but there was no sign of anyone in there. We started to go through the opening and we heard a creak on the floor behind us, but just as we both started to turn it felt like my head exploded and I went down. Apparently this old woman had been hiding in the shadows with a wooden club or a bat of some kind and just started swinging. I heard Deena scream, but then I hit the floor and passed out for a few seconds."

"So, she didn't say anything before she attacked you?"

"Nothing," Jack said.

"And you didn't have your pistol drawn at that point?"

"No, like I said. It was in my jacket pocket and I never took it out."

"Okay, go ahead."

"When I woke up, this crazy woman had chased Deena into this weird room and was beating the hell out of her with this board. She was trying to protect herself but taking a lot of blows. It was like this woman was on crack or something."

"Can you describe her?"

"She looked like a witch," Jack said, thinking quickly. "Like you would expect a witch to look like; grey hair, old dirty dress that looked like it was supposed to be white, crazy eyes. She was a nightmare."

"What happened next?"

"I just ran and tackled her, trying to get her away from Deena, and when I did, her foot smashed the lamp and sent burning kerosene across the floor and up one wall. We wrestled on the floor and she was clawing at my face and trying to bite me. I lost my grip at one point and she took a bite out of my cheek." Jack pointed at the bandage on his face.

"Ouch," Nolan said, wincing in sympathy.

"That's how the fire started, and once it did, the house went up like torch. We were both still trying to fight this woman off, but we were terrified we would burn up before we could get out. The old woman didn't even look like she gave a shit. She was hell-bent on killing us, I guess. We could barely breath, but I kicked her in the chest and she fell backwards, just when part of the ceiling gave way and collapsed on her. Deena and I were both bleeding and fighting to breathe, but we made our way to the stairs and, partway down they collapsed under me and I ended up falling and breaking some ribs, but we both managed to get out, barely. I didn't look back, but the old woman didn't make it out."

"You didn't see or hear her after that?"

"No," Jack said, looking down. "The house was a furnace by that time. The only glass left in one of the windows shattered from the heat, I remember that."

Officer Nolan paused and looked back over his notes.

"So, neither of you did or said anything that this woman might have perceived as threatening?"

"Hell, no," Jack frowned. "When I called out, before we went in the house I said that we didn't want any trouble, that we were just hikers looking around. She just attacked us for being there, as far as I can tell. Once she started trying to beat us to death we were screaming at her to stop, and everything after that was self-defense."

"It sure sounds that way. Well, I can tell you we don't get many homeless squatters around Benton, but out in the county there are more abandoned structures and we've seen some strange cases. And some of these people have serious mental health issues. It's not a stretch to think one of them could get that violent."

"What about the murders," Jack asked, with the proper effect. "My friend Andy and the others we found in the well? Isn't it possible the old woman was the murderer?"

Nolan sighed and shook his head. "It's impossible to say at this point. What I can tell you is that with everything you've given me so far, this is going to be a much deeper and broader investigation than I had originally thought. We may end up bringing in some state resources, depending on what our investigators find. In the meantime, I'll leave you my card. There's a link to our portal, if you could upload the photos you showed me and any others you have from the scene, ASAP, I would appreciate it."

He stood up and adjusted his belt, considering something as he closed his notebook.

"I'll speak to your friend as soon as she's up to it, but I need to ask what your immediate plans are, I mean when you're discharged."

"You mean am I planning on leaving the area?"

Nolan nodded. "More or less, yes."

"I think that depends on how Deena is doing," Jack said, all pretense gone. "How long they keep her and what condition she's in when they discharge her. As long as she's here, I'm going to be here. After that, I couldn't tell you."

"I can appreciate that. We *are* going to need you to come to the department as soon as you're able and walk through this in more detail with a couple of our folks. It'll be a lot easier if you're in the area, at least for a few days. After that, we can talk to you remotely or arrange an in-person as needed. We would ask, however that you keep us informed if you or your friend are going to be traveling out of the area, and particularly out of the state."

"I understand," Jack said, but even as he did, he dreaded the thought of being the central figure in yet another slow-moving police investigation. He had suffered through it once at an age when he should have been playing in the woods and watching TV. He had no desire to do it again.

Jack studied the young man's face.

"I guess you have no idea how long an investigation like this would take."

Nolan shook his head. "Not unless I was psychic. But as long as what you've told me is accurate, and you haven't done anything wrong that you're not telling me about, I'd say your part in it will be wrapped up in a few weeks."

The officer's words hung there in the air as a sick feeling washed over Jack and he wondered what the hell he had just done.

Officer Nolan extended his hand and Jack shook it but could not manage a smile.

As soon as he was alone again Jack hurriedly pressed the nurse call button, more anxious by the minute to get free of his IV tether so he could make a bee-line to Deena's room when they released her from the ICU. When a voice from the nurse's station asked over the speaker what he needed, Jack mentioned the IV and his pain medication. The voice said someone would be in shortly.

Tick-tock, tick-tock, he thought.

He found some comfort in knowing that the hospital didn't allow visitors in the ICU. It would likely keep the police away, at least for a little while. He only hoped it would be long enough.

When Nurse Ronda came back in, she was carrying a paper pill cup and humming something Jack did not recognize.

"I'll get that IV out for you," she said. "I hope everything went alright with the...with your visitor."

"It was fine," Jack lied, as he turned away, just in time for the jolt of searing pain in his arm as she pulled out his IV rig. "It was just routine."

"You've got some water, so go ahead and take these," she said, pushing the pill cup across the bedside table towards him. "We'll get you more in a couple of hours, depending on when the doctor wants to discharge you."

"Thanks," Jack said. "And can you let me know whenever they move my friend Deena out of ICU? She's been through a lot and I really want to see her."

"Oh, I'm glad you mentioned that," Nurse Ronda said as she leaned over him and began fiddling with the wire leads that were stuck to his now-shaved chest. "I was mistaken about your friend."

The beeping on the heart monitor sped up, as Jack braced himself.

"They've already moved her out of the ICU. She's on the third floor of the east building."

Oh, shit, he thought, fighting the panic that was rapidly rising.

"I'd like to go see her. I'll be careful, but I'd really like to see her now."

"That's fine, if you're careful, but you'll need to wait until that young officer is through talking to her."

"What?" Jack said in disbelief. The cardiac alarm went off again, but he didn't even notice the pain as she pulled the adhesive EKG pads from his skin one by one. After another moment the alarm fell silent as Jack reeled.

"Damn things are so sensitive," she complained as she worked. "Yes, it was good timing. He was on the way out when I talked to the third floor nurse's station. I was just able to catch him and let him know so he headed over that way. I'm sure they can let me know when he leaves and you can go and see her. How does that sound?"

Jack had turned away to hide his despair and could only nod.

We're screwed now, he thought. *Well and truly screwed.*

CHAPTER 22

The exchange between the head nurse at the third-floor-east nurse's station and Officer Nolan had been polite, but tense. She had cautioned him that, while Deena was well enough physically to move to a patient room, she had been severely traumatized and was in a very fragile emotional state.

The no-nonsense woman had agreed to let Nolan talk to her for a few minutes (a few minutes only) because he had pressed the issue (she knew he was from out of town and had no jurisdiction in Winston-Salem) by telling her that Deena was a key witness in an active murder investigation. The nurse had let Deena know that he would be coming in, but had encouraged her to tell the officer when she needed to stop, and to press the call button if she needed a nurse to step in.

In his room in the adjacent wing, Jack had been given some generic box-store clothing (that did not come close to fitting) because his had been turned over to the Benton police as evidence. And even as he was struggling through the intense pain of trying to get them on as quickly as his broken ribs would allow, Officer Nolan was introducing himself to Deena.

Nurse Ronda seemed dubious of Jack's efforts to walk so far across the hospital so soon, and suggested that he give himself a little longer to recover, but Jack was adamant. He turned down her offer of a cane, insisting that his legs and balance were fine, and after he proved this by walking down the hallway and back outside his room, she relented.

Jack tried to appear calm as Nurse Ronda gave him directions to the east wing, but his mind churned over what Deena might be saying to Officer Nolan. He had no idea what and how much she remembered about their bizarre ordeal, but even the smallest detail could blow a Mack-truck-sized hole in the flimsy yarn he had constructed for Nolan, instantly wrecking their credibility and buying them one-way tickets to the top of the "likely suspects" list. As he made his way through the halls and rode on two different elevators, he kept to himself and tried to push down the dread he felt, but it was nearly pointless. All he could do was brace for whatever happened.

When he rounded the corner on Three-East, Jack was nearly out of breath. His ribs were throbbing and he felt mildly dizzy. It did not help that several rooms past the nurse's station, he saw Officer Nolan emerging from a door. Nolan closed it behind him and turned to head down the hallway, but then looked up and saw Jack approaching.

"Jack," Officer Nolan said. "You're up and around?"

Jack took a couple of breaths and gritted his teeth against the pain. "Yeah, they told me Deena was in a regular room. I wanted to get over and see her as soon as possible. You talked to her?"

Jack searched the young man's expression for any sign of trouble, but saw none.

"For a few minutes," Nolan said. "She's in pretty rough shape, but she gave me enough for now."

"She did?" Jack asked, bewildered that the officer was not taking out the handcuffs.

"Yeah, she more or less confirmed what you told me. Not in exactly those words, but she...well, like I said, she's in pretty rough shape."

Barely able to conceal his astonishment and profound relief, Jack blinked and for a moment had no words. Finally, he managed to speak.

"I'm just glad she's out of the ICU. And I'm glad, ah, you got what you needed."

The young man lightly patted Jack's arm.

"Take care, both of you and we'll be in touch," he said and headed off down the hallway.

For a moment Jack watched him go, wondering what the hell Deena had said that even remotely supported his version of events, but only for a moment, then he hurried to her door and went inside.

She was propped up in her bed and attached to the same array of monitors and equipment that Jack had just been freed of, only she had a hard splint on one forearm, from the elbow to the wrist, and a thick soft bandage on the other arm, extending from her wrist to above her elbow. A deep purple bruise ringed one eye and there were scratches on the side of her face.

Her eyes lit up when Jack walked in the door, but as he went to her bedside he saw tears well up and spill down her cheeks. He leaned over and carefully wrapped his arms around her as she cried.

"I'm so sorry," he whispered in her ear. "But you made it. We got you out of there and you're going to be okay."

"I'm so glad to see you," she said through her tears. "I thought I was going to die. And I'm so sorry. I tried to stop but she was..."

Jack gently shushed her with a finger to her lips. "It's okay," he said, then lightly kissed her. "Don't think about that. I've got you back now, that's the only thing that matters."

"That police officer was just here," she said. "He was trying to ask me questions, but everything is such a blur. I don't think I was much help."

"Yeah, I saw him on the way out," Jack said, as he sat on the edge of her bed and gently took her hand. "He said you did fine."

"He asked me about an old woman," Deena said, wiping her eyes with the back of her other hand, "I told him she wasn't an old woman; she was the devil. I told him all I remember is being so afraid that she had hold of me and wasn't going to let me go. I remember being terrified that she was going to kill me in that awful house and that you saved me from her. I don't know, it was all so horrible..." She began to sob and Jack did his best to comfort her, but he knew that despite her narrow escape, her road back would be a long and difficult one.

And he understood then how Officer Nolan had taken Deena's comments to mean what he did. By some miracle, she has said just enough, and in just such a way that Nolan had made a critical but mistaken assumption; one that Jack hoped would make all the difference.

Jack was discharged several hours later, and although he rented a hotel room by phone at a nearby Holiday Inn Express as a place to shower later, he had no intention of leaving Deena. Heavily medicated for pain, she slept for long periods while he camped out in a chair in the corner of her room, but they talked when she was awake; mostly about how she was doing and what she needed, but occasionally about what had happened at The Farm.

It was obvious to Jack that her memory of the previous two days was muddled and had diminished rapidly as the demon had gained increasingly more control of her mind. By the time she had attacked him in the attic of the house, there had been so little of her consciousness left that she remembered almost nothing.

Jack let her take the lead and did not push her, despite his own burning curiosity about what she had gone through; and as the hours passed and she became more alert, he saw signs that her mind was waking up. She would sit in silence for long periods, lost in thought.

After one such silence, just as he was filling up her water cup again from a Styrofoam pitcher, she turned to Jack with tears in her eyes.

"You found him, didn't you? Andy? I thought for a while that it was another dream, but now I think I'm remembering. He was there, in the well, wasn't he? You had already discovered him down there, hadn't you?"

Jack felt his cheeks burn. "Yeah, I had. Early yesterday morning. I hiked back down there and found the well, and they were there. Andy and the others. I tried to call you but there's no damned cell service, so I couldn't reach you. By the time I did...well..."

He stopped, not wanting to state the obvious, but she finished his sentence, staring blankly at the corner of the room.

"I wasn't me anymore. I was her."

Jack just waited as more tears flowed down Deena's face and she wiped at them with her wrist.

"It was so awful. I can't even begin to explain what it feels like to have thoughts and memories in your head that aren't your own. And they were horrible."

He put down the pitcher and sat on the edge of her bed again, gingerly wrapping an arm around her shoulder.

"At first you know they're not your thoughts, your memories, but they get stronger and there's more of them, and then you're feeling things that you know you would never feel; hatred and rage and the urge to...do terrible things. Before long you're not sure anymore what's you and what's not. Then you're not even sure who you are."

"I can't begin to imagine what that would be like," Jack said, shuddering at the thought, and at how terribly close she had come to disappearing completely.

"But then, in an instant, they were all ripped loose from my mind," she said. "They tried to hold on, she tried to hold on. I could feel it, like I was being pulled apart. It was like how the suction from a huge tornado pulls everything out of a building in a split second. Then I was there again. I was me." She turned to look at him again. "And you were there. Oh, my God, and you were hurt...I'm so, so sorry."

"Stop. It's okay. I'm okay," he said, pulled her into him, despite the pain, and gently rubbing her back. "Don't think about that. We got you back, that's all that matters."

She sniffed and took in a couple of shaky breaths.

"Am I?" she asked, a note of fear in her voice. "Back, I mean? Do you think she's really gone?"

"I do," Jack said, with genuine conviction. "I'm certain of it."

"How did you do it?"

Jack was silent for moment, then smiled. "I didn't do it, Andy did."

Deena furrowed her brow. "What do you mean?"

"It was the beads. They told us where to look. I'll tell you more about it later, but I met a very interesting man yesterday; a genuine Chockowan Tribal Elder. It turns out that the indigenous people of that area knew a great deal about the evil spirits and demons that tormented their people, including how to banish them. It also turns out that what was binding this demon to that valley all those years was the bones of the Chockowan shaman who cursed the valley at the time of the massacre. They must have been kept somewhere else before William McNeill built the house, then after the demon possessed Margaret, she hid the bones behind the wall of the attic, where they've been ever since. This man I met said it was simple; burn the bones and the demon's power in the physical world is gone."

"You burned them, in the wall?"

"Yeah, that's how I know she's really gone. I watched it happen. I saw you come back."

"Thank you," she whispered, leaning her head against his. "Thank you so much. I know how hard it must have been to see me like that."

He exhaled deeply. "Yeah, it was. It definitely was. And not for nothing, but remind me never to piss you off. I mean, just saying..."

She chuckled quietly and the sound warmed Jack's heart like a spring thaw. And at that moment, he knew she would be okay.

"Since we're on the subject," he said, pulling slightly back to look at her, "I need to fill you in on a conversation I had with that cop."

"The one who was in here?"

"Yeah," Jack said. "I had to tell him something about what happened; something he would stand a chance of believing and that wouldn't drop us both in it. I figured that if they start poking around in what's left of that house they might find some incriminating things. And I didn't exactly have a lot of time to think something else up."

"Oh, shit," Deena said. "That's why he was asking me about an old woman?"

"Yeah," Jack winked. "You know, the crazy one who attacked us?"

After a moment of confusion, he saw the realization dawn in her eyes and she nodded. He shrugged and they fell silent for another few moments.

"So, what do you think is going to happen next?" she finally asked, wincing as she ran her fingertips over the padded bandage on her left arm.

Jack sighed. "Well, we've both got some healing to do and that may take a while."

She squinted one eye at him. "You know that's not what I mean."

"I know," he said with a heavy sigh. "I think this is going to blow up into a very big thing, especially when they link it to a twenty-three-year-old cold case and the McNeill family tragedy. And for better or worse, I think we're going to be right in the middle of it...at least for a while."

"I was afraid of that," she said, and they sat in silence for a moment. "Do you have to leave? I mean after we get out of here?" Deena asked quietly.

"I've got the summer off, and I'm not sure about going back to teaching in the fall, but I can't stay in Benton," he said. "I'm sure we'll have to do a bunch of interviews here with the police, but present company excepted, there's nothing but baggage and painful memories here for me now."

"I get that," she said, turning away, but he knew that she didn't want him to see her tearing up.

"But I hear Black Mountain is beautiful this time of year," he said, clearing his throat.

Deena turned and looked at him with surprised eyes.

"I hear the leaves are supposed to be gorgeous up there," he mused, "And I've been wanting to do some antiquing."

She could not suppress a grin.

"I hear there's a really great Antique shop over there. They say the owner is a little crazy but..."

She cut him off with a kiss.

CHAPTER 23

The days and weeks that followed were difficult ones for Jack and Deena, but they leaned heavily on each other both physically and emotionally. The Benton Police interviewed each of them no less than a half-dozen times and they would later be called on to give depositions for the State Bureau of Investigation. Officer Nolan offered to let Deena notify her father initially about the discovery of Andy's remains and with some encouragement from Jack, she agreed. He had broken down on the phone at the news and they had cried together for several minutes, until he tearfully confessed that he did not have the strength to identify Andy's body and begged Deena to do it. She had agreed, but had seen it as a final unforgivable act of cowardice on his part. The last time they would ever speak would be several months later, after the authorities finally released Andy's remains and they held a small private ceremony at Oakmont Cemetery.

Jack's prediction that the case would be a "big thing" proved correct, but for a mercifully short time. Initially, when hints of the contents of the well and its ties to the unsolved disappearance of Andy Redmond twenty-three years earlier reached the press and social media, the case briefly became front-page news on nearly every paper in western North Carolina. And when photos from the well and some of the initial forensic findings were leaked on the internet (despite the Benton PD's attempts to ensure a "tight lid") they went viral and fueled an intense media firestorm.

It was revealed that, apart from the remains of Andy Redmond, authorities discovered the complete skeletons of two young children and the partial skeleton of one adult (the skull was missing). Jack and Deena had been horrified at that revelation, privately speculating that in addition to the atrocities Margaret had committed on their children, she had apparently beheaded William's corpse and done something else with the head. The most lurid media attention arose from the leaked close-up shots of the rough stitching over the mouths of the dead children, fueling intense speculation of cult ceremonies and human sacrifice at the remote farm, although the Benton PD was quick to denounce such speculation as baseless rumors.

Unnerving discrepancies in forensic results began appearing soon after the investigation started and the bones at the scene were carbon dated. Despite all the juvenile victims having identical injuries, inflicted by identical implements and using stitching cord that any medical examiner would testify came from the same source, it was determined that the other two children had lived and died nearly a hundred years before Andy Redmond was even born. This effectively ruled out a single killer and raised the first of what would become many unanswered questions.

While the carbon dating gave investigators enough context to locate a recorded land purchase for twelve and a half acres in the river valley in June of 1923, by William Gregory McNeill, census records for Randall County (as Jack and Deena knew) were incomplete during those years, and that left them unable to determine the identities of the other children. In part, because they never learned of the existence of William McNeill's journals.

While Jack and Deena had been deeply conflicted over what to do with them, they knew that the journals would only undermine their statements to the police and would cloud an already impossibly complex criminal case by introducing demonic possession as a factor. They also knew all too well that it was the journals that would have ignited the real media firestorm. The dreadful narrative of the McNeill family's descent into terror and murder would have proven a gold-mine for the press and social media, with viewers and readers hungry for tragedy and scandal; the grislier the better. They knew that apart from providing possible identities for the dead, only harm would come from turning over the journals, so with little fanfare and few words, they quietly burned the books in a barrel behind Deena's house one moonless night that fall.

Early in the case there had been predictable skepticism on the part of the Benton Police about Jack and (later) Deena's unusual account of what happened that night at The Farm. However, in the weeks that followed their rescue, arson and crime scene investigators combing through the remains of the farmhouse located partial human remains in the form of charred bone fragments and determined that kerosene had in fact been the accelerant that started the fire. While both of these facts supported their statements to police, they did not rule out that someone had been murdered in the house the night the fire started. Jack and Deena were not charged with a crime, but remained possible suspects until a month later, when forensic experts in Raleigh were able to carbon date the bone fragments from the house and informed the Benton PD that they were between five and six hundred years old.

This threw the case into further confusion because, while it directly contradicted the existence of a mad squatter woman who had supposedly attacked Jack and Deena before perishing in the fire, it also meant that there was no evidence a death had even occurred that night, much less a murder. And it raised more troubling questions about what five-hundred year-old bones were doing in a hundred-year-old house at all.

When they were pressed to amend their original statements, Jack and Deena refused, and the police briefly considered charging them with obstruction and arson; however, the county attorney advised them against it. She insisted that they had no credible evidence of obstruction and that burning a hundred year old crumbling wreck of an abandoned house, for which there was no living owner of record, was not grounds for an arson indictment. She argued that by burning the shell of a house, Jack and Deena had actually done the county a favor.

While Deena's name stayed largely (and mercifully) out of the press, after Jack was mentioned as one of the hikers who discovered the bodies, it did not take media researchers long to connect the dots and dredge up the old news stories that put him squarely in the frame for Andy Redmond's disappearance. Several of the legacy stories even implied that the only reason he was not charged was the lack of evidence. These resurrected speculation about his possible involvement, but given all the details that had come to light, the police quickly squelched those rumors by stating that Jack Crawford was not considered a suspect in Andy's death.

Jack returned with Deena to Black Mountain, where they spent time recovering from their ordeal in Benton and, with Tanya's help, got Stella's Antiques up and running again and open for business. They each struggled with their own wounds, both physical and psychological, and frequently had trouble sleeping, but they regularly talked with Millie and they supported each other in ways that only people who have experienced a shared trauma can. And, over time, they both began to heal.

At Deena's urging, Jack attended Mel Redmond's memorial service, as did Jack's mother, who he had finally contacted after they had been discharged from Saint Marry's. Jack had given his mother the lite version of events, convinced that the unabridged saga would have given her a stroke. She had been stunned by the news of Andy and The Farm, but radiant at learning of Jack and Deena's blossoming relationship.

Despite her initial prodding for Jack to keep the house on Wildwood Lane, after everything that happened, Jack's mother never mentioned it again, fully supporting him when he hired a contractor to renovate the interior and put it on the market six months later. The day it sold, Jack felt as if a great weight had been lifted and a door closed on the darkness of his past.

Good riddance. Its someone else's problem now.

After going to the closing together, he and Deena went out for dinner and raised a glass in a symbolic send-off and the start of a new beginning.

Several weeks after they returned to Black Mountain, Jack decided to pay another visit to Josiah Red Wolf, to thank him for his timely and crucial help, and to follow up on something that had been bothering him since their first conversation. The idea that the Chockowan had suffered such terrible atrocities at the hands of Spanish explorers in that valley, and that the incident had been forgotten and conveniently swept under the carpet of history, seemed an unacceptable injustice to Jack, and he had been cultivating an idea to help rectify it. But when the two met again, Jack had been pleased to learn that the Tribal Elder had shared his concern and had already begun working with the North Carolina Office of State Archaeology to launch a formal investigation by their department into the justification for designating the river valley as a "site of historical significance."

Josiah thanked Jack for giving him the chevron bead that night and explained that it was the bead, more than anything else that supported his claim and convinced the OSA to move forward with the investigation. In the months that followed, archaeological teams from the OSA would discover further supporting evidence that the valley was in fact the site of a Chockowan massacre, and petitioned the state to declare a large portion of the valley, including the site of The Farm, protected under the Native American Graves and Repatriation Act of 1990. Their petition was eventually granted, and in what he would later call the greatest honor of his life, Josiah Red Wolf would consult with the State of North Carolina on the excavation and return of Chockowan remains to the tribe for traditional burial, and on the development of a memorial park in the valley, complete with a monument to the indigenous people who perished. As part of the park development, what remained of The Farm would be bulldozed and a terraced garden of wildflowers built on the grounds. The site was eventually deemed significant enough to warrant a state grant of funds to build a greenway from Jack's old neighborhood to the valley.

And after hundreds of years of darkness and isolation, people began coming to the valley, walking the paved, manicured pathway that had for so long been a rutty, overgrown road bed. They came in twos and threes, or by themselves, emerging after the long wooded walk into the expanse of the river valley. They came to see the monument and contemplate the weight of history, to enjoy the beauty and solitude of the park, or to put down a blanket by the river and enjoy a picnic. And they stood on the hilltop that overlooked the valley, admiring the beautiful terraced flower gardens that spread out around them; unaware that The Farm had ever existed.

No suspect in the murders was ever named, and three years after it began, the case was quietly moved to the cold-case file, where it remains to this day. Soon after, following some debate among local officials and a donation of three burial plots in the Oakwood Cemetery by the Hawthorne Funeral Home, the remains of the other victims in the well were finally buried under a single headstone, inscribed with the family name "McNeill."

EPILOGUE

It was a cool spring morning in the mountains of western North Carolina, and cotton-ball clouds drifted lazily across an impossibly blue sky before disappearing behind the ridgeline that bordered Tanshaney Memorial Park. The fields by the winding river that snaked through the valley had fully greened and the rippling water glistened in the sun. The only visitors to the park this day were two dozen of the Eastern Chockowan Tribe, dressed in traditional ceremonial clothing, and their special guest, Jack Crawford.

The greenway and the park had been closed to the public by the Park Service for a special event, and a ranger had been stationed at the entrance to the greenway to keep out the curious. At the request of the Daniel Warton, the Principal Chief of the Eastern Chockowan, no press had been allowed.

As he watched from his vantage point on a bench in the terraced flower gardens on the hilltop overlooking the valley,

Jack felt privileged. This day was the culmination of two years of work on the part of Josiah and the other members of the Tribal Council, and it was an emotional moment for the Chockowan as they brought closure and healing to a terrible chapter of their past. The Cleansing Ceremony was an ancient one, involving the burning of cedar and medicinal herbs and the pouring of water, as well as a traditional dance and prayers to Onatlavahee, The Great Spirit, to purify the valley and protect and release the souls of those who died there.

It made Jack smile to see Josiah Red Wolf among the men and women of the tribe, dressed in colorful traditional ceremonial clothing circling the granite monument at the center of the park, moving in unison as they danced and prayed to rhythms of drums, bells, and shell rattles.

He had come to believe that the indigenous people of the Appalachians understood the universe and natural world in ways that modern western civilization never would. And as he thought about the power of their ceremony to heal, and about the hundreds of their ancestors who had died there, Jack reflexively ran his hand over the brass nameplate on the back of the bench, *his* bench, and said a silent prayer for his childhood friend. He and Deena had donated the funds for the bench, which was constructed of cedar, considered a sacred wood by the Chockowan. The plate was inscribed with the words: "In Loving Memory of Andy Redmond."

When the ceremony was finished, Jack stood up and walked down the gravel path as the members of the Tribe began to gather their things and file up the steps toward the greenway. Josiah's eyes were misty but he bore a wide smile as he greeted and embraced Jack. Then, one by one, as they passed, each member of the Tribe shook Jack's hand and spoke briefly to him. In the many months since his and Deena's ordeal, word of what happened there had quietly spread among the members of the tribe and it humbled him beyond words to see the expressions of gratitude and something bordering on awe on their faces as they regarded him. Josiah had often commented that Jack was the only person in living memory who had seen and done what he had, but it wasn't until that moment, that Jack understood how much it meant to them.

Josiah stood with Jack and watched the others as they made their way along the greenway and into the woods, beginning the long walk back.

"Want to head back?" Josiah asked. "I'll walk with you."

Jack thought for a moment and looked back toward the bench.

"No, thanks anyway. You go ahead. I think I'll stay for a little while."

Josiah smiled and put a hand on Jack's shoulder. "I understand. We'll talk soon."

As his friend walked away, Jack turned and walked back up the hill to the flower garden and made his way back to Andy's bench. He sat for a long while, listening to the breeze and the chirring of the crickets and the birds all around him. He didn't know whether all the souls of the dead had really been trapped here all those years, and whether they had finally been freed, but he deeply hoped so. He hoped so for Andy's sake.

Finally, Jack reached into his pocket and pulled out the cricket, rolling it over in his hands and thinking about how long he had kept it, part of him wanting to try it again one last time, but part of him being afraid to. For a brief time, it had somehow reconnected him with Andy, and even though he knew what needed to happen—that Andy needed to move on—it felt oddly like losing him all over again. It was hard to think about; but the cricket made it real.

Even without the dilapidated buildings of The Farm as landmarks, Jack knew the terrain of the hillside, and he knew that Andy's bench sat very close to the site where the old house had stood. Not twenty yards from the now-filled, sealed well.

What more appropriate place?

Jack sighed and stood up, holding the cricket out in front of him and closed his eyes.

Click-click.

Jack waited, reflexively holding his breath, but the only response he heard was the wind rustling the trees and the babbling of the river below him. He wiped the tears that had begun welling in his eyes as he nodded his approval and put the cricket back in his pocket.

Deena was waiting for him at the entrance to the greenway and wrapped him in her arms before they climbed into the car to head out of town. When they turned onto King Street, Jack asked Deena to make one last stop by Oakwood Cemetery. There they walked the familiar path that wound among the sea of headstones until they reached Andy's, which sat near the base of a spreading oak. Deena stood while Jack knelt in front of the granite stone and looked at the new inscription, "Andy Redmond, Beloved Son, Brother, and Friend."

"Best friend," Jack whispered as he touched Andy's name with two fingertips. After a moment he pulled the cricket from his pocket one last time and placed it on the base of Andy's stone before standing up and taking Deena's hand. Together they turned and walked back to the car and drove out of town, in the direction of home.

AUTHOR'S NOTE

While the events and characters in this story are fictional, The Farm was a very real place and was an iconic part of my childhood, growing up in Boone, North Carolina.

It, along with the beautiful but strangely isolated river valley in which it sat, was exactly as I have described it in this story, including the old farmhouse and what we kids called "the attic," a dark and unfinished part of the upstairs behind a broken wall, with an opening that we were never brave enough to go through. The pervasive stillness and melancholy of the place was also very real, as was the unnerving sense of being watched.

My brother and I spent countless hours wandering the valley, looking for arrowheads (we found quite a few), exploring The Farm, and shooting cans with our father's twenty-two rifle. Much like Jack and Andy, we tried to spend the night in the old house, but the unnerving noises of the dry tree branches on the rusted tin roof, and the odd sounds in the darkness of the attic (yes, those were real too) eventually drove us out. We retreated to the field by the river and built a bonfire, where we stayed for the remainder of a cold and sleepless night.

The Farm was a mysterious place to us, likely built in the 1800s and abandoned sometime in the early part of the twentieth century; but built by whom and abandoned for what reason, I was never able to determine.

We continued our visits to the valley and The Farm for years, until it was discovered by a group of troublemakers from our school, who first began to vandalize the old house and eventually burned it to the ground.

Years after I grew up and moved away from Boone, the valley became the site of a beautiful park and the Don Kennedy Trail, a network of greenways that borders the river. The longest of these follows the path of the old roadbed in my story, along the ridgeline, from my old neighborhood to the former site of The Farm.

You can go there if you like.

ABOUT THE AUTHOR

Jeff McEntire was born and raised in Boone, North Carolina, in the picturesque Blue Ridge Mountains.

He is an author and an artist.

Jeff lives with his wife, Jen, and their dog Gretchen in Durham, North Carolina.

Also by Jeff McEntire:

Dangerous Ground

Carver's Hollow